I0761844

PARADOX TRILOGY: BOOK ONE

PARADOX

JAMIE RIPP

INK STREET PRESS

ISBN: 978-1-7336261-0-1 (ebook)
ISBN: 978-1-7336261-1-8 (paperback)
ISBN: 978-1-7336261-7-0 (hardback)

Published by Ink Street Press
support@inkstreetpress.com

Edited by Alan Brown and Blair Thornburgh
Cover Design by Alexandra Purtan
Formatted by Lorna Reid

BOOKS BY JAMIE:

PARADOX TRILOGY

Paradox
Revelation
Ascendance

EXCLUSIVE BONUS CHAPTER:

Forgotten Journal

www.jamieripp.com

Dedicated to my family.
My husband, and my beautiful children,
My mom and dad, and my sister and brothers,
My grandmother, and my Editor,
Whose enthusiasm of my story encouraged me to write and inspired me to finish.

PROLOGUE

The Dark Ages were a time of raiding parties, conquest, and strange occurrences. Vikings were responsible for creating and launching what we now call the dawn of vampires. Savage and brutal, they would cut out the hearts of the leaders of any village or tribe. Eating the heart was thought to prolong the life of whoever consumed it. Sadly, they did this to every town, tribe, or group that they wandered upon.

I always thought these stories were hogwash. Whoever heard of men eating men? These stories and ideals were not generally brought up in civilized conversation. I dragged myself out of bed early in the morning as the roosters crowed and the animals stirred. This morning felt different to me. It was still cold out, although we were on the brink of summer. I bundled up and went out to finish my chores before breakfast. I gathered the eggs, milked the cows, slopped the pigs, and fed the livestock, all before sunup. When I slumped into the old wooden chair for breakfast, my wife was putting the final touches on the meal while my two children played noisily on the floor. I was too tired for all the clatter. I yelled at them to stop and told them to sit down and eat their breakfast. I didn't yell often, but there was something off about today that made me a little irritable. My kids, on the verge of tears, quietly sat down, and were careful not to make eye contact with me. My heart sank. I apologized, hugged them, and went out to finish my daily work. I wanted to get an early start before the sun came up and it got too warm. I sometimes envied those in the village, with their effortless responsibilities, while I was out in the field, day in and day out, working for the food they ate. My kids, running by my feet, asked if they could work in the field with me and were disappointed when I told them no. The looks on their faces broke my heart, but the fields were no place for a four- and six-year-old. The air was cold, and the soil was warm, making a cloud form over the ground. It was hard to see the plow. Plowing the fields was tedious work—no wonder when all you did is follow a horse and keep the furrows straight.

Half-asleep, I was jolted awake by screams off in the distance. My home and village were burning; large billows of smoke engulfed the village. The horse reared and pranced. It knew something was wrong. I untangled myself quickly from the reins. I ran as fast as I could, and as hard as I could, but no matter how hard and how fast I ran, it wasn't fast enough. All I could think about was my wife and children stuck in a burning house, and I wasn't there to help them. The kids must have been so scared, and my wife so helpless. Emerging from the chaos, I came to my home practically in rubble. Still, I approached, knowing what I might find. I pulled the wreckage away piece by piece, exposing the bed shared by my kids. I hesitated for only a second, afraid of what I might see. I pulled back the wood, and to my heart's relief, there was nothing there.

I raced through the rest of the house, looking for any signs of my family, but there were none. Panicked, I heard a small whimper. Just outside I saw my wife and kids huddled in a ball of fear. Something was wrong. It was not natural for them to be this way. I ran to them and scooped them up in my arms. My wife laid there, lifeless and stained with her own blood. My son and daughter were struggling for air, fighting for their lives. As the tears ran down my face, my daughter opened her eyes. I could see the agony as she smiled at me, and then, with a quick flash of fear in her eyes, she was gone. Her beautiful hazel eyes were now dull and bleak, her red hair pasted to her head with blood. My son, panting short, shallow breaths, grabbed my hands, and then slowly met the same fate as his mother and sister. I screamed. I had just lost everything. My children hadn't even had a fair chance at life. And I was to blame. I didn't listen to my gut, and now my family was gone. I pulled them closer, holding them as tight as I could, praying that this was all a nightmare, that I would wake up any second. The smoke was dying down, and the scattered screams and yells faded into the distance as I held them for the last time. Everything went blurry and wavy as I sobbed uncontrollably. Their fate was my fault. I would never forgive myself. My heart ached as I reluctantly pulled away, and, with one final look at my family, anger for their deaths rose inside me. Now I wanted justice. My sorrow was engulfed by rage. The chase was on. I was going to get revenge. I was my family's protector in life and death, and while I may have failed them in life, I wouldn't make that same mistake in death.

Friends and neighbors lay strewn about, most of them in pools of their own blood. They had not just been killed; they had been brutally attacked, savagely ripped apart. That is when I realized I was the only one standing. My entire village had been laid waste, yet I was somehow spared. The grief consumed me, and I vowed I would have my revenge for them as well. Thereafter, I wandered the streets of distant cities, just daring anyone to taunt me or otherwise engage me.

Replete with the rage and sorrow of losing his wife and children, Nicholas hunted the Vikings to settle the score. When he found them, they were not like ordinary people. They were fair-skinned, thin, and sickly looking, their mouths permanently stained with blood and their teeth were sharp and jagged. While the unholy tribe sat around the campfire and swapped stories, Nicholas snuck closer, but a man grabbed him and held him fast, bringing him to the others. Adrenaline running through his veins, Nicholas was able to fight free for only a second. The leader of the Viking clan, with stature and authority, came forward and roared at his clan for teasing their food. He placed a strong and powerful hand on Nicholas's shoulder, and pushed him forward. A young man with a wide toothy smirk and a crushing grip held him, bent down, and roughly bit his neck. With a sharp, stabbing pain, Nicholas quickly lost consciousness and fell limp. Yet this was not the end of Nicholas. The leader, thinking him too weak to kill, left Nicholas for dead, bleeding, to see his own life dwindling away.

Nicholas had too much anger to die. He watched the clan until morning, when they packed up and left in search of another village to annihilate. The way these creatures disregarded life, like it was no more than a weed beneath their feet, infuriated Nicholas. He grew stronger and stronger every day, and as he did, he learned his abilities and mastered the art of their use. With each passing night, Nicholas regained his former strength and then some. The Vikings had been unaware of the repercussions of biting Nicholas. The venom left behind mutated Nicholas into one of them, leaving him with an unsatisfied thirst for blood. Half of the desire was created by his obsession to settle the score, and the other half was from the bite, the same thirst for blood and power possessed by his maker.

After a century of wandering, Nicholas realized his abilities were too strong to be merely human. His prolonged lifespan left him to conclude that he would never die. With a scorned heart, he hunted the clan of Vikings down, finally meeting the leaders haunting pale face. His opponent seemed to have aged and grown weaker; the once brave and powerful appearance was now saggy and feeble. Nicholas took advantage of the Viking leader's frail state and finally gained his revenge. As the Viking breathed his last, he spoke to Nicholas in no more than a whisper.

"I have been waiting for you. I am not the one you seek, but I saw you coming the day we left you for dead—a mistake, I admit. One I never should have allowed. You have gained power with my death. But you will lose that power when one of us, one not governed by our rules, yet one who shares our same fate, will find you. They will find you and they will destroy the power you have created."

Before Nicholas could ask him what it meant, life left the man as nothing more than dead remains. To ensure The Old One's death, Nicholas ate his heart to consume his power. His words disturbed Nicholas, for it was he who he thought he sought, and he vowed to remember them. He had to keep the power he had assumed, as well as the strength to overtake the clan. Weighing the odds, the clan bowed at his feet, and they remained faithful, serving him for years to come. Unlike The Old One, Nicholas never aged. His face remained thin and distinguished and his hair stayed white. But his eyes, once a beautiful blue, turned dark with the fury and pain that consumed him, sagging with gray bags from the ever-present weight he bore. His thin and muscular frame stood tall, and he carried himself well, projecting power and authority when he spoke. Whether or not you wanted to, you listened in fear. No one else aged, either. Every one of his subjects stayed precisely as they did when he attained power. Frozen in time, they became ageless and immortal. Believing no one equal to himself, Nicholas was not unlike his maker. He was just as brutal and merciless. He savagely killed anyone who crossed him, making sure all felt the same pain he had. He hunted the streets by night to keep anyone from seeing the agony and hatred in his soul. The sun soon burned every time he faced it, another inescapable frustration.

The clan moved from nation to nation, leaving their mark of terror on the places they came upon. No one dared to cross Nicholas, especially those who served under him. A few would test the line, but they were brutally corrected. But Steven, who was smart and posed an unsuspected threat to Nicholas, broke the rules and fell for a human he came upon in one of the villages. It was love at first sight, hid the girl under the floorboards, and fought to keep her safe until the time came when he was able to escape. Time passed, and Nicholas grew more and more powerful until Steven finally found the perfect opportunity to leave with her. Steven had been one of the original Vikings and Nicholas, noticing a change in Steven, watched him even more closely than usual, and found he had not only fallen for the girl, but also gotten her with child. Believing the child would fulfill the prophecy, Nicholas ordered their death.

Steven and his love, Ava, fled with their child in their arms down the streets of London. Nicholas ruled with death and fear, and Steven knew they must get away. Steven knew what Nicholas was capable of. He had seen Nicholas demolish defenseless villages, burn his fellow vampires alive, and kill anyone who got in his way. Steven and his new family would have to disappear and never be found again.

The cobblestone streets were barely visible through the dim mist that hung over the city before daylight, but Steven knew the streets better than anyone. He hunted along them at night and walked them during the day. Thus, Steven and Ava handily outdistanced their pursuers until they turned down a dead end with a steep wall. Steven forgot Ava did not possess the ability to jump the wall. He grabbed the two most precious things in his life—the girl he had unconditional love for and the baby he knew was unique—and leaped over the wall. Landing in the water on the other side, Steven grabbed the baby and swam to shore, but his one true love was drowning in the water's deadly undercurrents. Hoping to save Ava, he quickly bit her in hopes that his venomous bite would bring her back to life.

She too now lived a life of immortality, but the chase was not over. Steven and Ava knew they would be hunted for the rest of their lives. Overjoyed at making it even this far, vowed to keep their daughter from ever knowing their secret as vampires. They would raise her as a human in hopes that Nicholas would never gain control of her. Assuming the identities of Roger and Emily Stone, they built their lives around their daughter, making sure she would be safe.

ONE

I splashed through the glossy, rain-soaked, cobblestone streets. I ran as fast as I could along the misty, dark alley. The moon cast shadows that danced and played as I felt fearful of being followed. I could hear my pursuers' soft-thudding footsteps closing in, and the sounds of exchanging orders. The terror of being captured taunted my thoughts. I could feel the cool breeze against my skin as a storm threatened to thwart my escape. I hid behind a barrel on a dock in the harbor, and I could hear a cold-hearted laugh from a man who approached my hiding spot. I hoped and prayed that the man would not find me. Then, out of nowhere, I was grabbed from behind. The grip on my wrist was firm but not crushing. The moment I realized I was caught, I was swung around, to come face to face with…

This is 95.5 KWNR. Good morning, Las Vegas!

My alarm woke me. I placed my hands against my thundering heart and looked around. Seeing I was still in bed, I breathed a sigh of relief. A cold sweat dripped down my temple, and a shiver ran up my spine. Looking down at my wrists where the unknown assailant had grabbed me, I still felt the pressure of his grip as I resisted him.

"*These boots were made for walkin', and that's just what they'll do…*" Turning over, I hit the snooze button. *Another song I will be humming all day, no doubt*. Grudgingly, I rolled out of bed and opened the blinds. Traffic was backed up as everyone rushed to work after leaving their houses five minutes too late and trying to make it up on the road. The honking horns and obscene yells coming from the endless row of cars on the freeway made it just another hot day in Las Vegas.

As I rounded the corner to the kitchen for breakfast, I saw Mom was flipping pancakes. Her red, shoulder-length hair was neatly pinned up and ready for the corporate world. My mom, Emily, was dazzling. She was the epitome of perfection. If I looked long enough, I would find myself getting lost in her blue and opalescent eyes like a sailor to a siren, her gaze mirroring my own emotions. She had the supermodel look down to a T, but without the attitude. She was slender and taller than me. Her face was thin and elfin, but she held herself with stature and poise. As her daughter, I always felt overshadowed. I had always been jealous of my mom and her looks, hoping that I could one day be like her.

After pouring a glass of milk, I was about to sit down when my dad walked in. He poured some coffee in his mug, placed a black golf bag against the wall behind his chair, then sat down. Dad was in his casual clothes, a simple pair of slacks and a short-sleeved, button-down shirt. His hair was carefully styled to appear disheveled.

"Good morning, dear. How did you sleep?" Mom's tiny voice swept through the kitchen as she smiled at me.

"Fine, thanks. Where are *you* going?" I asked my dad, pointing to the clubs against the wall.

"I'm playing golf after work with Phillip." Dad was a man of few words, but those few words carried meaning and force. My dad, Roger, was an engineer for the government. He was tall, too, and although he tried to fit in, he was far from average. His deep brown eyes were dark, wise, and burnished, hiding his every thought and emotion like a stone wall. His hair was meticulously and expertly tousled; he took pride in his looks and himself, always dressing to impress.

"Oh, okay." I smiled at Mom. "Hey Mom, Mark is picking me up from work and taking me to the movies. Can you drop me off so we won't have to swing back and pick up my car?"

"Yes," Dad said, piping up before Mom could answer. "You need a new car. It'd be better if you took that beat-up old metal heap to the dump." His words spoke volumes.

"Your father is right, dear," Mom said. "I don't understand why you won't let us buy you a new car."

"I just don't think I need one. She manages to get me where I need to go with little problem," I said, digging into a small stack of pancakes.

Dad sighed and pegged me with a disapproving glare. Although he and I always disagreed, I was just as stubborn, if not more so, than he was.

"All right, dear, if I'm going to take you, we'd better be off." Mom turned off the stove and griddle while I grabbed my purse, and we left the house.

Once in the car, I immediately saw my work schedule sticking out of Mom's briefcase. I closed my eyes and shook my head, chuckling. My mom drove, weaving in and out of traffic like she was Mario Andretti.

Absently, I thought back to how I ended up working at the credit union. It was easy, really: Mom was the CEO, and although I could have chosen to do anything, the credit union sucked me in like a black hole. Any and all dreams of moving away from home were squished like a spider under a shoe, just like that.

We pulled up to the credit union. Mom waited for me to walk in before she left.

As I entered, Catherine, my manager, greeted me. She was a petite lady, about five-foot four, and wore glasses that usually sat near the end of her nose. Her features were mouse-like, but those looks were deceiving. She projected power and confidence. She, like my parents, had the same flawless composure. Her eyes were brown and lively, and although she was strict and professional, you could see there was another side to her, a side that was fearless and adventurous. She dressed in suits and dresses that accentuated her figure. She was my mom's best friend.

"Good morning, Catherine," I said. Today, Catherine was wearing a yellow and pale blue print dress that looked like it was designed just for her. Her high heels added a few inches. I clocked in and took my drawer out from the vault.

"Good morning, Arri," she replied in her high-pitched voice.

I liked Catherine. I had been working here for three years, and not once had she mixed her business with her personal life. I finished counting my till and headed to my desk to log in.

When I sat down, I noticed there was something different about my desk: my typewriter pen cup was still to the far right, my drawers were still locked, the brown fake wood surface was still clean, but something was off, and I couldn't place it. I paid no attention to it. I cleared my workspace of my purse and keys and set up for the day.

"Who are they from, Arri?" Catherine asked. I jumped in my seat.

"You startled me." I readjusted myself. "Who is what from?"

"The flowers, silly! How did you move them and not see them? I swear, child, how is it you have the memory of an elephant, but can't see what is right in front of your nose?"

She was right. There could be a storm going on around me, and unless I was looking for it, I would miss it. I was usually oblivious. I hadn't even noticed the flowers on my desk. I merely moved them out of my way and began the day.

"I don't know. I guess I wasn't paying attention." I read the card out loud. "I look forward to making your acquaintance." That was all it said.

"Does it say who they're from?" Catherine's voice was noticeably edgy.

"It doesn't. The card makes no sense. Who am I supposed to see? It must be a mistake."

Catherine reached for the card.

"The handwriting looks familiar," she muttered and furrowed her eyebrows.

"What is it, Catherine?"

"Nothing, dear. Just a little déjà vu." She smiled. With a wave of her hand, she entered her office and closed the door behind her.

I hated it when people hid things from me, especially my parents and their friends, and it was getting to be quite the little habit of theirs. I shook my head, headed to Catherine's office, and entered without knocking, just hearing the end of her phone call as I barged in.

"I know his handwriting; it is definitely Nicholas. Emily, I am telling you, he sent the flowers to her just to toy with us. He knows where she is, and this proves it!" There was panic in her voice. As soon as she saw me, she hung up the phone. "Can I help you, Arri?"

"Yeah, what's going on? I've seen this look on your face before, and I know it means something."

"It's not important, Arri. You have nothing to worry about."

"I didn't ask if there was anything to *worry* about, Catherine. I asked what's going on."

"In due time, dear, in due time…"

I realized I wasn't going to get anything out of her. I thought about standing my ground and demanding an answer, but it had never worked in the past, so trying it now was no use.

After I left her office, I buried myself in my work and the day went by quickly—almost like normal.

TWO

After the last customer left, I managed my drawer, clocked out, and texted Mark.

Me: I'm off and ready. What is your ETA?

Mark: I'll be there in two, just turning onto Sahara now.

As I waited by the back door, Catherine approached me.

"Hey there. You okay?" She put her arm around my shoulder.

"Yep. Just waiting for my ride," I said, not looking at her.

"Who's coming?"

"Mark. We're going to the movies. Apparently, there's a new film he wants to see." I said the words with no enthusiasm.

"Oh? Why do you sound more like you would rather have a bone marrow transplant than see the movie?" She giggled.

"It's probably a great movie, but Mark has been acting a little weird lately, and honestly, I was going to call it off with him after the movie. I'm pretty sure he'll be upset. He doesn't like it when things are not in his control. He likes everything—including me—just so: no opinion, no thoughts, just kind of mindless. I don't think I'm his kind of girl, and I'm not really looking forward to his temper."

"Mark has a temper?" Catherine cocked her head.

"You, Mom, and Dad set us up. I would have thought you guys would have known everything about him right down to his DNA sequencing."

"Yes, but…he never seemed angry." Catherine's eyes became distant as she thought.

Just as she opened her mouth to say something more, a honk blared from just outside the door.

"Well, there's my ride. See you tomorrow!" I called to her as I bolted for the door. I didn't know what was worse: hanging out with Mark, or telling Catherine about my personal life.

I got in Mark's car and let out a small sigh as I took in his scent. The smell of his liberally doused cologne mixed with the smell of the leather cleaner was enough to make a person gag. I crinkled my nose briefly, but smoothed out my expression before facing him.

"Hi there, babe." He leaned over the console to kiss my cheek. Mark and I had been dating for a little over three months, and it was three months too many. I fought the urge to clench my jaw in annoyance and offered him a small but polite smile instead.

"Hi."

"Are you ready? I invited a few friends, if that's okay."

"Yeah, of course. Anyone I know?" I asked, as a conversation starter even though I had never met any of his friends.

"No, not really." Just like that, the conversation was closed.

The rest of the car ride vibrated with awkward silence until we arrived at the movie theater. I had the feeling that tonight was not going to be the quiet night I was hoping for. It would be even harder for me to dump him with all his friends around.

After we found a parking spot, Mark took my hand and we approached the ticket window.

"Yes, two adults, please."

The woman behind the ticket counter glared at me with open contempt and looked at Mark as if he were the king of Versailles. Mark's light, almost platinum, blond hair was a striking contrast to his copper complexion.

The woman took his card and gave him our tickets, making sure she brushed her fingers against his skin as he took them. At her touch, Mark looked up, smiled, and winked.

In any other circumstances, this would have surprised and upset me, but this was usual for him. Mark was a womanizer.

After securing popcorn and drinks, we sat in the tiny theater. The lights dimmed and the only the illumination was the screen. Since this was a small theater, I wasn't surprised to see that we were the only ones in the theater, as we so often were.

"I just got a text from my friends. They're here!" Mark turned around just as the doors to the theater opened and blinding hallway light blasted into the room. All I could see were the shadows of six football-player-sized men. Pasting on a fake but polite grin, I rose to meet them.

"Arri, these are my friends," Mark said, and rattled off their names like I actually cared. "Guys, this is Arri. She's the one you've all been giving me crap over," he said, smiling at me. The guys whistled and nodded as they looked me up and down. I couldn't tell if they were sizing me up or checking me out.

"Hi, it's nice to meet you. I was starting to wonder if Mark had any friends." I said, joking.

"Ha, ha, Arri. Very funny," Mark said, with no humor in his voice.

"Same here," said the tallest one. "I was wondering if you even existed. Our man Mark here has kept you all to himself. And I can see why," he added and ran his finger down my arm.

Trying to hold my temper, I balled up my fists and shook him off.

"Oh, you'd better watch out, Mark. This one is feisty."

"Nah, she's as docile as a house cat." He brushed a lock of hair behind my ear.

"Yeah, well—" I started, but then the screen came on, and the previews came to life. "Oh, look! The movie!" I turned around, sat down and opened my Red Vines.

"Here, I'll go get you guys some snacks while you keep Arri company," Mark said, as he squeezed my fingers in assurance.

The theater doors closed and the guys took their seats. Two sat in front of me, two sat behind me, and two sat beside me, one on either side. The opening credits ended and the screen went blank. It took me a moment to realize something was wrong. Instantly, two of the men grabbed on my arms and hoisted me up.

"What are you doing?" I demanded, flailing my arms and legs.

"Not on your life, sweetheart. You're coming with us, so you can stop your fighting, because it's useless." Their grip tightened, shooting pain up my body.

"Ouch!" I kicked harder and started to scream when a heavy, calloused hand covered my mouth. I flinched. The emergency exit door was open and Mark was in the doorway, motioning to his friends.

"Come on, guys! Let's get her out of here before someone sees us." His usually polite and confident expression had been replaced by an angry, desperate look.

"She's not going anywhere!" I heard a husky voice say. A good handful of men stood just inside the theater doors. The heavy-handed man tightened his grip, but the men holding my legs let go.

"On your way, buddy. This is none of your business." The grip on my arms loosened.

"Oh really? Then why does it look like you're trying to take this young lady against her will?" the husky voice said.

"Again, I say it's none of your business. Now get lost!" one of Mark's friends said.

The husky-voiced man at the door laughed.

"I'm pretty sure you have no idea who I am," snarled another of Mark's friends—the tall, lean, and bald man who held me.

"I know who you are, and what you are. But do you know me?" said the husky voice.

"Does it look like I care, chump?"

"No, but you should."

"And why is that?" Acid dripped from his words.

"Because if you did know me, then you would have already guessed that there is no way you're leaving here with her," the husky voice drawled, and the man speaking narrowed his eyes. Then, without hesitation, he and his men charged my captors head on like a scene from Gladiator.

As the fight raged, time seemed to slow, frame by frame, like a flashing strobe light.

I used the seats to my advantage, kicking off them and falling back onto the men holding my arms. With great effort, I pulled free from them in the struggle and dashed for the doors behind me. I heard Mark yelling through the fight.

"I'm not done with you yet, Arri! I will get you when you least expect it! I promise!" As the last word left his mouth, I heard a loud, grunting exhale. Looking over my shoulder, I saw a few motionless bodies thudding to the floor, and five people standing in the middle of the aisle, staring at me. I sprinted from the theater. There was something definitely going on, but I wasn't going to stick around to find out. As I passed the ticket booth, I noticed Little Miss Flirt wasn't there. As I reached into my back pocket, I froze. My cell phone was gone. In its place was a small pink slip of paper.

There is no running from fate!

—N

My heart was lodged in my throat, and I gasped for air. Tears streaked my face. Glancing back, I saw a black Escalade following me. Taking off in a full run, I headed to the strip mall next to the theaters and hid behind the carts in Walgreens as the SUV slowed and crept by the front of the store. I couldn't see into the tinted windows, but a sinking feeling pooled in my stomach. After the SUV pulled away, I found a pay phone just outside the sliding glass doors and called my parents.

"Hello?" When I heard my dad's voice, my throat tightened.

"Hi, Dad?"

"Arri, honey, where are you? What's wrong?" Hearing my dad's frantic voice made it harder to speak.

"I… movies… Mark…" was all I could sputter out.

"Stay right there. I am on my way."

I nodded, unable to find words, and hung up the phone. As I turned to watch for my dad, I saw the black Escalade parked next to a nearby gas pump.

It seemed like forever, but when my dad finally pulled up and got out of the car, only ten minutes had passed. I ran and threw my arms around him. After I stopped trembling, he placed his hands on my shoulders, pulled me away, and looked in my eyes.

"Are you hurt?" he asked, stern but compassionate.

"No, I don't think so." I looked down and took a few shaky breaths to contain my delicate composure. Dad walked me to the passenger side, buckled me in, stared at the SUV, and nodded.

THREE

When we got home, Mom came running outside. She pulled me from the car and cradled me, wiping the tears from my cheeks. Dad was right on our heels as we entered the house.

"What happened?" Mom asked.

Looking between the two of them, I told them about Mark, his friends, and the fight that broke out. The people that walked in and saved me, the SUV that followed me to the store. As I recited the events of the evening, Mom was dumbfounded, and Dad's usually expressionless features were shadowed with hatred and anger.

"Oh honey," Mom said, smoothing my hair out of my face.

Dad paced the floor, then knelt before me.

"Did you see who else was there? Any faces or names?" he asked. He looked so frantic and angry. I thought back and nodded.

"Who?"

"Just two. Tomas and Drake, I think. They were friends of Mark's." At the mention of their names, Dad pounded his fist on the coffee table, breaking the table into shards of wood, and hoisted himself up. I jumped.

"Roger!" Mom's stern voice reverberated through the house. "Watch your temper."

Dad glared at the table, then back at me, then grabbed his jacket from the coat rack and left. Mom's voice cut through the silence.

"No worries, dear. He'll be back. He just needs to blow off some steam." With a forced breath, she stood and took me upstairs. I was still in shock, and I felt like I was watching myself from the outside looking in. I had no emotions, nothing. I felt empty, like a hollow shell of myself.

"Let's get you in the bath," Mom said, as she turned on the water, checking its temperature.

"No thanks, Mom. I just want to go to bed."

Mom didn't say anything. She just watched as I crawled into bed without changing my clothes or taking off my shoes. Clutching the stuffed animal I'd named Scratch, I pulled the covers over my shaking body and stared at the wall, praying for sleep.

When I woke the next morning, I felt tense and stiff. Noticing the time, I shouted, "Ten-thirty?"

I sprang up and rushed to the bathroom to get ready. I was officially one hour late for work. After taking a shower and fixing my hair, I tore out of the bathroom and skidded to a complete halt.

My mom's tall, slim silhouette shadowed the doorway. She had unintentionally posed, as though she were a runway model. Her red hair flowed over her shoulders and outlined her slender, elfin face.

"You let me sleep in!" I cried, as I scampered around my room looking for my clothes.

"I called Catherine this morning. I didn't think you would be up for working after what happened last night." My mom's expression showed concern.

All night I had been haunted by Mark's words and the note signed by the mysterious "N."

"Are you okay?" Her voice shook me from my thoughts. I hung my head and raked my hands through my unkempt hair before I finally broke down and accepted what happened. I still couldn't truly believe Mark did what he did. Maybe part of me hoped it was a dream.

"Why would Mark kidnap me?" My voice shook. I stared at my mom's worried eyes, and just like that, it hit me. "The flowers, Mark and his friends…" I said, sorting it out. "They're all connected. Mark was going to take me to see whoever sent the flowers." I looked up at Mom. Mom's expression was as shocked and deep in thought as I felt, but I barely managed a glimpse before she concealed her trepidation.

"What was Mark thinking? He knew a stunt like this would start a war," she said to herself, frowning just slightly. As soon as she saw me staring, she sucked in a deep breath and steadied herself.

"What stunt? What war?"

"Oh, sorry, dear. Look, we're going to handle this. You're safe now. Just never mind what I said. You need to concentrate on recovering from last night and leave everything else to your father and me."

"Leave *what* to you and Dad?"

"Nothing. Just you rest now."

"I'm so tired of you guys hiding things from me. Mark tried to kidnap me and all you can say is *nothing*. My life has been full of secrets, and quite frankly, I'm tired of it. Every other time something happens, you all flip out, but now you have nothing to say when I am nearly abducted."

I should have known it would only be ignored. I stood and paced the floor as Mom sat quietly, watching me.

"You've been bent on protecting me, deceiving me, and keeping me from anything that might hurt me. I wish you were bent on helping me understand things rather than sheltering me from them."

"Honey, I don't know what brought on this attitude, but it's not necessary…"

"Have you been listening?" I interrupted, completely taken aback, and without even the slightest hint of emotion, Mom shrugged. Frustrated, I threw my hands in the air.

I grabbed my purse and ran downstairs. The intensity of my anger scared me. I yanked my coat off the rack, and without looking back, I stormed out of the front door. I heard my mom faintly calling out behind me, asking where was I going. I didn't care. I was exhilarated by my final stand, even if my freedom was only going to last just a few moments. I turned the key to my car and nothing. Knowing my mom was just a few seconds behind me, I decided to try again, and this time, it tried to turn over. Finally, on the third try, the engine growled to life.

I didn't know where I was going, but I didn't get far before I saw my mom's car behind me. After the attack last night, I really should have thought this through a little better before I just took off. I mean, as far as I knew, Mark was still out there plotting and planning his revenge. I can't imagine his failure to capture me went well with his boss, if he had one, and here I was running around like I had no sense.

I pulled into the closest restaurant and went inside, knowing Mom would never follow me in and risk making a scene. After being seated next to the window, I could see her sitting in the car waiting for me. Her face was annoyed, but I didn't care. I had to admit, I did feel satisfied with my false sense of victory. I knew it wouldn't last long—I lived at home, after all, and unfortunately my parents still controlled a lot of things. I ate slowly, reading my book, and enjoyed every moment. I took small nibbles and made sure the experience lasted as long as possible. Two hours had passed before I finally gave in to the inevitable and drove home.

As I pulled into the driveway, Mom parked right behind me.

"What was the meaning of that?" my mother said in her most excited tone, which was still mostly calm. "You are under no circumstances to ever leave like that again! Am I clear?"

"Do you hear yourself, Mom? I'm nearly nineteen, and you're telling me I'm grounded. You're telling me, yet again, that I am a prisoner in my own home." I wasn't done, but she raised her hand to stop me. She closed her eyes like she needed to steady her temper.

"This…" She stopped and exhaled hard. "I'm sorry. You're right. We do need to give you more leeway." I could see that she was trying hard to sound at least half-sincere. I knew it was a false attempt at a promise, but we headed into the house nonetheless. At least we agreed to disagree for now.

We walked into the living room to find my father and a young man seated on the sofa—a colleague of my father's, judging by the conversation. They were talking business. When they saw us walk in, they stood. My dad held out his arm to me, as he introduced the man to me, then to my mom. The gentleman bowed to both of us.

"This is—"

"Erik." The gentleman finished Dad's words and waited for us to be seated before seating himself. His voice was smooth and arrogant. He had blond, shoulder-length hair and a gentleness to his face. My presence here was useless. I knew the routine. My parents and their guest would talk about obscure subjects like South America borders and power output in the Himalayas. Mom and Dad had a habit of talking over my head. I looked up just as Erik addressed Dad.

"I will be leading the watch in the northern territory to keep the rebels at bay. We can't afford the interruption and need to show everyone we can keep the peace. I highly doubt they will present a problem, but I want to be safe."

"Do you think you can handle it?" my dad replied.

"Of course, my lord," Erik said without hesitation.

"I have already sent a team down that way." Dad's stern and demanding voice gave no invitation for dispute. "They will meet up with you and your men tomorrow."

I looked over at Dad, puzzled. "Did he just say *my lord*?" I asked. That wasn't a phrase that came up in general conversation very often.

"Yes, dear." Dad never embellished or said more than he had to. Seeing that I had lost today's battle due to an unexpected guest, I conceded, knowing the fight will have to continue tomorrow.

"Well, it was a pleasure to meet you, Erik," I said. "I need to get going." I stood up to leave, and Erik, along with my dad, stood as I left. Offering a placating smile, I headed up to bed.

FOUR

That night, my dreams were a little weird. I dreamed I was in a small town, a place I had never been, but I still felt it had a sense of significance. Shortly after arriving, I was running for my life.

"How did you sleep, Arri? You look exhausted." Mom's voice floated from behind me when she entered the kitchen from the pantry as I sat down for breakfast.

"I didn't sleep at all." I told her about my dream, laughing.

"That's what you get when you read all those paranormal books. Do you think it meant anything?" My mom was a firm believer that all dreams had a meaning.

"No, just a weird dream that ruined a perfectly good night's sleep." I yawned and stretched my neck.

"Arri." My mom paused. "I want to remind you that we are having dinner with Catherine and her husband." Mom knew I hated to go out with my parents and their friends. It was bad enough I was constantly subjected to the company that bombarded our home, let alone having to go out and be tortured in public.

"Really? Do I have to?"

"Don't whine, dear. It's unbecoming of a lady. And yes, you have to go. I thought you liked Catherine and Phillip."

"I do." I scowled at her before finishing my last bite of French toast.

After work, and a long, lifeless dinner, we finally pulled into the driveway. Just as I was getting out of the car, I could see the shadow of a tall, broad figure in the night's shadows. But when I spun around to see who it was, it disappeared.

"Arri, dear, what's wrong?" Dad asked with concern.

"Nothing. I thought I saw someone, but..." I cut myself off. "Sorry, I'm just tired. My mind was playing tricks."

My parents exchanged wordless looks. The last few days had been more than stressful, so we finished the evening with some ice cream, and I went straight to my room.

I was getting changed for bed when I swore I saw another shadow out on the back lawn. This one was a little more distinguishable and didn't disappear quite as fast. I managed to take a second look before it was gone.

On Friday morning, I left my room with a book and sat on the back patio in the fall sun. It was getting a little chilly, and I loved the change in temperature. I was lost in the pages of my book when Dad came out and joined me. His brown hair was stylishly disheveled as usual. Dad was not a personable man; he always had an unmistakable and commanding presence everywhere he went. He never yelled, but when he got involved in my life, it scared me.

After what felt like a staring contest, I broke the silence.

"What's up?"

"Your mom and I are going to London to see an old friend. If there are any problems or anything out of the ordinary, call Catherine. She will be here if you need her."

My parents always traveled: Paris, Africa, Jamaica, and that was just in the last six months. I wished that I could go, too. My parents had traveled the globe and back again several times, always leaving me behind. It was like they lived this alternate life that I was not a part of. One trip they took, they went to Egypt, and Mom spoke about riding camels and the ruins of the Karnak Temple and the Valley of the Kings. I wish I had a life of unexpected voyages and taking risks. Instead, I went to work and came home.

After saying goodbye, they left immediately, leaving me alone, or at least an artificial version of alone, once more. I was never really by myself. Catherine would come over every few hours in the evening to check on me, which was fine, because I was still seeing those shadows and figures in the dark. As they randomly appeared and disappeared, I felt watched.

On Monday, I came home from work, and as usual when I was alone, the house was dark. Apart from the front window ajar, and the house feeling freezing, nothing was out of the ordinary. I paused in the doorway as the eerie feeling of the kidnapping still lingered. Mark had fooled and deceived me and my parents for months before he finally let his true colors show, and now with my parents gone, I was a bit apprehensive about being alone. What if the shadows I'd been seeing were him and his buddies toying with me before he broke in?

That night, I was startled awake. Someone was watching me. I sat up and saw a shadow flicker in the corner of the room. I screamed and switched on the light, but nothing was there.

Work was beginning to feel like a break from the terror I felt at night. But I wished my parents would come home.

The following night, I set the alarm like every night, and a few hours later, just like every other morning for the last four days, it was turned off yet again. I was deciding whether or not to call Catherine when I heard my parents drive back up.

A fresh sense of stress emanated from them as they walked through the door.

"The meeting went that well, huh?" I asked.

"Yes. Looks like our plans have been sped up a little." Dad looked a little pale and on edge as he went beneath the bar for a glass of maroon liquor. It was strange to see this side of him. I thought nothing could upset him, mainly because nothing ever had.

"Oh, don't mind him. What have you been up to?" Mom walked in behind him and poured herself a drink.

"Nothing, really. I picked up a new book on vampires and Celtic folklore." I loved to read about the unnatural. It was an escape from my mundane life.

"I don't know why you read all that nonsense. No wonder you have all those crazy dreams." My mother's voice was disapproving. She would have preferred me to expand my interests. "We need to find you a hobby. Obviously, you have too much time on your hands."

She gave me a simpering smirk, and the two of them headed off to their room to get unpacked as I wandered off to work. As usual, they didn't elaborate on their trip any more than to say that they were not too pleased with the outcome. Later that evening at dinner I told them about the shadows, and they brushed it off like it was nothing, but the looks they gave each other told me it was more.

That night, my parents took turns standing guard outside my door. Something must have happened while they were gone. Something was definitely wrong. It was just a matter of retrieving information. Life was too stressful now. I had gone from bored to paranoid in a matter of a few weeks. I guess that is why they say *be careful what you wish for*.

My weird dreams returned that night. This time, I was dying, and my throat stung as something warm burned its way down. I was twitching, trying to escape the torture, too weak to fight. I stopped breathing. The whole thing was like an embedded memory, but it felt so real, so scary. Finally, I panicked and tried to wake up. I gasped and clutched my blankets to my chest, relieved I was still tucked safely in bed. Lying back down, I was about to close my eyes when I heard my parents in the hallway.

"Are you sure Nicholas has sent them to spy on her?"

"Yes, Emily. She is almost nineteen. She has stopped growing, and her features are frozen in time. If there is a chance she is one of us, now is when she will show her true colors." As my father's voice rose and faded, I could hear that he was pacing outside my door…

"She *is* one of us." My mother again. "I can't lose her, Roger. I won't allow my little girl to be enslaved or…whatever else he would want her for. I won't allow him to have her." She was crying now.

"Her obstinacy and temper show she is changing." Dad steadied his nerves; I could feel the tension and stress seeping through the door. "Look, Emily," he went on, "I understand what you are feeling, but we already know what he wants for her. He wants to make sure that she poses no threat to his position of power. He knows that she is special and that she can put our world back in its place, and now we know he is after her."

There was a long pause. "Emily, do you remember what I told you when we first left him? When we held her in our arms, scared because we had nowhere else to run, and the footsteps behind us were getting closer? I told you I would never let anything happen to our little baby, even if I had to die for her. I promised you that she would be safe. Again, now, I am making that promise." My father's voice faded. "This can wait 'til morning. We need to contact her guardian now."

FIVE

I sat on my bed with a new science fiction novel in my hands. My eyes skimmed over the page but I couldn't concentrate on anything. All I could do was contemplate the weird things that were happening. My parents' nervousness was permeating the house; it filled the air like an ocean fog over rough terrain. What could they have possibly meant by *one of us*? Ideas and frivolous thoughts about them being aliens, mythical creatures, even FBI agents filled my head. The shadows were just people stalking them to find our Achilles' heel. But I knew my parents, and they may have traveled for business, but they were way too dull for any of that, which brought me back to my original question.

What is *one of us*?

Work wasn't making this week any easier on me. I dreaded work because of one particular credit union member. He was tall and sickly thin with ashen hair and a grimacing smile, like he was smelling a fart. He started coming to the branch about two weeks ago, right after the night with Mark. He wasn't rude or curt; he was just overly nosy and prying. Today was Friday, which meant payday and no breaks. The day so far had been packed. I felt like an ATM. "Account number? Withdrawal or deposit? Will that be everything? Have a nice day." As the day dragged on, my voice became monotone, like a drone.

"Hey, Arri, your boyfriend's back," Sheila said in a teasing sing song voice, leaning over the middle partition between our workstations. She was a quiet brunette with braces and a high ponytail. We'd worked together for the last year and she was as much as a homebody as I was. I glanced up.

My heart sank. Cold anger rose and my blood pressure skyrocketed. There he was, Mr. Inquisitive, the man I had hoped would give up on this game of twenty questions and not come in today, but I was out of luck. Carefully, I looked around for any excuse. I finished the transaction and sent my current member on his way, then grabbed the roll out of the receipt machine and ran to Catherine's office to hide. I closed the door behind me, not even checking to see if Catherine was there. I was too busy concentrating on my escape.

"Can I help you?" Behind me, Catherine sounded irritated as I peered through her office blinds.

"Oh! I'm sorry, Catherine." I spun around. Catherine had a large oak desk, on top of which sat a gold engraved nameplate: *Catherine White*. To me, at just five feet tall, the desk was huge. "I was trying to hide for a moment. D-do you m-mind?" I stammered.

"Trying to hide from whom?" She seemed intrigued. I figured she thought it was a guy I liked. I pointed to the second person in line and shivered.

"See that man there? He has been hounding me all week." I threw my hands in the air. "If I have to help him one more time, I just might hurt him. I swear he is intentionally trying to upset me, pushing every little button he can, and as soon as he thinks I'm getting even the slightest bit frustrated, he pushes even harder. It's ridiculous. I mean, I'm not saying I have the patience of Job, but I am generally a pretty patient person, and I am about to lose it." My temper was rising, and toward the end of my tantrum, I realized I was raising my voice, too.

"I would calm down unless you want him to hear you," Catherine said calmly and sat me down. I had been pacing as I talked, too, I realized. "You definitely are your mother's daughter! You would get excited about the price change of milk. I really wish you would have told me about him sooner, though." She sighed and grinned at me. "Is there anything specific he is asking for?"

I tried to think, but shrugged. Then it all hit me at once. I gasped.

"Are you okay?"

"Yeah," I said, meeting her slightly panicked stare. "It just dawned on me. The questions he was asking me were not to get me mad, they were to get information from me about the branch, the security systems, and schedules." I gasped again, as if I'd run out of oxygen during my exhale of information. "He was asking me when I worked, if I opened alone, and if we all arrived at different times!" I was yelling now. I shook my head again. "I can't believe I missed it. I feel like such an idiot. I had paid so much attention to the fact that he was annoying me. I didn't see the obvious." I covered my face with my hands.

I had worked for Catherine for almost three years and had never been promoted. I didn't have any intention of moving up, or in any other direction. Things were fine: Catherine was happy, I could count, and she always trusted me to open and close. Even though I didn't hold a managerial position, I still had all the codes and combinations to the vault, computers, and even the alarm system.

Catherine looked out of her office window to see if the man was still there, but he was long gone.

"Arri, go home." Her voice was stern.

She was talking to me, but clearly her thoughts were elsewhere. Catherine was practically shoving me out her office door.

"Oh, and be careful!" she yelled after me. She closed the door behind me.

"Emily! We have a problem." I heard through the door. "Either it is a coincidence or he's up to something." Catherine was silent for a minute. "I'm sending her home now."

I heard her hang up.

Catherine made sure that for the next few days I was not on the schedule. Mom and Catherine were up to something. Tired of all their games, I took it upon myself to go to work. I was fifteen minutes early when I called Catherine and told her I was there. My colleague Andrea was already there, reading the office manual, waiting for someone with a key to open. Andrea was just out of high school and still a drama queen, which went well with the other young, snobby girls. She had brown hair and brown eyes, stylish clothes, and clearly no issue with money. She only had to work because her parents thought it built character. But she was new and scared to death of the new computer system. She tried to hide it, but I'd seen it the moment we started training.

I knocked on her car window, startling her. The manual flew out of her hands as she gave out a small squeal.

"Are you ready?" I asked.

She grabbed her purse. We walked to the back door together: It was protocol to open and close in pairs, which never quite made sense to me. If we were going to be robbed, it was just as easy to rob two as it was to rob one. Especially two girls—not saying we were weak, just more vulnerable. The credit union wasn't even officially open for another hour, giving any robber more than enough time.

I unlocked the door, turned off the alarm, and relocked the door behind us. The morning routine was the same every time and kind of monotonous. After I turned on all the computers, opened the vault, and finally got out my drawer, I put us at our assigned teller stations. But today, someone was pressing their face up against the front window: a gentleman in a long trench coat, knocking. I swore I knew him from somewhere, as crazy as that sounded. His build and the light facial hair reminded me of someone. A sinking feeling settled in the pit of my stomach. Something was amiss.

The first rule of banking was never to let anyone in but your coworkers, so I pointed to my watch and held up my fingers to indicate that we opened at ten. But the man kept tapping on the window. I was smart enough not to approach the door, so I kept on with my work and tried to ignore him. I was in the middle of counting out my change when a soft knock came from the back door. Megan and Sally, two other tellers, stood at the door waving. Just as I headed toward them, I saw that the man in front had stopped tapping; he seemed to have vanished. I quickly hurried the girls in and watched each of them carefully. Megan came in behind Sally, and as she passed me, I saw a man emerge from behind my car out in the parking lot. Noticing me, he curved his mouth into an evil smile that gave me the cold creeps, and then, with a simple shake of his head, he disappeared.

As the girls and I counted and set up, the man reappeared at the front doors. This time he wasn't alone; two other men were with him. He signaled to the first, who gave him a curt nod then disappeared from sight. The second was given an order as well, and he too left, but quickly returned with a cell phone in hand.

I addressed the girls. "Hey guys, any chance one of you knows the man at the door? He seems pretty determined to come in."

The girls looked, shook their heads, and went back to their discussion, back to magazines and the hottest guy in Hollywood. Their shallow habit of judging people irritated me. They were so wrapped up in their conversation that they didn't notice the beating on the door getting louder. As I turned my attention to the front doors, the back door shook as the third guy pulled and tugged.

I hit the panic button under my desk.

The alarms screeched. The back door shattered. The men in the front pulled and banged the doors, setting off yet more alarms. The overhead lights went out, leaving the flashing alarm lights the only source of illumination. One second the men were there, and the next they were gone.

The girls, oblivious to the source of the alarms, screamed and ducked with their hands over their ears. I ordered them into the vault and followed the last girl in, locking the door behind us.

"What's the big idea?" Sally hit the vault door with her fist. "You realize we're locked in here, right?"

Sally had blonde hair to her elbows, a twenty-year-old Barbie who thought she was better than everyone else.

"Really?" I said. "Did you not see or hear the pounding on the doors? The shattering glass? Anything?"

A light thudding sounded on the other side of the door. No one heard it; they just looked at me like I was crazy.

"What are you talking about?" one of the girls said.

"Was it necessary to lock us in here because someone was hitting the door? I don't think he *meant* to break it." Megan's response was just as airheaded as she was. She was the epitome of a blond stereotype. "Now the vault door is locked, and, I would like to point out, we are on the wrong side!"

I rolled my eyes as the girls hit me with every possible question. I had no answers—at least none that any of them would understand.

In record time, the police came, and Catherine was there to let us out. The confusion on her face was a strange relief. I could hear the cops explain to Catherine that there was no one in the bank except for the ones in the vault. The money remained untouched, which confused the police. They did another thorough check and even viewed the video surveillance.

"Oh, excuse me, ma'am." A tall and thin police officer approached Catherine. "I was going through the security videos, and I did notice that there was a slight glitch in your camera system. It recorded four people entering before it went blank. I would have a technician look at it to eliminate any future problems."

Catherine nodded, then glanced over to me and gave me a slight hint of a smile.

After the police left, Catherine pulled me into her office to hear my side of the story. She had already called the other girls in, and now it was my turn. I was debating whether the girls really were that oblivious to the banging or if they'd heard it and just not been as scared as I was. Catherine was aware of every aspect of my life, and I was sure my mom had kept her updated about the shadows I had been seeing and the issue with Mark.

"So, care to tell me your side?" Catherine's curious tone was unnerving.

"Well, I would say that it was an attempted burglary, but the fact that we still have all our money would say otherwise." I chanced a glance at her then quickly returned my gaze to my fidgeting hands. The hem of my shirt had seen better days. I plucked at stray strings.

"Oh, I would have to agree with you. I don't think they were after the money. I think they were after something even more valuable." Catherine's voice was intrigued. My head shot up.

"Excuse me?"

For a moment, worry flashed on her face, but her expression swiftly changed from fear and concern to understanding, as if she had known something I had not.

"You said it yourself. They're not after money." She looked at me with interest.

"What are you trying to say, Catherine?" My mind instantly went to Mark, and I shivered.

"You have had quite a morning. Why don't you go home? I will see you first thing in the morning after the door's fixed."

"Are you kidding? After what just happened, you just want me to go home? No answers, no explanations, nothing? Just accept it and go?" I stared at her with my hands on my hips waiting for an answer, but Catherine was like a vault. She gave me a look that left no room for arguments.

Without another word, Catherine gestured toward the door and excused me such that I had no choice but to comply. I left her office feeling frustrated and annoyed. This wasn't over. I needed to know more. Like why was everything happening now, out of the blue, and if it was a coincidence that I was involved or if there was more going on. I went back to my station to put my drawer in the vault. I glanced behind me to see if Catherine was watching. She was. As I was leaving, I overheard Megan, Sally, and Andrea talking about me.

"She is so weird. I don't think he meant to break the door," Sally said, pointing a glare in my direction.

"Right? Like, you heard the police! The video showed nothing at all."

"Catherine's sent her home early a lot in the last few weeks," Megan mused.

"I think she's getting fired, and Catherine is only using her until she can fill her position," Andrea said. They all glared at me one last time.

With the girls' indifference to the attempted break-in and their animosity toward me, I felt alone. I was just stalling the inevitable of telling Mom about today, but I stopped on the way home and got one of my favorites, chicken and dumplings, for lunch, which made me feel a bit better. But I was still uneasy about what had happened. By the time I pulled into the driveway, Mom was on the porch waiting for me.

"Mom." I threw myself into her arms, with so many conflicting emotions I felt numb. I was scared it was one of Mark's stunts, confused why the money wasn't touched, and worried about what Catherine meant when she said the men wanted more than money. What does a bank with no safe deposit boxes have that is worth more than money?

"Catherine called me on my way home. Are you okay?" She sounded genuinely upset.

"I'm fine. I think." I pulled away and smoothed out my hair. "Nothing happened to me, just to the bank." I pulled my purse back up on my shoulder and tried to shake it off as Mom walked me into the house.

We sat in the living room and talked about why it took me so long to get home. After I calmed down, I told Mom everything that went on this morning: the man at the window, the broken door, and the girls thinking I was getting fired. In the back of my mind, I was still focused on the video surveillance. After we went over everything twice, Mom let me go quietly without hesitation.

Upstairs, I changed and grabbed a book to read for an escape from my own mind. I was trying to concentrate, but the lingering question kept repeating in my head: were they after me—and if so, why? I was saved from my own thoughts when Mom knocked on my door.

"Can I come in?"

"Sure," I said, knowing the previous conversation wasn't over. But to my surprise, I was wrong. Utterly wrong.

"Where is my little girl?" my mother said haltingly. "I miss her. You know, the little bubbly girl I once knew. She somehow has turned into a hermit who stays in her room and cuts everyone out of her life. There is more to life than burying yourself in a book, you know." She took a deep breath. "Is this about Mark?"

For a moment I was perplexed. "Yeah, well, that and everything that has happened in the last month. It's like a chapter out of a mystery novel. All the events that come together before the final reveal, but this time, there *is* no reveal."

Mom looked confused.

"I mean, the shadows I have been seeing, and the men at the door...that's a lot to be a coincidence. And they weren't there for the money. Not a penny was taken. They were after something else. But why did they leave without it?"

I looked at Mom, then lowered my eyes to the empty words in the book.

"Oh honey, I know it seems like everything is falling apart, and you are caught in the middle, but I promise, your dad and I are handling it. I know it's hard, but I need you to let it go."

I stared. She actually believed I would let it go and that was it. I chuckled.

Mom let out a little musical laugh. She took my hand.

"Let's go all girly. Get some ice cream, go shopping, and maybe catch a movie."

Before I had a chance to think, Mom kidnapped me for the day. She took me to the movies and dinner. We had our nails done and finished the night with the ice cream, as promised.

We stayed up all night catching up, and talking about all I had been going through. It had noticed that many of the conversations my parents hid behind closed doors or out of the room were much too far away for me to normally hear. Over the last several weeks, since Mark and his men attacked me, my hearing had become remarkable, and not just a little. Astronomically better. I could hear the scraping of silverware on dinner plates and conversations from the other couples five tables away, even the rough and course rasping of a paper clip grating over the fibers of a document seemed to be at normal volume. I felt strange like a side of me had woken up, or that something stirring inside me was bringing it to the surface. I thought of telling Mom about my new discovery, but the advantage of this was far too high to tell anyone.

SIX

Raindrops keep falling on my head…

I lay in bed and stared at the ceiling, my head ringing in protest to waking up. Ignoring the numbing headache, I thought back to our girls' night. It had been so long since Mom and I had fun that I'd forgotten what it felt like. The sugar consumption alone had been enough to bring down a horse. In the bathroom, dragging my heels a bit, I looked in the mirror and saw Medusa staring back at me. My long brown hair looked like it had been in a blender, and my dazed storm-gray eyes looked oddly out of place against my porcelain complexion and soft red lips. I stared at myself until I faded into a blur and all I saw was a Picasso of me.

I sighed, managed to tame the disaster, and headed downstairs for breakfast. As I turned the corner, I heard some mumbling from the kitchen. With each passing step, my parents' heated discussion grew clearer. I waited in the hall outside the kitchen to listen.

My mom sounded upset. "I don't think she's ready! She can't face him now. She may be strong and stubborn, but she is still a child. She wouldn't have a chance against him! Are you sure he wants her?" My mother's voice was a little shaky.

"We'll finish this conversation later. I need to talk to Alex now. But yes, he wants her." My father's voice, by contrast, was firm.

"Hi, Mom. What's for breakfast?" I said in a chipper voice that was completely contrary to how I felt. The tension in the kitchen was thick and suffocating. "Is everything okay?" Mom looked flustered.

"I'm fine, dear. How about pancakes?" Her voice was still iffy. This was a side of her I rarely saw.

"Sure, pancakes are fine."

Dad was already gone by the time I finished breakfast, and by the look and size of the briefcase he had been carrying, he would be home late. I was running a little late and got into my old, beat-up CRX. As I turned the key, she backfired in protest. A loud bang from the rear sent my heart jolting to my throat. I had been having trouble with the car for almost six months and desperately needed a new one. But I turned the key one more time and she started right up. I made it safely to work, only stalling once on the way.

I arrived at work and launched into my new tasks immediately. Sally, Megan, and Andrea were about five teller stations away, and it looked as though they were still angry with me and taking bets on how long it would be until I got fired. The rest of the branch had already forgotten about it, chatting about the new branch openings. The credit union updated the new postings every month, creating a lot of excitement. Everyone seemed a little more riled up than usual.

I logged on and pulled up the postings to see if there was anything unusual. Just a teller position in our branch and few listings in other states.

I stopped. A teller position, here? Because of my mom and Catherine, I usually knew the inner workings of the branch before anyone else. Were they letting me go? I knew these last few weeks had been a little different, but Catherine seemed to understand better than anyone. I scrolled down and glanced at the other positions. There was nothing out of the ordinary until I came across a posting for Richfield. I mulled it around for a moment. The name looked and sounded familiar, almost like I had seen it before. I clicked on the assistant manager position, just to see if there was a picture. The job would be available in three weeks. In the middle of the page, a photo of a small quiet town shone up at me. Something about the photo was uncanny, like déjà vu.

For the rest of the day, I would periodically glance at the picture. I had always wanted to move. I didn't like or dislike my simple life—well, the simple life I had until recently—but I had always hated this lifeless, desolate desert in which I unfortunately resided. So I wanted to move, more than anything.

That afternoon, Catherine called me to her office. As I crossed the foyer, every teller in the branch stared at me. My knees wobbled, and every breath became an effort. I had never been fired before, and with all the rumors, I was scared witless. When I got to the office, Catherine gestured to the chair nearest me and closed the door behind me. She sat down at her oversize desk. What was only a few seconds seemed like a lifetime. Her face was impassive as I waited for her verdict. She must have noticed my anxiety, because she smiled.

"Nervous? Out of all the times you have been in my office, have I ever reprimanded you?"

"No," I replied.

"Okay. Then relax. I was curious—how are you holding up in the loan department?"

I took a deep breath, let out a sigh of relief, and my heart resumed its regular pace.

"Fine, I guess. I haven't run into any snags yet. Why?"

"Well, as you might have heard, there is a teller position available in our branch."

"Yes, I saw. The consensus among the girls is that I'm going to be f—"

Catherine burst out laughing. I'd never heard her laugh before, not like that. It scared me at first. Her laugh was high-pitched, just like her voice, like chimes in perfect harmony. Startled, I looked around her office, and saw all the employees and members looking through Catherine's window. Catherine realized everyone was staring at her and quickly closed the blinds, sat back down, and faced me.

"Arri, my dear, I'd never fire you. I was going to offer you a new position, actually. Karen quit this morning. If I promote you, then your teller position will be open, won't it?"

I stared at her for a moment. "A promotion?"

"Yes, if you will accept it." She smiled, knowing well I would not turn it down.

"Yes. Yes. Yes!" I cried. My fear changed into excitement, and Catherine let out a small, enthusiastic laugh.

"I heard about the girls' bet. What do you say we have a little fun and make them sweat?"

I never took Catherine for the devious type, but I liked this side of her. It made her a little more likable. We walked out of her office. Andrea, Sally, and Megan were all watching me like hawks stalking their prey. I went over to my teller station and slowly placed my personal items in a box. Their eyes gleamed with satisfaction. I looked a little sad, trying my best to play it up. Halfway through cleaning out my station, Catherine stopped me and cleared her throat loud enough to get their attention.

"I have an announcement to make…"

The three girls exchanged a satisfied smirk.

"As you have seen," Catherine went on, "there is going to be a new teller position open. I am pleased to announce that it's Arri's. I have finally decided it was time to let her go…" She paused for a moment to catch her breath and let the girls simmer. They looked utterly triumphant. "…as a teller and promote her to loan officer." With that, Catherine hugged me and gave me a nameplate with my name italicized in delicate cursive. Normally, Catherine would never do draw attention to an individual teller like this. It *was* a little much, but I still couldn't help but throw the girls an *I told you so* look as I unpacked my things at my new desk.

Later, I could hear them gripe about how unfair it was to promote me after everything I had done, all the chaos I had caused in the last few weeks. Still, the day went by so fast. I hadn't looked at the clock 'til I noticed all the other tellers getting ready to leave. Catherine locked the door and announced closing as usual. The great thing about being a loan officer was that there was no cash drawer. If I needed to deal with cash, I took it to a teller, and they would deal with the transaction, leaving me cashless. The most time-consuming part of being a teller was counting my drawer at the end of the night; the rest was easy. Now I just grabbed my purse, logged off my computer, and left, beaming with gratitude all the way.

I was disappointed when I found out Andrea, the recent high school grad, was my leaving buddy. We were the last to depart, and as much as I didn't care for her, I wasn't going to let myself get all worked up. As I put the key in the lock, the air felt eerie and ghostly. Then Andrea gasped, and I spun around to see why.

Three men were walking out from behind my car. We froze.

Since we were almost robbed, Catherine had been fanatical about safety, so I carried my cell phone at all times. I reached into my pocket, hoping more than anything that they would just keep walking, and leave us alone, but I lost hope when they stopped and gave us a menacing grin. Their faces were perfect, handsome except for their crooked smiles. I hesitated mid-step, and my legs were twitching with the impulse to run, but I couldn't move. Andrea, meanwhile, screamed, then ran. One of the men darted after her with unnerving speed, but stopped in his tracks when another spoke up.

"Leave it. We're not here for her." His voice was raspy and deep. He lumbered toward me. I thought about running like Andrea, but two things were stopping me. One, my legs *still* wouldn't move, and two, the man admitted that they were here for me, which meant running would be a futile attempt. So I stood there, waiting for them to make their move. One was about fifteen feet from me when a low rumble came from behind me. I was still frozen in terror. My body gave a painful jolt, and all I wanted to do was just give up and cry. Even if I tried to move, my feet were planted and weren't going to take me anywhere.

I turned slightly, trying to see what was making that guttural noise. Without taking my eyes too far off my pursuers, I assumed it was more of them. I didn't have enough time to react. At my side, the shadow of an enormous dog grew along the pavement and stretched up the parking lot wall. I could swear my heartbeat tripled, hurting my chest. My knees were getting weak as I shook in fright.

The two men who stayed back were now advancing, flanking their friend. The man in front curled his lips again, his teeth shining in the light, and let out a growl. The two other men followed suit. Yet more growling came from behind me, as more wolf-like dogs surrounded us, all humming in unison, the throaty rumbling was so deep it sent vibrations through my body. I didn't know if the men and the dogs were on the same side, or if they were on opposing teams and I was caught in the middle.

Something cold and wet nudged my fingers. Two enormous dogs

stood beside me, crouched, bracing for an attack. I let out a scream as four more dogs advanced, enclosing us.

"Now wait a minute…" the leader of the men said. "We are not here to quarrel. We just came for the girl." I knew he wasn't talking to me, but there was no one else here except the dogs, and they didn't exactly speak. I looked around for more men I hadn't seen but it was just me and the dogs. The white dog to my left side barked, positioning himself between the men and me. The black dog to my right did the same, and the rest of the dogs made a low rumbling sound that was threatening enough to send a shiver up my spine.

Then the man in front leaped across the gap between us.

He was barely an inch away when a flash of black streaked in front of me and I stumbled back. Suddenly the two other men advanced as well, but three of the dogs surged at them and pinned them to the rough rocky pavement. The white dog next to me nudged me toward my car.

"I'll get you!" one of the men said as I got in my CRX. The car flared to life on the first turn of the ignition, like it knew I was in trouble. I had no time to play games and tore off at full speed.

As I turned the corner, I looked back. The fight seemed to be dissipating. Two lumps in the parking lot—the wingmen—laid motionless. Only one was still fighting. The black dog looked up at my car, as if making sure I was safe, but as it did, the remaining man, seeing an opening, jumped from under the dog and made his way to me. I was not about to take any chances. I gunned it, cutting people off, running stop signs and red lights. I was horrified to see that the man was running after a moving vehicle and somehow still gaining. I rammed the gas even harder, now flooring it, willing my old car not to give up, hoping it could go faster. The man seemed to slow, and then darted out from behind me taking a left onto another street. I wanted to look back again, but at this speed, I would have hit someone. I was a great driver, but I wasn't exactly prepping for the Indy 500. The ramp to the freeway was backed up, and I was not about to stop. If I did, the man would definitely get me. The exit was coming up fast. I had no choice: I had to use the shoulder. But at the end of the ramp, the freeway was backed up as well, for at least a few exits. I was stuck. There was nowhere for me to go. But I couldn't stop now. I passed a cop waiting in the traffic, and instantly I saw his lights behind me.

This can't get any worse.

There was no way out, whether I pulled over or not, and getting in trouble was better than losing my life. How I was going to explain what happened to my parents before the police hauled me off to jail? I passed the accident that seemed to be slowing traffic and moved over to use a lane instead of the shoulder. I was weaving in and out of the vehicles when the cop caught up beside me and signaled for me to pull over. He swerved to the side, closing the gap between us, signaling me once again—

—and then his car disappeared.

A loud crash split the air behind me, my rearview mirror reflecting with smoke and fire. Too scared to look back, I jammed the gas pedal harder. The faster I went, the longer it took to get home. I was three exits away, then two.

Something flung my car to the left. I slammed into the guard rail. The leader on the outside of my car had punched through and broke my driver's side window.

My car spun out of control, swerving in and out of lanes, hitting several vehicles as I tried to correct myself. The creepy man was almost within reaching distance when a streak of white flashed in front of my window. I raised my hands to block the shower of broken glass, but none came. Just growling. The white dog had fastened its jaws around the man's neck. I grabbed the steering wheel, gaining control. When I swerved, the white dog tore into the man, who yelled in pain. The man and the dog tumbled from side to side as they fought on the hood 'til finally the man lost his grip and let go. They fell from my car, hitting the concrete hard before rolling off onto the shoulder.

I wasn't going to stick around. After they disappeared, I seized control of my car, sped up, and finally, minutes later, made it home.

Stunned, I sat in the driveway for a second 'til I realized how unsafe that was and darted into the house.

I slammed the door behind me, backed up, and stared at it,

waiting for something else to happen. Something shuffled behind me, and I whipped around, ready to defend myself. It took me a moment to realize who it was: my mom and dad, staring at me, confused. With one look at my mom's face, I ran and threw my arms around her and closed my eyes. Finally, some relief. After a moment, she pulled away and asked what had happened. I was reluctant to let go, but she was insistent.

"Arri?" Dad said.

My eyes filled with tears and I fell to my knees and wept as my parents bombarded me with questions.

"What happened? Why are you shaking? Is everything okay?" Dad was relentless, maybe even getting frustrated with my silence as I sobbed.

"There… I was… Andrea… dogs… my car," I sputtered and mumbled.

My father had never been the most patient man. Mom, meanwhile, got me a soda from the fridge, then pulled me to the couch, sat patiently, and waited for me to steady myself.

"Arri!" Dad pounded his fists on the coffee table, earning a scowl from my mother. I tried to explain what was going on, but it all came out in gibberish. My parents stared at me.

"Arri, Arri, Arri. Slow down. You're not making any sense. What's this about dogs on the freeway? Let's slow it down and start again." Mom put her arm around me.

I mentally reviewed the events of the night, calming myself until I could finally talk about them: the men, the dogs, the fight. My head spun. As I finished, Dad, unusually huffy, stormed outside. When he came back in, he slammed the door, yelling into his cell phone.

"I don't care what happened." There was a long pause. "At least she's safe. For now." He flung his cell phone down on the tiled entryway, shattering it. Mom shot him a glare. "Roger, is that really necessary?"

"There… he… I…" He never finished, just threw up his hands and went upstairs.

"Where are you going?" Mom said.

"To make another call." He disappeared down the hall.

"What was that?" I asked.

Mom exhaled. "Nothing, dear."

"What was all that? Why would they be after me?" I stared at her in panic. "Oh crap, do you think the police are looking for me? How am I going to explain all this?" I shuddered. "This is bad."

"Arri stop!" Mom's sharp tone yanked me out of the panic. "Your dad and I will figure this out. Now, was there anything specific you can remember? Anything about the guys that seemed different?"

"He yelled 'I'll get you,' and when Andrea ran, one of them ran after her. And the other said they weren't here for her and to keep their eyes on the job. Does that help? What do you think he wanted? Why me?"

My mother's face fell, her concern warped to anger. "I don't know, dear. Maybe they wanted you because they thought you had codes or keys to the vault. The most important thing is you're okay." Her words sounded sincere, but I felt her guilt.

"Oh Mom, what am I going to do? I'll need to tell the police *something*. That cop chased me forever. He probably called it in to the dispatch." My stomach turned at the thought.

"You'll tell them nothing." Mom's lip twitched as she ran her hands through my perfect hair. "I don't know what they wanted, but I'm sure your dad and the District will fix it."

We sat in silence for a moment while Mom thought. Then she finally broke the stillness.

"Well, why don't you go upstairs and wash the makeup off your cheeks and I'll get dinner ready?" She kissed me on the forehead. I rose to leave just as the phone rang.

"Hello?" Mom had answered the phone in the kitchen. "Arri?"

"Yes, Mom?" I was already halfway up the stairs.

"The phone is for you. It's Catherine."

I came back down and picked up the receiver in the living room. "He—"

Before I could finish, Catherine's voice rushed from the speaker. "Arri." She sounded panicked. "Are you okay? Andrea called and told me about the incident. I went back to the bank, but when I got there, there was no sign of anything except that Andrea's car was missing. I was hoping you got away. But who took her car? You know what?" She had barely taken a breath. "I'm coming over and then, we'll talk." Before I had a chance to put a word in otherwise, Catherine had already hung up.

"Mom?" I yelled.

"No need to yell. I'm standing right here." Mom magically appeared at my side.

"Catherine is on her way over. Sorry, but I couldn't stop her."

"That's all right, dear. Don't worry about Catherine. I'll take care of her."

When I reached the top of the stairs, Dad came running out of his home office. Seeing me, he stopped. He cupped my face with his hand, and a tinge of concern hardened his eyes.

"Arri," he whispered, much like a faint sigh escaping his lips. He opened his mouth, shook his head, and without another word, kissed me on the forehead and rushed downstairs. Outside, his car started and the screech of tires shrieked down the street.

A few minutes later, I stepped out of the shower and into my favorite pair of yoga pants and a small tank top. The smell of dinner wafted through my open door.

As I entered the dining room, I heard Mom and Catherine talking.

"Emily, I don't think it's safe here anymore. No matter how normal we try to make her life seem she's smart and knows that something is up. They've obviously found her. I think we need to get her out of here." My mom seemed to want to interrupt, but Catherine rushed on. "At least 'til we figure things out. We know Nicholas is after her. You know what he is capable of, and how far he is willing to go. He already compromised Mark!" Her voice was downright pleading.

I froze. This was the second time I'd heard the name Nicholas. Who was he? Why was he after me? I paused to listen, not revealing I was there.

"I'm not sending her anywhere," Mom said. "If they found her here, it is only a matter of time before they find her somewhere else. Arri is my daughter first, and only when I know she is safe can she be whatever it is you think she is destined for." Mom was not happy with Catherine's request, and it showed in her voice.

"What if we sent her to Jessie in London? He's a prominent figure in the District. We can keep Nicholas's men occupied here, for at least a little while. I fear she'll get caught unless we do something, Emily. Nicholas's men already know where she works, lives, even her favorite bookstore. The best we can do is get her to where she will be safe. This isn't about us, Emily. It's about what's best for her."

"Yes, I know, Catherine. But Jessie?"

"Why not him?" Catherine said curtly.

"Well, do I really want to trust him with… her?"

"Emily, please. I am begging you."

Catherine's plea lingered, unanswered. Unable to resist the siren song of food, I finally entered in the kitchen and went straight to the stove to grab a plate and scoop my food.

"Hi Catherine," I said, my voice thick.

"Arri!" Catherine squealed. "How are you feeling?" She flew from her chair and took me in her arms then pushed me back out to assess the damages. "You look tired."

She wasn't wrong. "I'm okay now, now that I have calmed down."

This was so surreal. As we ate, there were no further conversations about Jessie, London, Nicholas, or the evening's events—at least in my presence. After I left the kitchen, my mom and Catherine were already devising a plan to get me to London.

But I had the upper hand. I had information, and they had no idea.

SEVEN

With the events of that fateful night still fresh in my head, and the thought that there was someone after me, my dreams were more freakish than usual.

In my dream, I was running away from three men, toward a mansion. The men's faces were familiar, like a painted doll's faces with no creases or flaws. Their teeth were straight and white, making their masks complete. When I got to the mansion entrance, just as I could feel the door handle in my fingertips, one of the men caught the back of my shirt, tripping me and pulling me to the ground. I tried to get up, but couldn't. My fighting was useless against his brute strength. The man had pinned me down, and his evil grin turned into a wicked snarl. There was a frightening look of excitement in his gleaming eyes. I could hear the other men laughing and bawling with encouragement. They paced back and forth like hungry wolves waiting for the hunt. Then, when my captor leaned in toward me, I felt his warm, erratic breath drift across my neck. My heart pounded, and chills ran down my spine. His lips parted, and his teeth grazed my skin. The pressure on my neck increased. Right when I thought his teeth were going to sink into my flesh, the mansion door flew open. All the men backed away and tried to drag me along with them. From behind the mansion door, a hand grabbed me. There was a tug-of-war until finally the men were overpowered and released me.

The stranger pulled me into his arms and saved me from the men. With my heart relieved, it was strangely comfortable to be in his warm embrace. "I can't hold them off for long. Why are they after you?" His voice was seductive, refined, like velvet to my ears. I might have melted into his alluringly irresistible grip, but his question held me at bay. My mind was blank. *I have nothing to offer anyone.*

Suddenly, my alarm sounded with a deafening blare of music, and I was freed from my own nightmare. The clock showed 6:00 a.m., and the sun was just rising over the mountains. Lying in bed, I pondered the dream and the chase from last night. There was no way I was going to return to the place I was attacked, barely escaping with my life. My car was destroyed. I couldn't explain what happened, and even if I did, no one would believe me.

After getting dressed, I went downstairs for breakfast. When I entered the kitchen my mom was in her usual position: as always, she was on the phone. When she saw me, her voice suddenly changed to an officious tone.

"I understand, but I still don't think she's ready." There was a long pause, and her demeanor and expression changed. "Are you sure?" There was another pause. This time shorter. "I'll see what I can do." She hung up and then looked at me with a sullen face.

As my mother placed my food in front of me, I asked, "What's going on?"

Clearly seeing my concern, my parents exchanged a brief, uneasy glance. Initially, I didn't see my dad sitting across from me. I must have been preoccupied with my mom and overlooked him. After last night, I figured my dad would have been gone longer.

"Oh nothing, dear, just District stuff." She pasted on a smile, but there was a burden behind her eyes.

"Well, you made the front page of the newspaper," Dad's amusement was apparent in his voice. He carefully threw the paper in front of me with a headline that read *High-speed Pursuit Ends with Police Officer's Death.* Under the headline was a picture of the charred and mangled police car on the freeway. The flipped and torn vehicle was gut-wrenching. *That could have been me.* I read the caption beneath the photo.

At 6:18 p.m. on October 4th, a car chase transpired as a woman in a late model CRX was clocked at ninety miles per hour on the shoulder on the 215 freeway between Tropicana and Russell. Officer

Law Concade engaged in the high-speed pursuit and lost control, officials say, after the CRX allegedly swerved, resulting in a fatal, fiery crash for the officer. The unidentified woman is still at large. Police are seeking public help. If you have any information on the whereabouts of this woman, please contact the police immediately.

"This is bad, right? How am I supposed to go to work now? It's obvious. It was me! One look at my car and all the damage and it would be like me flagging down the police at every turn." I looked at my parents in horror.

"Don't worry; we pulled your car into the garage this morning so nobody will suspect you. You'll just have to take my car in the meantime." Mom's voice was as balanced and logical as mine was panicked.

"Mom, I can't go back there, that's crazy."

"Yes, honey, but if you don't, it will look even more suspicious. The District has taken care of the police, but you still need to go. Act like nothing happened."

"Are you kidding me? I almost died. A man chases me at ninety miles per hour on foot, and you think I should go back to the scene of the crime? How does that make any sense?"

Silence. Finally, my dad rose from his chair. "Your mother's right. You go back to work and let the two of us worry about whom and what they wanted." With that, he exited the kitchen, leaving no room for argument.

After breakfast, I called Catherine immediately.

"Hi, Catherine? Do you think you can find someone to cover my shift? I'm not ready to come back yet." I was hoping she would magically be on my side. I stilled, waiting for her response.

"No, dear I'm sorry. I would have to agree with your parents on this one."

Scowling at the phone, I hung up, slamming the phone down on the side table. I went into the garage to view the full extent of the damage. I looked over the bent and tangled metal. The actual handprint of my attacker was indented in the roof. The shattered window stirred the dread in my stomach. Broken glass peppered the seats and the floor. My dad would undoubtedly use this to convince me to get a new car. I walked back in the house just as he was walking out. My dad looked at me with loving eyes, then looked to my car. The regret and sorrow I saw in him last night returned. I smiled and thanked him again, and we went our separate ways.

After giving into my parents' insistence that it would look too suspicious not to go back to work, I borrowed my mom's extra car for the time being. As I drove to work, my thoughts kept returning to the conversation between Mom and Catherine the night before. They were willing to ship me off, as they put it, without regard to my input. I drove in silence, glancing in my rearview mirror more often than needed, and gripping the steering wheel like it was my last lifeline, until at last, I slipped into the parking lot of the branch. After parking, I sat there for a moment as my heart raced and pounded in my ears. The fear practically consumed me. With caution and great effort, I got out of the car and darted to the back door.

When I entered the branch, there was a nervous buzz about the place, as all the employees talked and gossiped, each one giving their interpretation of what might have happened last night, and who the men were. The moment they noticed me, they were instantly quiet. I could have heard a pin drop as everyone watched me with each meticulous step I took toward Catherine's office. Andrea ran up to me.

"Sorry, Arri. I'm not sure what came over me. I ran as fast as I could and didn't stop until I was several blocks away. I called Catherine from a pay phone and told her you were in trouble. Arri, I'm so sorry." When she finally stopped, she was panting. She sounded truly repentant.

"Well, it definitely was an exciting evening," I said, trying to make light of the conversation and not giving into suspicion. I smiled and gave Andrea a hug, telling her it was okay. I really wasn't angry with her. I would have done the same thing if my legs had moved. As I walked away, she called after me.

"How did you get away? What did they want?" I closed my eyes and kept on walking and acted like I hadn't heard anything.

When I finally came to Catherine's office, she opened her door, and without a word waved me in. I sat down at her desk and waited impatiently. She closed the door and gave me with a concerned look.

"How are you?"

"I'm fairish, I guess. I don't understand what I'm doing here, though."

"Yes, I know, but it was necess—" Her words were cut short when there was a knock on the door.

The door slowly opened. Courtney poked her head in, her red hair pinned up nicely in a bun. She took in Catherine and me talking and grimaced.

"Sorry to interrupt, but there is a man by the name of Colton here to see you?"

"Yes, thank you, Courtney." Catherine frowned as the door clicked shut. "It must be my ten o'clock interview." Her words were quiet and to herself while she fiddled with a few papers on her desk.

"Oh, Catherine," I said. "When you have a moment, I would like to talk to you about a position in Utah."

Catherine turned around, raised one perfect pencil-thin eyebrow, and beamed with interest. "Yes, what about it?" She couldn't hide her curiosity.

"Well..." I bit my bottom lip and twisted my hands together in my lap. "With all the trouble going on here I thought it would be better if I left. Maybe a change of pace?"

"You know, it might be a good idea."

"Yeah, well, with what happened last night, I need to get out of here." *Hopefully, I'll get the position, and maybe if I leave here I won't have to go to London.*

"Arri, I have absolutely no question you will get the position."

I have been through enough in the last few days to occupy a therapist for years. I'd thought about it throughout the day, and I was certain this is what I wanted to do. I had always hated it here and had been dying to get out of Las Vegas for as long as I could remember, and with everything that had happened, now would be a perfect time.

I was pretty confident, as usual, until I had to face my parents. After a full day of nerve-racking stress, I met my parents at Tony's Bar and Grill. I was fidgety and unsure how I was going to do this. I mustered up the courage that hit me before, and I entered the restaurant with a new found self-confidence. Mom and Dad were already seated and ordered some appetizers and drinks. I sat down next to them, and to my surprise, they were in a fantastic mood. Dad had even turned off his cell phone. Before I knew it, dinner was winding down.

"Arri? You have been awfully quiet. Is there something on your mind?" my dad asked. "What are you thinking?" My parents knew me better than I did. As my mom would say, I wore my emotions on my sleeve. I laughed nervously as I exhaled.

"Do you think you could keep an open mind?" I said, not sounding too confident.

"Sure, hon," Dad said, as he looked at me curiously and skeptically, and my mom nodded. This was it. This was my chance to tell them I was applying for the job and if all went well, moving. No pressure, I just needed to do it in the right way.

"Well," Mom said, "what exactly did you have in mind?" They exchanged looks and focused their attention back on me.

"I was thinking of taking a new position at work." I stopped it there, waiting for their reaction. It dawned on me that my mom was the CEO of the credit union, and if she didn't approve, she could smash my hopes in just seconds.

"And what position is this?" she asked. "Weren't you were just promoted?"

"It's a new assistant manager position. The only thing is…it opens in three weeks." I bit my lip, cringing.

"Arri, I don't know of any assistant manager positions opening here," my mother remarked.

"Well," I paused. "It's in Utah." I held my breath and waited for the rain to come. I had expected them to put up a fight.

After a long tormenting moment, I hung my head and accepted my defeat.

"Arri, why are you so upset?" My dad's voice was soft and sympathetic.

"I don't know." I faltered for a moment before adding, "Please, I am begging you to at least consider the possibilities this could have for me." I gave them a half-smile.

Dad signaled the waiter, and we left the restaurant without another word.

I could sense that he was still pondering our discussion. It wasn't his usual silence, but his casualness and the distant look on his face was what gave it away. My mom had already logged it away and didn't think about it again. When we approached the cars, Dad placed his hand on my shoulder and gave it a small squeeze.

"Emily," he called, "I'll drive Arri home. I don't like her being alone." He gave me a wink and opened the driver's side door.

Mom looked at Dad suspiciously, like she didn't trust him. He looked like he had something to get off his chest. We were on our way out of the parking lot when he directed me to go left. He gave a few more directions, and we ended up in the Target parking lot.

"Uh, Dad?" I asked. "What are we doing here?"

He didn't say anything as he got out, traded places with me, and raced off. As we drove, Dad spoke, but never made eye contact. He merely swerved in and out of traffic like a NASCAR pro.

"How important is this position to you?" he asked. There was no emotion in his voice.

"Extremely important, Dad. I was almost killed the other night. I don't know if you realize I am nearly nineteen, and in all fairness, I think you and Mom are way too protective. But with everything going on, even *you* can't protect me. It's getting to the point where I feel like a prisoner in my own home." I rubbed my face. "Dad, the man that ruined my car is not going to give up. Why did he attack me? And let's not even mention the dogs. I mean, really?" I paused to look at my dad, and his eyes showed nothing. "That's not all. I can see and hear the fear and worry the two of you carry around with you. I can feel it too. Literally! I know there is more going on than either of you are telling me." I exhaled. Finally, I was able to talk, and not be ignored. Dad looked at me and smiled.

"You know, in this case, you're right and quite perceptive. Arri, there is something you have to know. Your mother and I feel extremely guilty. We thought it was best to protect you from our way of life, but regardless of our efforts, it's caught up with you."

"What are you talking about?"

Dad adjusted his seat and faced me. "Arri, there's a lot you don't know."

"Like what?"

"Arri, you are a part of something big, and these attacks are a result of Emily and me not telling you. We aren't exactly your average Joes. We are very different from other people. We—"

I interrupted. "Will the attacks ever stop?"

"No, I'm sorry." His expression fell, and I could feel the sadness in his heart. "I know your mom will want to send you somewhere else, but I will be on your side. I have seen you change right in front of my eyes, and I see great potential in you. You are stronger than we ever could have expected, both mentally and physically. You may even be the key we have all been hoping for." He paused for a moment, deciding whether or not to tell me what he was thinking. "Your mother and I are very different, and I think you are too."

He started the car, and we drove home in unbroken silence.

"Like what world would this be?" I asked at last.

Dad laughed slightly.

"It means…" he struggled with his words. "It means you are part of an elite society." He winked.

This was like the Twilight Zone. Like my parents were secret operatives of the CIA, and I got caught in the middle. I wanted to know more.

I was sad to see the ride ending as we pulled in our drive. Dad and I had never been able to talk so freely.

"Remember, not a word," he whispered.

My mom came out immediately and gave my dad an angry glance. Putting her arm around me, she asked me where we went.

"To get some ice cream." I said, in a deceptive voice.

As night fell, I went to bed, closed my eyes, and quickly fell asleep.

I was in the middle of a large grassy area waiting for someone.

When a few men came out from the woods, they were laughing.

"Is that it? Just that one little girl? This will be a snap."

Staring at them, I felt no fear, anxiety, or worry, just the anticipation of getting it over with. The men start advancing, and just as they reach me…

I was jarred awake when my alarm woke me up. My parents were already in the kitchen when I came downstairs.

"I still think we should let her go." Dad's voice was low and gruff.

"No," Mom hissed.

"Come on, Em, we can't keep her here forever. You are only postponing the inevitable. She'll be nineteen in a few days, not eight."

"Yeah, but she is not like others her age. She is in far more danger than the average nineteen-year-old," she spat.

"All the more reason for us to let her go. We can give her a head start by leading the hunters off her trail. It is the last thing they would expect."

"Rog, I can't let my little girl go. She needs protection."

"Yeah, but who better than her guardian?"

"Me, that's who." Mom's voice was angry and cold.

"Nicholas is not stupid. He would not expect her to leave without us. This is the perfect opportunity, Em. We need to think about her and not our selfishness. It would be easier for her guardian to protect her while we find out how to stop this. Besides, she knows something's up. We can't keep pretending nothing is wrong. She will be the one to pay the price."

"Oh really, Roger?"

"Yes, really. Did you have a better plan? You know she is stronger than you give her credit for. Just think about it."

"Were you talking about me?" I entered the kitchen and grabbed a bowl and a box of cereal. I sat down and poured my breakfast.

"You are in a good mood," Mom said, as she flashed a skeptical look at my dad. "Besides, what makes you think we were talking about you?"

"I heard the two of you chatting."

"Honey, I think you are hearing things. We were just sitting here waiting for you," Mom said. Dad smirked and then winked at me.

“Well, I had better get going if I am going to make my meeting,” Mom said. “Do you need a ride to work, Arri?”

“No thank you, I’m good.”

Mom scowled and mumbled something incoherent to Dad, then left the room. He elevated his brows and chuckled before he stood to leave for work.

“Dad?” I asked after him.

“Yes, dear?”

“Thank you.”

“For what?”

“Supporting me.” I smiled, and Dad flashed me a suspicious looking grin before leaving.

EIGHT

It had been two days since I brought up the assistant manager position and one day since my parents' awkward conversation in the kitchen. The air between my parents was beyond tense. As I rounded the corner of the kitchen, I was surprised to see that my dad was the only one home.

"Arri?" Dad asked. "I..." His expression was doubtful. "How did you know I supported you yesterday?"

I bit my bottom lip, thinking.

"Are you going to tell me?"

"Yes, sorry." I tensed, just hoping Dad would understand. Seeing Mom was not there, I continued.

"I heard the two of you arguing over me going away. You said, 'who better than her guardian.'" At his surprised expression, I gave him a weak smile. "Do you have to work today?"

"Yes, why?" Dad looked at me curiously.

"Well, do you think you can call in, and you and I could go out?"

"Sure. I'll see what I can do." He took out his cell phone and made a call that he wrapped up quickly.

Smiling, Dad opened the front door and held it for me. "So, where to?"

"How about Egg Works? It's close and serves breakfast."

A quick nod was his answer. As we drove to the nearby restaurant, the ride was relatively quiet. Once we arrived, as usual, Dad asked that we are seated away from everyone else. He seemed tense.

"Dad?"

"Yes, dear?" He was busy surveying our surroundings. Another fun little surprise I noticed about myself was not as easy to pin down. It was like feeling emotions that weren't mine. Right now, the ones I was feeling… were his. Although his physical demeanor was nonchalant, a whirlwind of emotions exploded under the surface. The changes were as erratic as a stormy ocean. With a small sigh, I looked up, and Dad turned his attention to me, his gaze shadowed with curiosity. The tension I had felt had melted away, and now he was simply worried.

This was too confusing. I really was able to feel what he was feeling.

"Dad? When you said I was different, what exactly did you mean?"

After what felt like a lifetime, he answered. "That's a hard question."

"Yes, but it's an important one."

"Why do you ask?" he sat back in his chair and placed his hands in his lap, trying to look relaxed.

"Well, over the course of a several weeks I've noticed a few things, and not just the odd chases and shadows."

"Let's do this: you tell me what you've noticed, and we'll go from there."

I felt like I was on a Ferris wheel and dad and I were just going in circles. I didn't want to tell him in case he thought I was crazy, and he didn't want to reveal more than he thought I already knew. I decided to cave and go first.

"Nothing too spectacular, but…I guess I sort of heard you and Mom yesterday when you told her you thought I should go." I wanted some sort of sign that indicated I was on the right track—and I sensed my father's hesitation.

Despite my excitement—*I was right*—I had to choose my words wisely.

"Go ahead," Dad said at last.

"Well, this isn't easy for me." I dug deep for the part of me that said this was a good idea.

"Why don't you go ahead and tell me whatever it is you wanted to tell me?" He held up his hands in surrender. "No judgments, I promise."

"Thanks, Dad." I absently rubbed my legs. "I noticed it a few weeks ago. It was small but sudden." I paused. "It was most noticeable when I heard Catherine and Mom talking about sending me to London while I was in the far hall." My voice faltered a bit. I was still hurt. I couldn't believe that my mom and Catherine were plotting and planning my life without so much as taking what I wanted into account. It was like I was a canine rather than a daughter, being told to go, sit, and heel. With a deep, shaky breath, I continued. "Did I hear that right?"

My father gave a shallow nod. Hearing the strain in my voice, the tips of his mouth turned down to a tender frown. I expected to get scolded for listening in on their conversations, and figured my eavesdropping days were over, but instead, he felt proud of me. Even though he physically showed no reactions, I could sense it.

"Then there is all the whispering around the credit union that Catherine didn't expect me to hear." No reaction at all from Dad. "Do I sound silly?"

"No, dear. Is it a possibility you are exaggerating it slightly? Anyone can hear from an adjacent hall?" It sounded more like a challenge than doubt.

I raised my eyebrows at him and smirked. "But it's more than that. It's like I can hear from far away rather than just the other hall, and almost like I can zero in on certain conversations rather than the crowd as a whole. For instance, the couple on the other side of the diner, next to the kitchen, are arguing about paint colors to paint the guest room. She wants it pastel blue with roses and he wants it yellow with bluebonnets, his mother's favorite."

Dad laughed and nodded with satisfaction. "Have you told anyone else?" Now he looked a little nervous and his emotions confirmed it.

"No."

"Good," he said, grinning gently.

I was relieved to hear that Dad understood me. Through my own haphazard emotional turmoil, his were just as erratic as mine. It was like a spinning pinwheel, and the constant changes were making me nauseated. When I initially told dad about my eavesdropping, I felt fear, worry, and apprehension, but now I felt pride and a small sense of relief. It was like every time I answered, I got a different feeling in response. His emotions were telling, but what did they mean?

"Well," Dad said, interrupting my thoughts. "It looks like you have been doing just fine. You are coming along nicely. I figured it was only a matter of time. I can see you'll fit into our world very well." He had the typical *proud Dad* look on his face.

"Coming along nicely? Fit in just fine?" What were you expecting, for me to turn into a Jedi?" Dad scowled at me playfully. "In all seriousness, when you say *different*...exactly how different are we?" The words came out and Dad drummed his fingers on the table as he thought about what to say.

"Can I take your order?" A waitress by the name of Amber came up to the table with her order pad in place.

"Yes, the sausage skillet with seasoned potatoes and a Coke for me." I looked up at my dad who was still staring at me. "And I guess just a coffee for him."

Amber nodded and left stopping at another table.

"Dad? Earth to Dad!"

My dad's composure faltered. Though I couldn't see what he was feeling, I could feel it. He was indecisive. Finally, he broke the silence.

"I must be honest. I am having a hard time deciding how much I can tell you. You need to understand—it's not because I can't tell you. It's simply that I fear the more you know, the more danger you will be in. Giving you too much information is just as dangerous as not giving you enough. Your mom and I were hoping if you knew nothing, you would be safe. But I now know this is not the case."

"But you *need* to tell me something. I mean, people are chasing me. The bank has been vandalized and you guys are talking about something called the District."

"Yes, well, there's more to you than you think. Your being chased because we are different. I made a very risky decision a long time ago, as a result, you have become a target, but we will protect you. In time, you'll understand it all, but the District is already on it. And your mom and I won't stop until we know you're safe."

"Who is the District and how are they going to help me? Dad, you said so yourself, these attacks won't stop. They already know where I am. I'm not going to lie. I'm a little scared. I am not prepared for this.

Dad ran his hand through his untidy hair. "I am truly sorry you have been put in this situation. I will help you the best I can. I can't tell you much, but I can tell you about the District."

"All right, here we go. We have a sausage skillet with seasoned potatoes and a Coke for the young lady, and a nice hot coffee for the gentleman." Amber, our waitress, interrupted as she set my plate down in front of me then placed a mug in front of my dad and filled it to the brim. Before leaving, she smiled down at me then gave my dad an appreciative once over. "Is there anything else I can get for you?" she directed the question to my dad.

"No thank you, Amber, I think we're fine." My dad said, not looking up at the waitress. With a slight frown, Amber left, and Dad waited for me to show him I was ready, so I nodded. Digging into my breakfast, I listened.

"The District is much like the secret service. It was established to safeguard and shield other people from our differences. Only they are not limited by boundaries. They work alongside us every day, but you don't see them. They help keep the peace, so to speak."

When dad didn't expand beyond that, I threw my hands up in the air.

"Really, that's it? Is that all you're going to tell me?"

My dad grimaced and nodded, then took a sip of his coffee and checked his watch. By this time, I had already made a pretty big dent in my food. My stomach was full, but I there was no real answer. Just another riddle.

"Come on, let's go."

After paying for our meal, Dad and I left. I felt just as lost as before breakfast started. If I had only paid attention earlier and not been so clueless, I would have seen that my life was not so boring after all.

NINE

The next day, I felt confident. Just before lunch, I had told Catherine I was applying for the position. At the end of my shift, I logged off and clocked out as usual. I was just leaving when Catherine pulled me into her office. After I sat down, Catherine made me wait while she finished signing some papers. My stomach was in knots, and my insides cringed just waiting for the shoe to drop.

"So Arri." Her voice was its usual high-pitched chipper tone. "I was talking with your mother today while we were having lunch. You told her you were applying today." I didn't know whether she was stating a fact or asking a question.

"Yes," I answered, my voice unsteady. "It's quite a drastic move, but I'm hopeful. Dad seems to be okay with it." I left Mom out on purpose. She did not share my same enthusiasm about me moving even as far as next door, let alone three hundred miles away.

Catherine's face went from stern to gentle when she saw my distress. She had always tried to keep business as business and friendship as friendship, but this was skirting the line between them. It was mixing the business side of taking a job and the emotional side of dealing with friendly advice from someone that you had known for a long time. Catherine took my hands from across her desk and looked straight into my eyes. Her voice was kind and steady.

"As a friend, I can't tell you what to do, but Emily and I had a good talk today, and after heavy persuasion on my side, we've taken the opportunity of submitting a personal recommendation from the both of us." She paused and looked at me for a response.

"And?" I asked, impatiently.

"You have been offered the position. If you accept it, call Mary"—she pushed a piece of paper toward me—"the office manager, and you will have two weeks to move. If not, you may decline. No pressure either way."

Her expression was unusually upbeat as she waited for my reaction. I was stunned. I was not expecting this when she called me in her office. When I didn't immediately react, Catherine asked if everything was okay.

"Yes, I'm just surprised." I breathed steady and slow, smiling but was otherwise speechless. "So I have two weeks?" I said after another short while, a little less shocked and a little more like a screech.

"Yes, I know it's sudden, but what do you think?"

"Well, I think I'll take it!" I let out an excited squeal.

I had considered myself someone who never really took chances, but now, I was going for it. It scared me to think I had to move away not only to gain my independence and freedom but also to find out who I really was. Before I knew it, I was almost home.

I pulled into the drive and sat in my car for a moment. Was moving really going to solve my problems? My head was spinning. When I was done arguing with myself, I walked in the door and went straight upstairs. Just as I set my purse down and took off my shoes, my mom walked in.

"Are you busy?"

"No." I moved over, and she took a seat next to me at the foot of the bed. There were so many things I wanted to discuss, but the most pressing was for me to find out exactly why she didn't want me to take the job. She was not only my mom; she was also my best friend and role model. She was everything I wanted and hoped to be. So as dumb as it sounds, I would never dream of going up against her. I would never want to lose her as a mom or a friend.

"Catherine called me into her office this afternoon. She said the two of you had lunch."

She smiled and broke my concentration. "Yes, Catherine mentioned that you have been a little distracted lately. And that you two have been discussing the position on and off, but nothing official."

I was relieved that she had initiated the discussion. I was afraid she would not be open to discussion, and I would definitely need more than her approval. I would need her support and help.

"I have decided your dad and Catherine were right. I can't keep you all to myself, not forever. You are a grown woman now, and I need to start treating you that way. I am so proud of you, Arri. You have been so patient with your overbearing mother, and still managed to grow up into a responsible young lady."

"Mom? Why didn't you agree with me leaving in the first place?" My heart wrenched, and my voice broke. Her voice was calm and soothing, but there was heartache and tears in her eyes.

She let out a deep sigh. "I just figured if I held on to you as long as I could, I would never lose you. I promised your father we wouldn't tell you, so let's keep it between us, but…"

Being in the middle would really make it hard to keep my stories straight. My mom went on.

"Your father and I were going to let nature take its course and allow you to find out a few things on your own while giving you guidance and support. But if you left, your father and I would not be around to help you through it all…"

Mom was babbling. I cocked my head.

"Through it all…like what?" I asked.

"Well, needless to say, your father and I are a little different than the average parents. Only a specific type of person is allowed in our community, and you are one of them."

"One of them? One of who?"

"It is not easy to tell you, so please bear with me if I stumble over my own words." Apologetically, she smiled at me. "Arri, I know most parents tell their children they are special, but Arri, you really *are* special. You are destined to do great things, and if that pressure was not great enough on its own, you might have abilities others don't. You are the first, so you are alone."

I leaned over and hugged her. "I think I understand part of what you are telling me." Maybe it was time to tell my mom I knew. "I have noticed a few things lately, but I wasn't sure what they were. When you and Catherine were in the kitchen talking about shipping me off to London…I heard it. Not the whole conversation, but I heard lots from the stairs. I understand that I was not supposed to eavesdrop, but why were you going to ship me off to London?"

Mom looked remorseful and shocked as she looked down at her fiddling hands. "It's not that we wanted to, but since the attacks, I thought if you went away 'til they stopped or forgot about you, then your troubles would be over, and you could return home." Mom hung her head and smoothed out the hem of her shirt. "Honey, I never really wanted to send you to London, but since you're moving, and throwing them off your scent, we won't need to send you anywhere."

"But who are *they*?"

"I know it all seems so strange and confusing right now, but you needn't worry. All I can say is you're different. You are one of us! But there are some of us that don't like change. What am I saying? Your dad and I have this all figured out and you're fine now." There was a short pause. "I'm sorry. I'm not doing this very well, am I?" Mom bit her lip.

"It's fine. I guess I wish I knew more, but I know you never really wanted to send me away. And you're right. I'm moving now, making a new start and hopefully even a friend or two." I smiled as the conversation lightened up. "I was hoping you would be okay with the move, because I have a rather large favor to ask." I paused to see her reaction. "I would like some help moving, if you are up to it."

My mom's expression lit up, and we were back to normal. The conversation bounced around in my head for a moment until she threw her arms around me and hugged me tightly.

"Anything!" she squealed. "Your wish is my command." She winked and pretended to take out a paper and pencil.

"Well, since I haven't ever moved so much as an inch, I was hoping you would be able to help me find a small place to stay: a decent apartment, a small house, or even rented space." I shrugged.

"Are you kidding? There is more to moving than just a place to stay, sweetheart." Her voice was incredulous. "There is the new wardrobe, the new car, and the new laptop, not to mention the furniture."

I had to stop her before she got too far. "Mom, wait a minute, you're moving too fast. I have a budget to stick to. I can't be spending money I don't have on things I don't absolutely need."

She wasn't listening to a word I said. She was still busy listing all the things she wanted me to have. "No worries, dear, I've got this."

I was relieved to see she was okay with me moving, but I was nervous about what she was capable of. Money was dangerous in her hands. She was never one to say no, or stop when the deal was right. Our house was full of little trinkets from garage sales to Saks Fifth Avenue. Some of the prices on these items were in the four-digit range. One was a small wooden box, and it was around seven thousand dollars, *and* it was empty. Mom was crazy when it came to money. So to make someone happy, money was never an issue.

The two weeks went by quickly. Periodically I heard my mom setting up a few things like power and water, but I wasn't entirely sure where I was going to live. My mom said the place was a little small, but I would love it. She gave me no other hints.

With only a few days left, I asked Catherine for a couple days off to pack and get ready for the move. Dad picked Mom and me up at the mall, from what she called "necessary shopping." She bought me clothes I didn't think I needed and what felt like enough shoes to wear one pair a day for a year.

When we arrived back at the house after hours of mind-numbing shopping, a familiar-looking man was waiting on our front doorstep. Dad handed me the keys, and Mom escorted me into the house and to my room. Typically, there was a formal introduction with wine and everything. We had more red wine in our cellar than the rest of Nevada put together; it seemed to be all my parents ever drank. This guest was different, though. He felt nervous and self-consciously unwelcome. After several minutes of hushed whispers and forced conversation, the man left the house in a huff. The front door slammed, he stalked away in a fury. When he reached his car, he gave me a pointed glare. I could have sworn that the air cooled a few degrees. Shivers ran down my spine as I stepped away from the window, tripped over a packed box, and toppled to the floor.

"What was all that?" I asked, pushing myself off the floor when

Mom opened the door to my room. I felt her heart jolt at my question.

"Well, in short, he broke tradition." My parents put tradition on a pedestal. To make sure I was always holding the proper protocol in any and all situations, I was taught time-honored traditions from China to England and from the twelfth century to now.

"What did he do wrong?" I asked, as we sat down for dinner. I tried to remember him. He looked familiar for one reason or another. But his face seemed like it should have been more shadowed and mischievous.

"Well, he broke the rules both by showing up unannounced and by not asking for permission from his elders." Dad's tone was flat. His features were tight with frustration, but other than his slight reactions, he was expressionless.

It seemed like there was a secret war, and I was the center of attention. I only thought this because I would hear my name mentioned while my parents were on the phone. This was not all that strange, but when it involved me not being ready, or not being strong enough to face him, I could only assume. I took these conversations and compared them to all the things that I had experienced lately, and I could only wonder what else there could be to know.

TEN

The day before I moved, my parents were on edge. It was like living in a small pressure cooker, just waiting for someone to break. From the small, confines of my empty room, I could hear my mom talking on the phone downstairs. I assumed it was Catherine. She was giving this person a play-by-play of my travels. I was able to tap into my hearing abilities quite quickly now. I used them whenever it would be to my advantage to hear what was going on around me, but I needed to be careful. I wasn't always able to distinguish one conversation from another, so I ended up hearing everything at once, resulting in a headache.

All my things were boxed and ready to go. It was a little depressing to see everything I owned in boxes. Not just the symbolism or idea, but the fact that the move was really going to happen hit me like lightning, as did the fact that everything I owned fit into just a handful of boxes.

I was sad when I found out how much I didn't own. I walked downstairs and went into the kitchen for a snack. In the kitchen, my suspicions were correct. I heard Catherine's voice on the other end of the phone. Mom's tone was light and frivolous. Her body language changed quickly when Catherine said they had an assignment. Mom hung up and called for my father. Dad was there in a flash. It still amazed me how fast they were. There was some truth to the expression *lightning speed.*

"Yes, Emily?" Dad answered. Mom's voice was unsteady, almost nervous. I could sense her excitement and anxiety caroming around in her like a bouncy ball.

"We have an assignment."

Dad's mouth dropped slightly. "When?"

"A week from tomorrow! Catherine said she and Phillip were on the assignment as well, and they leave tomorrow.'" I was a little unsure why I was allowed to hear this conversation, as opposed to all the others. Mom glanced at me. I thought it a little strange that Catherine would leave the credit union the day I was set to leave and Mom and Dad a week later. It was all rather sudden.

"Where are you going?" I asked, not knowing if they were actually going to tell me.

"Egypt. It has been ages since your father and I have been there. I am very excited to go." Mom would be jumping up and down if it weren't for her total self-control. I was a little jealous. I've always wanted to go with them, but I was told it was District business.

"Why did you sound nervous if you're excited?" I asked. Mom laughed slightly, and then, answered.

"Because the assignment is…well, let's just say the reason for the assignment is a little disturbing, and I would rather go there on vacation than for the reason we are going. Your dad and I used to visit there often, and it would be nice to go for pleasure instead." She said this in a matter-of-fact way, like I should have picked up on it or something.

A half-smile flickered across my father's face. "I'm hungry. I could use a little break, and I believe you need to pick up your last check from Catherine before you leave tomorrow." He and my mom exchanged a look of acknowledgment and then he turned toward me. "Why don't we all go to lunch and stop by the credit union? On the way home I have a little surprise for the both of you."

My mother's car was getting the windows tinted to a level dangerously below legal, and my car…well, to say the least, it was a total loss. I'd finally come to terms with junking it. Getting into my father's car, I placed my hands in my lap. My parents had extravagant taste and changed cars like people changed their socks. My father's Ferrari Enzo and my mother's Mercedes GTR were the two flavors of the month—two cars that were just for showing off, if you asked me, but in my parents' minds, they were necessary.

We went to one of my favorite places, the Olive Garden. I loved the Tuscan atmosphere and the illusion that you are in another place and time besides dry and hot Las Vegas. I had my usual tour of Italy and finished the whole plate—appetite has never been an issue for me. We were done with lunch and were waiting for dessert when a herd of people stopped by the table. As they approached, there was a sense of nervousness vibrating from them. It wasn't uncommon for people to be nervous around my dad, but this was taking it to a new level. When they finally reached us and gained their sense of confidence, they sang "Happy Birthday" in broken unison and served me a slice of German chocolate cake—my favorite. With all that had been going on, and trying to get ready for the move, I had completely forgotten it was my birthday. I was nineteen and didn't even feel a day older than yesterday. I had always seen age as nothing except a number, but it was still fun to have a birthday. I was shocked that I had forgotten entirely. I thought forgetfulness was reserved for the elderly, but I guess nobody is immune to it, not even me. My parents were much too happy to capitalize on my forgetting, but it was fun to be surprised like this.

"I was wondering if you were ever going to remember it was your birthday," Mom said, as I stuffed my face with the slice of cake. I was having too much fun with my parents. They were actually acting normal for once: no paranoid, edgy, or tense emotions. We were just a casual family enjoying the day together. I finished the cake, and we went to pick up my last paycheck.

We walked into the credit union and I was blown away by all the decorations. There was a mixture of *farewell* and *happy birthday* banners and decorations scattered throughout the whole place. Catherine was expecting me. She was front and center waiting for my reaction.

When I walked in, she yelled, "Happy birthday!"

Catherine was not concerned about what the members or other employees thought. To Catherine, I was almost as much her daughter as I was my mother's. Catherine had been there for me as much as my mom, almost every memory I had, she was in it. Past all the adornment, I couldn't help but see Sally, Megan, and Andrea sitting behind their stations with smug looks on their faces. It didn't take

Andrea long to fall back into the bad attitude of the credit union girls. Catherine leaned in toward me, and ever so softly she said, "I told the girls you were no longer working here, and when I saw how happy they looked, I left out the reason you were leaving."

I was happy to hear this news. I guess they expected a show from one of us. When they didn't get it, they retreated to the break room, and I was right behind them. Just before I entered, I could hear them discussing who won the bet. Sally was the winner, but before she was too confident in her winnings, I needed to smash the pedestal she thought she stood on. Typically, I was not vindictive in any way, shape, or form, but there was something about these girls that told me I was not too out of place. I could feel the satisfaction of the three knowing I was leaving. I walked in searching for a mug I had left.

"I'm sorry you're leaving us," Sally said, in a bad impersonation of being upset.

"Yes, me too," Megan added. I could feel that both of them were laughing on the inside.

"Me too," I said. "I loved this place. It has been my second home for a few years now. I was surprised when Catherine pulled me into her office the other day."

"Did you find another job?" Andrea asked, and I knew she assumed the answer was no.

"Oh, I don't need to find a new job. I'm being promoted to assistant manager and transferred to Utah. Did you think I was fired?"

Sally was shocked. She couldn't grasp the fact that she might have been wrong.

"You didn't win the bet, Sally. I did."

She was wrong, and I wanted her to know it. There was nothing else I could say. Proud of myself, I left the girls with their mouths wide open, all of them thoroughly humbled. Mom spotted me from across the room and shook her head, knowing what I had just done. It was not right for me to be so arrogant myself, but I felt better knowing I beat them at their own game.

After joining my parents and Catherine in the lobby, we adjourned to her office where she had a few wrapped gifts sitting on her desk. I opened the first gift, slipping my fingers under the farewell gift paper and gasping. I was surprised to find an iPad and a gift card for app downloads. Immediately, I opened the second one, wrapped in birthday paper, and this time found a two-thousand-dollar Visa gift card neatly tucked in a black velvet bag. The gifts were way too much, but I was grateful for the thought that came with them.

Catherine was a friend, and to leave her was heart-breaking. She was a great listener, and although she didn't mean to be, she was my key to knowing when something was really wrong. I would miss her very much, and tears rolled down my face as we said our last goodbyes and I gathered my gifts. As my family and I left, I took one last look at the building and sorrow hit me full-force. When I got into the car, I hung my head as the repercussions of my decisions hit me like a ton of bricks.

Dad and Mom were having no trouble with the emotional downpour that I was in the middle of. They weren't leaving—I was. Plus, they, in general, didn't show as much emotion as I did. I didn't know if they felt the full rainbow of emotions, anyway.

"Would it be okay if we picked something up from Tony at the lot?" my dad asked. Tony was the one they always bought their cars from. He had a back-east accent and a New York attitude. He was friendly, though. I only spoke to him on the phone, and he was never rude.

"Yo, Roger, my man." I could only assume it was Tony saying this as we pulled into the dealership. Unlike most people, Tony didn't show fear and apprehension when approaching my dad.

"Hello, Tony," Dad greeted his friend.

The difference in the way they spoke was amazing. It was *da Bronx* versus proper English.

Mom got out of the car, and I don't think there was even one man who didn't stop whatever it was he was doing, even tripping over things, just to look at her. I always thought my mom was beautiful, but there was no mistaking it when she was in a crowd. Her red hair, long legs, and obviously confident stance made her the perfect model and the ideal woman. Men would kiss the ground she walked on if she would only acknowledge them.

"Emily," Tony said, "a pleasure as always. Can I get you something to drink?"

"Yes, wine, if you have it." What? Mom was crazy. A car dealership isn't going to have wine. I was dead wrong; Tony nodded and asked Dad the same question.

"The same, please," he said, "and a Coke or Pepsi for Arri." Dad indicated the back seat, where I was still sitting. I didn't know we were going to be here for a while, but since we were ordering drinks, I figured I should get out of the car as well. Once I was out, Tony snapped his fingers, and a tall, skinny man appeared out of nowhere and took the car keys from my dad. He got in the car and pulled it around back.

"Thank you, Tony," Dad said, as he took his glass of wine that Tony had magically produced.

"Thank you," I said, as he handed me my coke.

Tony was staring at me. His eyes were glassy, and I was pretty sure he heard nothing as my parents spoke. I never considered myself too much to look at. I had heard several times that I mimicked my mom with her breathtaking looks and her perfect body, but there were also things that complimented my mom that didn't compliment me. She had red hair and self-confidence, and I had brownish-red wavy hair and no confidence. No matter how hard I tried, I always thought she was much prettier than I could ever be. Tony blushed and looked down. My parent's friends were so peculiar, but I was used to their odd behavior. Ignoring the men that were now tripping over things to get a closer look and the stares that were now directed toward me, I could feel Tony's embarrassment.

"So, are we all set, then?" Dad asked. Tony snapped out of his trance and focused on the task at hand.

I was missing something, something between the three of them that they were hiding from me.

I peered around the lot at all the new fancy cars that were for sale. I couldn't help but wish I had one of them. Out of all the fancy, overpriced, luxurious vehicles on the lot, I spotted a new Land Rover Discovery. It looked a little out of place between the cherry-red Corvette and the neon-yellow Lamborghini. If I was picking out a car for myself, the Discovery was perfect, but the simplicity of it didn't fit my parents' tastes.

While Tony and my parents talked about the old days and things I really didn't care for, I didn't see a problem if I was to just go take a look at the cars. In all reality, I needed one. I opened the door to the Discovery and sat in the driver's seat. It was much larger than my CRX and much higher. The seats adjusted just right, and it was screaming for me to take it. I was falling in love, imagining myself owning it. I would never buy the car, but it sure was fun pretending that I might.

"Are you planning on buying this?" Tony's voice was disgusted. I glared at him.

"Is there something wrong with this particular vehicle?" My voice was acidic. I may not have the same taste as my parents, but there was nothing wrong with this SUV. Granted, it was much newer than I ever would have looked at, but it was still a good-looking vehicle.

"No, not at all, my little *bambina*!" Tony exclaimed. "Just…no bling, no glitz, whatcha doin'?"

I understood his thought process. My parents' tastes were extravagant, and since he had never met me or really talked to me, he could only assume my inclination would be like that of my parents.

"Sorry, Tony, I had no reason to lash out at you like that. I guess my taste is rather different from my parents. I actually love this vehicle. If I could buy a new car, I would definitely buy this one." Tony looked puzzled.

We got out of the Discovery, and my parents and I examined the exterior. Tony disappeared for a moment and then returned with a little black box.

"Is this what you were here for?" he asked as we walked to our car that was now fully detailed.

"Yes, I think so. You'll take care of the paperwork?" Dad was acting somewhat evasive.

"I am afraid we needed to replace one of Emily's windows, an expense we will cover. There was a little scratch on the film, so it will be ready a little later today." Tony would have been shaking from head to toe if it weren't for the fact that his eyes were planted on me. He was probably trying to save face or hiding from having to meet my dad's gaze.

"No problem. You will deliver it then?" There was no doubt in my dad's voice that it would be done. We returned home, and finally, the day was over.

I couldn't believe I would be moving in the morning. I didn't know how I was going to get there, but I *was* going to get there, somehow, and start a new life for myself.

ELEVEN

I woke up to a brand-new morning. When I opened my blinds, the early traffic slogged past beyond the window. No congestion yet, but it would steadily pick up speed as the sun rose. Gradually, hustle and bustle would build into another unyielding day.

I was in the empty room where I had collected all my memories. I had grown up here. All of my hopes and dreams had been made here, in this house. The drawn and dated marks on the doorjamb showed how much I had grown from one year to the next. Everything I had done, collected, memories I'd made…they were all here. I didn't have much in the sense of materialistic objects, but what I did have made this room my home, my sanctuary, and safe place. I was emotionally attached to every object because each one of them triggered a specific memory of a time with my parents or a place I'd gone. The mere thought of leaving the only home I had ever known had me tearing up.

Mom came in just in time to interrupt my soon-to-be meltdown.

"Oh good, you're up." She bounced in. She was usually up before dawn, and couldn't understand why I needed sleep at all, let alone more than four or five hours a night.

As my mom stared back at me, my unstable heart wept in my chest. I was not ready to let go. I was prepared to face the world ahead of me, but I hadn't realized the cost of my decision. Mom was more than my mom; she was my best friend, my moral compass, my everything. I missed her already.

"Oh honey, don't cry." She hugged me, and then wiped the single tear that fell from my cheek, smooth and effortless as always. All the little things I overlooked before stood out now. "You're not gone yet.

Get ready and come downstairs. Your father and I are taking you to breakfast."

Her voice was even and steady. Even her perky personality was a mask. Emotionally, she was trying not to cry. The fact that she was sad broke my heart. After a pause to collect myself, I went to shower, brushed my teeth and hair, and packed everything I had just used. As I left my room, I turned for one last glance. It looked so sad and lonely.

"I'm sorry," I whispered and closed the door. I ached like I had just lost my best friend. Descending the stairs, flashbacks of my childhood set in with each step I took. At the bottom, Dad and Mom were waiting. I tried to smile. It was a little weak and broken, and a sad attempt at a grin.

"Are you ready?" Dad had a slight hint of excitement in his voice. It almost sound like he wanted me to go, but I was sure I was just being irrational, and I chalked it up to nervousness and grabbed my purse.

"Sure, why not?" My voice was monotone and grim. They were acting like today was no different than any other.

"Are you going to be like this the whole morning?" Mom asked. Her voice was cheery, but I could feel she was just as sad as I was. Still, I didn't want to be Johnny Raincloud all day. I needed to suck it up and play nice 'til I was gone and I could let the waterworks flow.

"No. I'm over it now. Where are we going?" I mustered up as much enthusiasm as I could.

"Great. Why don't you drive?" Dad handed me the keys. When I didn't seem too excited, they seemed confused, like I should have wanted to drive.

"Okay." I opened the door, and walked to where I had parked my mother's spare car, but couldn't see the black hunk of metal anywhere. In the place of the Rolls-Royce was the pearl-colored Discovery I'd been sitting in last night. I spun to face my parents' delighted expressions. For a moment, my mind was blank. I didn't understand. Then, it dawned on me. These keys didn't belong to the Rolls-Royce. They belonged to a Land Rover. Mom must have had a hand in the surprise, because on the ring was a little bow tied in red-and-white-striped ribbon—a detail I was sure Dad thought was ridiculous.

"Are you serious?" I screamed. They softened their expressions as I hugged them. My dad had been complaining about my eyesore car since I got it, and when it began to backfire, he had begged me to get a new car. He'd hated my old car, but I had bought it on my own, my first official act of independence.

"So do you like it?" Mom asked.

"Are you kidding? I love it. Is that what the whole Tony visit was about? You were trying to see what car I would choose?" I knew the answer, but Dad answered anyway.

"Well, you know how much I hated the CRX, so when it was totaled, it was a dream opportunity." His shoulders shook as he laughed, and I knew he was right. "Your mother and I thought it only appropriate that you had a decent vehicle for your travels, and a vehicle suitable for all seasons."

I clicked the beeper thing, unlocked the car, and jumped in. "You coming?" I called from the driver's seat as I revved up the engine. I pushed the little button on the ceiling, and the sunroof opened, letting the crisp autumn air wash over me. The engine hummed and purred.

A few minutes later, after pulling into one of our favorite diners, I gently pushed my car into park and squealed with excitement at the thrill of it.

We had been going to this place for what seemed like forever. We knew the manager and most of the servers.

"Good morning!" Janet, an older, kind-faced waitress, greeted us. She was tall and rather thin, but her friendly look was just a cover. Beneath the surface she was a tough old lady with a no-nonsense persona that demanded respect. "Mr. and Mrs. Stone, Arri. Just the three of you this morning or are you waiting for the Whites?"

"Just us, thank you. How are you this morning, Janet?" Mom asked, as Janet retrieved three of the menus. We were escorted to our regular table, in a distant, dimly lit corner.

"Fine thanks. Jeremy graduates in June, and he's my last." Janet placed the menus before us. "I'll have an empty nest when he leaves for trade school."

"That's great," Mom said, as she and Dad looked around and surveyed their surroundings.

As we ate our breakfast in relative silence, I was antsy. I wanted nothing more than to be with my parents a few moments more. I even wanted to rewind time. Eventually we finished our food and left with our stomachs full, but my heart was still empty.

"Now what?" I asked, as we hopped into my new car. My insides giggled as I tried to contain my excitement.

"Well, I thought we would get you packed and on your way. I don't want you driving in the dark." The clock in the dash read only eight o'clock. It felt like Dad was pushing me out the door. I had plenty of time to get there, and what were a few more minutes?

"Doesn't it only take like four hours to get there?" I asked.

"Six, actually, and you have never been there before. What if you miss a turn or get lost?" Dad replied.

He had a point, but still. I had at least four hours before I needed to leave and still be there before dark. But I didn't want to argue and ruin our perfect family time. So I lost the battle and headed home as Dad had wanted.

Dad should have been a Tetris pro: after he packed my car you couldn't fit so much as the blade of a knife anywhere. Up until now, I was nervous about the move. There was so much that had to be done that it was a constant stress. Then, packing and placing all my things into boxes until my room was an empty shell made it worse. Now the feeling of freedom and adventure loomed on the horizon. When it came down to it, I was as scared as ever. I felt alone and vulnerable, and I was not even out of the driveway yet. My mom smothered me as I said my last goodbyes and my dad smiled from the driver's side as he held the car door open for me. My eyes welled up with tears, and I held on to my mom tightly.

I hugged my dad goodbye. He was not the cuddly type, nor was he ever really affectionate, but as he hugged me, he gently whispered in my ear.

"Even if I never really told you, I love you. You are my pride and joy; you have made me so proud." With that, he stepped back.

Reluctantly, I got in the car and turned the key in the ignition. I backed out of the drive, crying softly as I watched my parents wave goodbye. I took one last look in the rearview mirror and took a mental snapshot. The house I grew up in got smaller and smaller until it disappeared around the corner.

It was official. I was on my own and had no ties to keep me here. My parents would be off to Egypt shortly, and I would not see them 'til summer.

This was it. I was finally leaving the place I hated more than anything—Las Vegas. It wasn't the city itself, but the attitude behind it. Only six hours to go and I would be in my new home. I could only hope the trouble won't follow me.

With a steadying breath, I plunged into my new adventure as I revved onto the freeway. I was out of Vegas, and crossing the desert, the one people joked gets longer every time they drove it. I had my new phone plugged in and was listening to my favorite songs, all sounding fresh and exciting as I drove to freedom. Just as I was really rocking out, my cell phone rang. "Home" showed on the screen.

"Hello?"

"Hey, sweetheart." Dad's quiet and authoritative voice came from the other end. "Your new address is programmed in your Maps app on your phone. Your exit is Elsinore. I know you're working in Richfield, but Elsinore is much smaller and only seven miles away from your new job."

His voice sounded foreign, like he was honestly sad I was gone.

"Thanks, Dad." Maybe this was just as hard on him as it was on me. He may not have shown affection, but with this strange newfound ability, I could feel that it—and other emotions—were there all the same.

"Sure, sweetie."

I closed my eyes momentarily, fighting the urge to turn back. Finally, with a low-spirited mutter, we said our goodbyes, and I went off on my way to my new home.

A while later, I neared Beaver. The trip had gone without a hitch so far. I pulled off the road and into the nearest gas station, where I filled up and bought some snacks. On my way in, I had taken a mental snapshot of my nearby surroundings. The pet area off to the left had a few dogs and one owner making a pit stop, and the actual pumps only had a small Honda and a decent-sized Ford truck parked at the far end of the stalls. I had parked at the first available pump near the dumpsters.

When I came back out of the convenient store with my bags in hand, the stalls were empty, and the dogs and their owner were gone. The parking lot looked deserted. It felt like a heavy fist had gripped my chest. Without a second glance, I ran the last few steps to my car and locked myself in. Putting my SUV in reverse, I started to back out. My rear alarm beeped, and just as I cleared the dumpsters, my heart stopped, and I froze. Right behind my car, a hooded man towered behind me only inches from the rear of my car. Slowly, he ran his finger along the length of my car, all the way to my front window. The shadowed figure's mouth turned up at the ends as a knowing smile crept across his face.

I gripped the steering wheel, letting my knuckles turn white and the pads of my fingers melt into the gel cover. He gave the door handle a quick tug. The door was locked, and I thought his efforts were pointless. But his eyebrows shot up, a look of intrigue lit his face, his smile changed into a warped grin, and his eyes sparked with challenge. My panicked heart tripled its beat, and without further thought, I slammed on the gas and screeched out of the parking lot, nipping the man in the hip as I went.

Shot through with terror, I turned and saw the man was gone. There was no sign of him anywhere. Heart pounding in my ears, my breath came in small, short spurts. My heart's frantic thudding finally lulled as I cleared my thoughts.

It was just random. It had to have been.

TWELVE

As I calmed down and drove for the next hour, the beauty of the scenery overwhelmed me. The color of the leaves showing the break from summer to autumn, the painted shades that splashed the mountains as fall hung in the air…reds, greens, browns, yellows, and oranges gilded the hills like only Mother Nature could arrange.

In all the years I had lived in Las Vegas, there were no real seasons; it went from blazing hot summers of one-hundred-five degrees to semi-mild winters that teased us with crisp and chilly temperatures. It was one of the things I hated about Las Vegas. Here, even the trees looked happy and peaceful, the stunning colors so captivating. If the vibrating bumps hadn't warned me I was on the shoulder, I would have driven off the road, distracted, but with a jolt, I corrected myself. *Forget all this beauty, I need to stop driving Braille and pay attention.*

As I'd seen many times before, a hitchhiker stood on the shoulder of the freeway and my happiness ebbed away at the sight. His anger seeped through the frame of my car as he stared at me with an iron fury. Not wanting to make eye contact, I turned away as I passed, but his hidden face sent shivers down my spine. He gave me the creeps.

After a few little towns on the way, finally a sign read *Elsinore—1 Mile.* My insides giggled, and even though nobody could see or hear me, I squealed with excitement. The journey to my new home was finally over.

At the bottom of the ramp, a small, older convenience store stood alone in a gravel parking lot. I parked, and as I walked in, everyone looked at me with awe and confusion. as if I were the only outsider they'd seen in a while. If it had been a bar, the talking would have come to a halt, and a mid-song record scratch would echo in the silence. The cashier was a blond teenager who looked too young to be working; if I hadn't heard her tell the customer in front of me that she had two kids, I would have never guessed she was more than fifteen. As her conversation with the young man about horses and cattle ended, the man sent me an appreciative look, then left, waving to the cashier.

"See you tomorrow, darlin'!" His baritone voice bellowed over the silence. The cashier looked at me, forced her lips into a half-smile, half-smirk, and eyed me skeptically. As I placed my Coke on the counter, I thought about asking her if she knew of the rental, but the look on her face told me I was better off finding the place on my own.

After I paid for my stuff and walked out, a man with snow-white hair held the door open for me, and I nodded my thanks. As I got in my car and looked for the address my dad programmed for me, the man made a quick exit as he spotted an elderly woman struggling to get out of her car near the entrance. He helped her out, and slowly they walked into the store. The older woman had a kind face, though she seemed frail. Still, her clothes were freshly ironed, and she was all dolled up even for a five-minute trip to the corner market. As he gathered a few things and helped her pay, she stood by the register holding onto the counter for support. After they left, he helped her in her car, loaded all the groceries in the back seat, and said his goodbyes.

I pulled out of the gas station and looked at the directions. By the looks of it, the house was just around the corner.

When I drove up, I was speechless. The house was beautiful: it had a white picket fence that separated the only two neighbors I had from my corner lot. A small anteroom lay behind the front door, framed by front windows with plant boxes that looked like they once held beautiful flowers. All I wanted was a small, simple place to stay. This was way too much. Mom had overdone it. After pulling around back, I opened the gate and drove in and parked by the back door, where a note read:

Dear Tenant,

I hope you like your stay here. I have always enjoyed this home and hope you will as well. It has not been lived in for quite some time and may need some tender loving care. I take it your mother and father have secured this house for you and have everything in your name. If there is any way I can make your stay here more comfortable, please let me know. I have compiled a list of neighbors that can help you if you ever need anything. Their names and numbers are on the counter. Again, I hope you like it here.

Sincerely, M.

The handwriting was old-school Palmer Method, and unfamiliar.

I grabbed the tissue-wrapped key my mom had given me from my pocket, slowly opened the back door, and stepped into a quaint, confined mudroom. The house was charming: a small two-bedroom cottage whose door creaked behind me as the old wooden floor protested with my every step. The age-warped windows were like peering through a wavy film .

There was something about this intimate abode that said home. The kitchen was loaded, the cupboards were stocked, and the dining table was set for a banquet. As I crept through the house, I found the master bedroom furnished with a king-sized bed, dresser, and a nightstand. Running my fingers along the nightstand, I paused. I had almost missed it, but there on the nightstand was another note. This one was written on pink floral paper and smelled of lilac perfume. When I opened the folded paper, the writing was familiar and feminine.

Arri,

I am hoping you like my decorating. I was having a hard time with the design. I realized as I was picking out your curtains, decorations, and furniture, we did not have the same taste. I tried to keep it simple, but there were a few things I could not resist. I love you, my dear child, and please remember to stay in touch.

Mom

The rest of the house was just as beautiful. I couldn't help but wonder when Mom had time to do all this—and from so far away.

Just as I was getting acquainted with my new surroundings, a soft knock sounded at the back door.

"Hello?" called a man's voice. I hurried to the open door.

"Oh, hi, sorry about that. I didn't realize I had left the door open. Please come in."

To my surprise, it was the white-haired man from the store and two other people. Up close, he looked to be in his mid-twenties. My heart skipped a beat.

"I apologize for my unannounced visit. I am Alex, and this is my brother Jonathan, and my sister Sarah. We live across the street." Jonathan looked slightly younger, I guessed, but Sarah was around the same age as Alex. I welcomed them in and introduced myself. As we engaged in some small talk, it was clear that Alex was the comedian of the family. Jonathan was quiet but polite, and Sarah was still a mystery. She gave off mixed vibes, her expressions were muted and masked.

After our little chat, the three of them said their goodbyes. I followed them back outside.

"So, I'll see you around?" Sarah asked.

"Yes, definitely. We'll have to do lunch or a barbecue," I said, looking at the back of my truck. "Well, when I get settled, of course." I stared at the over-packed boxes overwhelming the back of the Discovery and wished they would move themselves.

"Is this all you have or are the moving trucks on their way?" Alex asked, opening the back of the Land Rover.

"No, this is it." There wasn't much.

"Here, let me give you a hand." Alex picked up the first of the boxes with ease. "Light as a feather. If this is how they all are, then we are in luck." He disappeared into the house. Jonathan pitched in, picking up a few of the boxes himself. But Sarah was a different story. She grimaced and made no move to help. She was unlike her siblings in many ways. Her short skirt, tight crop top, and mile-high heels set her far apart from her brothers. Sarah seemed dangerous. I would have a hard time keeping any guy that got near her. While Alex was carefree, and Jonathan was relaxed, Sarah was different. She was shielded emotionally and physically; her expressions were calculated, her steps were measured, and her entire persona was controlled and guarded like she was hiding something. As a glint of amusement sparked in her eyes, she tried and failed to quell a smile with her hands. Then, her tone deliberate and distant, she excused herself.

"I'm sorry. I have to get going."

Something was definitely odd with her, but who was I to judge? I had never been close enough to anyone to have a friend, let alone know how they were supposed to act.

Getting back to unloading, I let Alex tease me with his exaggerated efforts as he acted like a few of the boxes were too heavy, making faces and grunting as he tried to pick them up. He pretended to lift a larger box and groaned and moaned, and then, standing up and rubbing his hands together, he backed up, puffed up his chest, and tried again. This time he effortlessly lifted the box, held it with one arm, and laughed his way into the house.

I liked him. He made moving as easy as he made me laugh.

"This was the quickest move I've ever helped with." Alex laughed and nudged me.

"Well, it's pretty easy when you own practically nothing." I grinned and tossed them each a Coke from my shopping trip. "Thanks for helping."

"No problem. It was easy." Alex smiled.

"Why is that?" Jonathan spoke up for the first time.

"Why is what?" I asked.

"You own nothing? All we unpacked were a few boxes of books, clothes, and miscellaneous things. Usually a girl has much more." Jonathan sat down on a rock by the back door.

"Well, I've lived with my parents 'til now. I didn't have a reason to have more. Everything was provided for me."

"So this is your first time on your own?" Jonathan said in disbelief.

"Yeah, it is."

"What do you think so far?" Alex asked.

"I don't really know yet. I just got here. How about you? How do you like living here? Have you lived here long?"

My new neighbors smiled broadly. Instead of an answer, Alex cocked his head, ran his left hand through his white hair, and shrugged. Speaking slowly, he asked, "Arri, have you ever been to a Harvest Festival?"

I thought. I had never been to a festival of any kind. "No."

"Well, there is a Harvest Festival in the park tomorrow afternoon, and at least four towns will be there. It might be fun. Maybe a little break from the ol' city life would do you some good. Would you like to come with us?"

Alex was sweet, and the gesture of a new friendship was irresistible.

"Sure, that would be great!" I found myself beaming too.

Alex's face lit up once more. "Great. We will pick you up tomorrow morning, around elevenish?"

It was hard to explain, but this place sparked a fire in me that I'd never felt before. After they left, I finished putting the majority of my things away. Now the house reflected me, a book-reading and plain-living hermit.

I put on a sweater, grabbed a cup of hot chocolate, and sat on the front steps, gazing at the field across the street where dirty white sheep huddled in the corner of the large pasture. The brisk air nipped at my nose, but I'd never felt so warm and at home. I tipped my chin to the night sky in search of the Big Dipper. I didn't know the night sky held so many stars. The never-ending span of space was hypnotizing, and tonight was especially beautiful. The breeze rustled through my hair, and the tree leaves sang as the music of the wind tickled the swaying branches, but fatigue was catching up with me. Reluctantly, I headed to bed. As I put my head on the pillow, I smiled, and my heart thrilled. I had done it. Finally, I had reached a new branch in my life with the freedom I seldom got at home. I felt proud of myself and my accomplishments.

For most of the next morning, I walked around the house, enraptured by the thought of a place of my own—no curfew, no parents hovering over my shoulder all the time, and no rules but my own. Music was blaring loudly, and I was basically strutting back and forth when a loud noise pounded from the back door

"Ahem."

Spinning around, I came face to face with Alex, Sarah, and Jonathan in the doorway.

"Oh, hi." My cheeks burned. "I was just..." There was no excuse for my goofing around that wasn't embarrassing.

"No, that's okay," Alex said. "It was funny." He tried stifling a laugh. "But if we are going to make it to the festival before all the good food is gone, we need to go."

"Sure." I gathered my things and we left. The festival was only a few blocks away, so we decided to walk rather than drive and try and find parking. It also gave me a chance to see the town a little. Jonathan was making fun of me, walking like a rooster flapping his arms about and strutting, every so often letting out a mocking cock-a-doodle-doo.

The town's main street was decked out in fall attire. The street poles were covered in large leaves that wound down the sides like a vine. The park looked lively, full of people like bees gathering in a beehive. Upbeat country music played in the background, and flags and banners in vibrant festive colors complimented the real trees surrounded the park. On one stage was cowboy poetry, and on the other, a country band and source of the music. Stands were selling all types of food and drink, and other booths sold homemade gifts and crafts. Outside of New Year's Eve on the Las Vegas strip, I had never seen so many people in such a small place.

Browsing the merchandise and listening to the music was delightful, and as I wandered about, and night fell, I realized I'd lost Alex and his family.

Plus, despite the distraction of the trinkets, my attention kept getting pulled to this guy who kept reappearing. His face was sweet and angelic, and his emerald green eyes were soft and seductive. Everything about him beckoned me, but I fought it. My heart raced. I didn't know if he was following me or if it was just a coincidence. I took a quick right at the taco stand and moved to the handmade doilies. Just when I thought we finally went our separate ways, he was standing next to me, examining a doily. Nervously, I scanned around for Alex as I tried to dodge my eye candy.

Alex, though, was nowhere to be found. It was getting late, so I walked home by myself. The festival was only a few blocks away, and streetlights lit most of the way. As I walked, I passed an old, vandalized machine shop that housed what seemed like a thousand birds. The dilapidated roofing, non-existent windows, and torn and missing shingles gave it an ominous appearance in the moonlight. Even worse, right in front of the old building, two streetlights were broken, leaving me vulnerable for a block or two.

And someone was following me.

Whoever it was wasn't obvious, but I knew the feeling—the eerie prickling on the back of my neck, the sudden chills—from the shadows in Vegas. Something was amiss.

Only two things followed in the shadows: danger and trouble. I ran toward the machine shop hoping that I could avoid them. I stepped over the broken wall and into the building. I was trusting the shadows would hide me until it was safe to leave. I leaned against a damp, splintered piece of wood. Fear instilled itself in my heart when the shaded figure turned the corner and stepped over the same fragmented wall. There was a masculine swagger in the shadow's walk as he closed in on me. When he turned and walked in my direction, I tiptoed to a new place and hid, but he seemed to already know where I was. His speed was impossible to escape. Every direction I went as I tried to evade him, he was there in front of me, waiting for me, beckoning and inviting me. After a few minutes of cat and mouse, he gradually and menacingly moved in, closing the gap between us.

My chest pounded, my breathing rough and fast. I tried to remember what I learned in self-defense class, but somehow, I also knew none of that would matter. I took a few steps back until I bumped into a hard rough wall. My attacker closed in. That sweet angelic face from the park was now taut with intensity, some dark desire. A few steps away now, he pinned my hands above my head. I was helpless. My attacker's face was only inches from mine. The moon's light illuminated his ashen skin, the depth and beauty of his green eyes scornful as he stared me down. He leaned in and smelled my cheek, then my neck. I was shaking now, breath erratic. His lips caressed my neck, and in spite of everything, his touch felt soft, gentle, like he was taking his time breathing in slowly. As he opened his mouth, I flinched, inhaling sharply.

My emotions were haywire. I was terrified, yet part of me wanted him to stay there with his body pressed against mine, and his soft breath kissing my skin.

But when I flinched, he moved back. His gaze still hard on mine, he loosened his grip. But no sooner did I fight back than his grip tightened again, this time harder.

Realization shone like a lightning strike.

"It's unlike a guardian to leave his post," he said, his voice seductive.

"No." The word barely managed to escape me. "Please, what do you want?"

"Is it not already obvious to you?" He touched his finger to my lips and sucked in a breath amused yet curious. My body sagged, arms limp in his tight hold, and my knees buckled. It was useless for me to fight.

His attention snapped to the right. "They're looking for you."

Then he disappeared into the shadows. Just as I regained my balance, someone spoke.

"Arri?"

Alex. I was safe.

From the looks of it, Alex suspected something was wrong, but I was too embarrassed to tell him.

THIRTEEN

I'd been in my new home for about three days, and all my clothes were put away, my books on the shelves, everything in its place. The great thing about not having too much was that there was not much to put away.

I started work the next day, and I was so nervous. The other employees had been there for years. Not knowing anyone made me uneasy. It was going to be a rough beginning, but hopefully I would integrate easily.

The same dreams had visited me almost every night since I moved in. Adrenaline pumping and chest aching, I woke up tangled in the sheets. They all started the same: me running to a large castle-like house buried deep in the mountains. The men who pursued me seemed to be after me for something, but I didn't know what. I held nothing: no money, no objects, just the dirt smudges I got from falling. At the castle, I waited impatiently for the door to open, and when it did, a faceless man appeared. Immediately, I was drawn to him. There was something about him that spoke to my soul. He would always reach out for my hand. I would take it and feel his skin against mine, feel the comfort and safety of it. Then I would awake, just inches from his welcoming embrace, yearning to stay.

These dreams were occurring more frequently and in more detail. I didn't know what they meant, but each night was more intense, more passionate, and more forceful than the last.

Like every other morning I awoke suddenly. I was so exhausted that a large cup of coffee would have been in order, but since I didn't drink coffee, I would have to settle for a refreshing glass of chocolate milk. After getting dressed, I sat at the large kitchen table and added to the enormous list of things I needed from the store. Each morning the list grew longer and eventually I would actually have to leave the house and chance a day in the outside world. The last time I tried that, I was pinned to a wall and ended up more breathless and enticed by the man than I was scared of him.

Driving on the small country road through the quiet town of Richfield, I looked at all the quaint storefronts lining the streets. It was just like the photos in the posting. When I got to work, I walked in ever so slowly. There were six teller stations off to my left, and four or five loan desks in their own cubicles to my right. A nook in the far left corner housed a small chest of toys and a little table where kids could play while their parents banked. As I walked in and studied the layout, a few of the tellers stood up straight, waiting to see which station I would approach. I had only made it halfway across the floor when a nicely dressed lady approached me.

"Hello, I'm Mary, the branch manager. How may I assist you?" She had the whole librarian look down pat. Her six-foot height was accompanied by plain-black heeled shoes that added only an inch and a half or so. Her long brunette hair was pulled back and pinned up with two pencils into a makeshift bun, with a few wandering strands of hair falling into her flustered face. Even her ironed and starched white blouse and knee-length gray pencil skirt screamed bibliognost.

"Hello, I'm Arri." We stood there for a while in silence 'til finally Mary smiled.

"Why don't we take this in my office?" Her office? I wasn't expecting to be a secret. As I followed her, I froze. The room was a mess: papers everywhere, an overflowing wastebasket, files on the floor. The path of a hurricane had nothing on this office.

After closing the door, Mary settled in her chair, brushing off a few stray papers toward the massive pile already on the floor.

"Oh, just push those off and take a seat," she said, waving airily. Tentatively, I did as asked and seated myself, nearly falling right over. The chair had a bum wheel, which would have dumped me on my rear if I had not grabbed on to the desk for dear life.

"Thank goodness you're here. I've been expecting you all week. I couldn't remember when I had told Catherine you were to start. I thought about calling her and asking, but I didn't want to sound disorganized."

Disorganized? All it would take is a surprise visit from corporate to have her fired. I practically grew up in the bank and knew enough to know that corporate would never allow a mess like this.

This was crazy. Mary didn't need me; she needed the man from Clean Sweeps.

"I requested to have someone sent a month ago," she continued, bringing me back to the conversation, "but the HR representative messed up the date on the position, and I didn't get you 'til today. As you can see, I need a little help keeping myself organized. There are records here from when I first started over five years ago. My last assistant was not too good at keeping me organized, but she had a way with the employees." She paused for only a half a second to take a much-needed breath. "It was too bad she left. She might have been a great manager one day, but what's done is done. I hope you are up for a challenge. So many of the girls wanted to be promoted, but I couldn't promote any of them." She leaned forward, her tone hushed. "They lack the leadership skills required to fill this position," she said, cupping her hands around her mouth, which was totally unnecessary since none of the girls dared to pass her office for fear of being swallowed by her mess.

"They are making bets on who will get the position. Now, is that the kind of leadership I need? No! I need someone who is trustworthy and not so catty." Mary stopped and shook her head and pursing her lips.

"I think I follow you so far," I said, "but what's with the secrets?" Mary paused for only a second, like she was going to go off again on another one of her really long explanations.

"No," she said. "I didn't have the heart to tell them I had already hired an outsider. Anna was more than an assistant manager to them. She was a friend."

"And she just up and disappeared?"

"Well, kind of." Mary's eyes darted to the door, then back at me.

"I'm sorry, but if Anna was their friend, then don't you think they've already figured out she's no longer here?"

"You would think so, but it turns out she said she was going on a vacation. Honestly, she didn't bother telling me she was leaving, nor did she tell anyone where she was going. No one has seen her for almost two months now."

"So why hire me if she is on vacation?"

"Initially it was going to be temporary, but as you might have figured out, this is no longer a temporary position."

It was extremely odd for an assistant manager to vanish and cause no panic within the credit union. A missing employee would undoubtedly scare everyone into assuming a possible robbery or heist, especially if the employee in question was an assistant manager. Back home, there was an act of vandalism, but it was less directed at the credit union and more toward me. With news like that, Mary seemed eerily calm.

"The girls have asked me if this was normal vacation time, but I told them not to worry."

Again, my words came out before I could stop them. "Obviously they saw the position posted or they wouldn't have wanted to be promoted." My outburst didn't faze Mary. She just shook her head. I was really curious why Anna would have left abruptly like that, and why the situation seemed so commonplace to Mary. Something was very odd about the whole thing…and here I was thinking I had left odd back in Vegas.

"Arri, I understand your confusion, but let me help you here. Every one of these girls had been asking me if they would be considered for the job if Anna didn't come back. She didn't return after the first week. Her house still had power and had not been rented or sold. I could only assume she just walked out and figured she would start new somewhere else. No one has seen or heard from her, but her bills are still being paid. So I placed her position on our website knowing I would have to replace her."

Even though there was something fishy about this story, I had nothing to prove she was lying. The missing Anna was strange, and working for such a secretive manager would keep me on my toes. I decided that not only did I have to act as an assistant manager, but also play spy to know what was going on.

"Well," I said. "Where do we go from here?"

Mary smiled. "We face the troops." Mary may have been long-winded, but she also had a good sense of humor. She showed me our lockers, the vault, really gave me the whole grand tour. We walked behind the teller stations, and she introduced me to the girls as a credit union observer, and the tension seemed to increase with each one I met. Mary waited 'til closing time to tell the girls who I actually was. She asked them all to see her about ten minutes before leaving, and when they were all around her desk, she called me over. It was like facing a firing squad.

"You guys have all met Arri." Mary gestured to me, including me in the meeting. "So, the credit union has sent us an assistant manager. Arri will be replacing Anna. I would like you to welcome her as a member of our little family." Mary giggled uncomfortably.

If looks could kill, I would be dead. Anyone of them would gladly volunteer to the deed as Mary told them Anna was gone and I was to replace her. The daggers they sent my way were murderous. Who would have thought I'd be trading one branch of vicious snakes for another? These girls didn't even know me yet.

When the day was finally over, Mary sent me home and left the girls to close up. I was only a few steps outside the bank when I suddenly felt uncomfortable, an almost vile hatred tainting the air. This was not me. Something or someone else was feeling this awful feeling, and I was unintentionally picking up on it. They had to be close. Was anyone around? No—no one. Just a few empty vehicles and me. I quickly got in my car and went to the store as I had planned, then, to the corner mart for a Coke. I was surprised to see Alex was already there and in line, waiting to buy a drink.

"Hi there," I said.

"Oh, hi, Arri." He stepped back and let the man between us go. "Just coming home from work?"

"Yes." I said. "It was awful." Alex looked amused. I waited for the cashier to ring up my drink, but all she did was stare at Alex. "How much?" I asked her, tired of waiting.

"He already paid for it," she said, rather sharply. Alex smiled and held the door open for me. There were only two cars in the lot: mine and the one of the man pumping gas.

"Thank you for the drink. How much do I owe you?" I asked.

"Nothing. I'm not really concerned over fifty cents," Alex replied.

"Do you want a ride home?" I asked.

"Would you mind?"

"No, not at all—please!"

Alex was silent the whole ride. It was very uncomfortable. I pulled between the two houses and asked if he wanted me to let him out here. He declined saying it was only twenty feet away and he could use the exercise. After opening the gate for me, he walked me to the door. As we approached the door, chills ran down the back of my neck. I could feel the anger and building rage coming from somewhere behind Alex, but Alex didn't seem angry.

"What's wrong?" Alex asked, alert.

"Nothing, just an odd feeling." I squinted as though it would improve my sight. "Would you like to come in?"

Alex hesitated for a few seconds, and then accepted. I'd realized that being home alone was a little scary. The dark house and cold floors amplified the emptiness. I made a mental note to leave at least one light on at all times. When Alex came in, I relaxed. I was just about to ask him if he wanted to stay for dinner when there was a knock at my door. It was Sarah and Jonathan.

"Oh, hello, Arri!" Sarah's voice was silky smooth as she pushed past me with her nose in the air, not waiting for an invitation.

"I saw Alex come in, so I thought I would invite myself. Jonathan was the only one left at home, so I pulled him along." Behind her, Jonathan simply nodded.

"So…who's hungry?" I asked, looking for something to say. Sarah glanced at Alex, then toward the back door. She wanted him to follow. It was apparent there was something they needed to talk about.

"Excuse us for a moment. I just want to talk to Sarah." They left, and I was alone with Jonathan.

"Are *you* hungry?" I asked. To my surprise, he nodded.

"Yes, actually. I am starving, but I think Sarah already ordered pizza, and it should be here in about three minutes."

"Don't you need to be home to get it?"

"Nah, it's on its way here." Jonathan plopped himself on the couch, and turned on my TV, making himself at home.

"Sorry about that," Alex said as he and Sarah walked back in.

Sarah glared at his back and curled her lips into a straight, thin line, looking absolutely livid. *I hope I never get on her bad side. She looks like she is ready to kill.* Softening her piercing stare, Sarah looked at me, but Alex chimed in before she could say anything.

"Now I believe you were asking if we were hungry?" Alex asked.

"Yes, I—" Before I could answer, the doorbell rang.

"I've got it!" Sarah sang as she ran to the door, pulling cash out from her back pocket.

I figured it was the pizza when I heard a man say, "That'll be forty-six dollars and eighty-one cents." I gathered some paper plates and napkins and placed them on the table.

It was like they all lived here. Like I had been quickly adopted into this little family.

The next few days were the same. I would go to work and lose myself in all the paperwork that Mary needed to be sorted and filed. I only briefly interacted with the employees, though the conversations indicated that I was envied by most of the other girls. I heard one of the girls mention Anna, and how they knew where she was, while she was on the phone. I couldn't hear the other side of the conversation, but I was able to listen to this side. It sounded like Tonya knew where Anna was and thought she might be returning. I was trying to focus more intently, but Mary interrupted with the quarterly worksheets.

After working there for a few weeks more, I realized why Anna might have left. Mary was no leader, nor did she have any management skills. Mary was the girls' friend, not their boss. She played the innocent role saying that I was sent by the board, and how she would have promoted from within.

FOURTEEN

Things were looking sanguine and promising. So far, no one was chasing me, so hopefully my troubles were behind me. Alex and his family were great; they were comfortable enough to come over whenever they wanted, and didn't bother knocking anymore. Like clockwork, I would come home from work, and they would be sprawled out in my living room, watching a movie, eating the goods from my last haul at the grocery store, and even rearranging my furniture 'til it suited them best. I would have to admit it was nice to have a change of pace. I was content. Most of all, I was happy it was my life.

Work could have been going better, though. It was becoming a necessary evil. There was a rumor that Anna was coming back, and Mary was beginning to annoy me. I had even found Anna's request for the leave of absence stashed in Mary's office. When I presented it to her, she was shifty. *But why would she hide Anna's request, and why hasn't Anna returned?* At least now I was getting a better idea how of who I was dealing with. Mary was not like a real manager. There was something going on and she was artful with whatever she was doing. .

That day, Alice, one of the branch's most talented tellers, called in sick, and I was in her teller position. Alice was one of those crunchy types; she ate only things that were organic or had come out of her very own garden. Something about her getting sick and calling in sick so often seemed a little odd. Being a teller again had brought up some old memories, but I was having fun, remembering how much I loved it. Yes, it was monotonous, but it was familiar, and in a way, it challenged me. I was on a mission: to prove to the girls and Mary that

I was unaffected by my current predicament and to prove to myself that I could do both positions without a second thought.

After what felt like forever, the day was only half-over. The girls had been giving me attitude all day—asking if I knew what I was doing, or pretending to give me hints and shortcuts on the computer. Good thing I knew better or they would have really screwed me up. If any one of them made one more comment, I was going to wring all their little necks. It was about ten minutes 'til I was to go to lunch and the next member in line caught my eye. Every day this past week he had been in my line. I stalled the transaction before him as long as I could to pass him off to someone else, but nope—I was it. He was debonair, and the casual yet compelling way he sauntered toward me made me weak at the knees. I was completely smitten.

"Good afternoon, how may I help you?" I needed to concentrate on every word. I was trying to be sweet, and not let him know I was jittering-June-bug nervous. I ensured I breathed at a reasonable pace, hoping it didn't match the rapid pounding of my heartbeat. He was gorgeous: long brown wavy hair, emerald green eyes, and a body that put a male model's to shame. His grace and poise intimidated me. Although I had never said so much as ten words to him, he always playfully flirted. Thank goodness I never saw him outside of work. I probably would have sounded like a blabbering idiot.

"Good afternoon Arri. I trust you are well?" Most people spoke with some type of slang, but this guy was well-spoken and probably well-educated.

"Yes, thank you. What can I do for you?" I pulled up his account that I had recorded to memory: Michael London. I had not only memorized his name and account number, but also noticed he came in at about the same time, and ninety percent of the time I was the one who waited on him if Alice was out. He wanted me to see him, but the movement of the line was even out of his control.

He smiled. "A withdrawal and a deposit please."

I nodded just as Mary walked up behind me and told me it was time for lunch. Michael's face lit up slightly. Silently acknowledging Mary's announcement, I kept counting back his withdrawal.

"Is there anything else I can do for you?" I asked.

He hesitated momentarily. His eyes implored me to do…something. I raised my eyebrows.

"Yes, Mr. London?"

With final resolve, he straightened his shoulders. "No, but thank you."

Something in his voice that told me he was holding back. He bowed, showing me his perfect, heart-melting grin one last time before he left. He reminded me of a jaguar with his precise and elegant movements. Blood rose to my cheeks. For a second there, I thought he might have had more to say. And secretly, I'd been hoping he did, just so I could look at him once more.

"I can't believe you!" Lilith, the teller sitting next to me cried. "If you date him, you will be envied by every girl in town. That guy is the most sought-after bachelor. Up until recently, he was rarely seen around town. No one's seen where he lives or knows where he comes from. It's weird how only now, when you are around, does he mysteriously appear." She snapped her fingers. "You're the only one he really wants to see. When you're not here, he walks in, then walks out!" She looked at me skeptically, like I had something to hide, but the truth was I had no idea who this guy was beyond his account number. It's not like we actually talked when I did see him. I blushed again.

When I left, Michael was still in the parking lot, standing by his car. He smiled, waved, and then got in his car and drove away. I was plain and simple, and he was immaculate.

When I left work, the night was different, unlike the happy feeling I usually felt when I drove home. An odd feeling of hatred settled in the pit of my stomach made me nauseated. The feelings increased as I got closer to home.

I pulled into the driveway, parked my car, and was about halfway to closing the gate when I decided to leave it open and head straight into the house. I was getting used to listening to my intuition. It was not like the gate locked properly anyway; it was a screw that held it closed.

I went into the house and put my purse down on the counter. Something was not right. I turned on the lights, and when they brightened the dark and empty kitchen, I was appalled. To my horror, it was a mess. Destroyed. Nothing left standing except the walls.

Stunned, I walked through the rubble that used to be all of my dishes. The glass cracked and crunched under my feet. Ripped and torn paper crinkled as I walked over it, giving the uneven ground a yet more slippery and unstable base. My books were scattered about with the pages torn out and discarded. My couch, the one thing I looked forward to after a long day at work, had been cut to shreds.

Who could have done this? I didn't think I had been here long enough to make an enemy. I went from room to room. Even the bathroom was beyond recognition. The toilet paper was strung off the roll and soaked, and the floor was flooded. The water from the toilet ran over the side of the tank, and the sink was stopped up with the water still running. I felt utterly shattered, betrayed, and violated. Mutely, I went back through the house again, getting a full view of the damage. There was so much destruction. What was I going to do?

Reaching into my purse, I pulled out my phone and called the police.

"911 emergency." A friendly female voice announced on the other end.

"Yes, um, my house was broken into?"

"Are you okay?" I could hear typing keys in the background.

"Yes. I wasn't home." My voice broke.

"You're okay. We'll send someone right out. What's the address?"

I told her my address then hung up the phone. I put my keys down next to my purse, placed my jacket on the counter, and did what anyone would do: I cleaned. I rolled up my sleeves and grabbed a few towels and rags, then got down on all fours and started at one end of the house. I had just begun picking up all the glass when Alex, Sarah, and Jonathan crept in behind me.

Alex chuckled. "Wow, I didn't know you were a party animal." His voice was playful, but he felt sympathetic and alarmed. Jonathan walked in, then walked right back out again. Sarah immediately came down to my level and took my hands in hers. I felt violated and couldn't look at any of my friends. My cheeks were stained with tears, my eyes were red, my skin was blotchy. Sarah led me to what was left of my couch and set me down. I tried to smile, but I couldn't. I stared at the floor. There was nothing left in me. There were no words that described this. I was lost. What did I do to deserve this? My mind was going in a thousand different directions at once. Alex was talking on the phone, but I couldn't hear what he was saying, just the rumble of his voice as he spoke.

As if lightning struck, I linked it all together. I was reading people's emotions. This is what I felt when I came home. The feelings of being followed and how I thought someone was after me. It was the same as Las Vegas. I thought I had left my problems there, but it was all right here in front of me. I must have had the look of a revelation, because Alex and Sarah stared at me, totally confused and curious.

"Is everything okay?" Sarah leaned forward cautiously.

"Yes, I'm fine." I smiled faintly. "I wasn't reading people. I actually felt them. I thought it was just me being nervous and paranoid, but it was them." I glanced back and forth between the two of them, expecting them to understand.

Alex raised one eyebrow. Sarah looked at me like I had bugs crawling out of my ears. They had no idea what I was talking about.

"Could you run that by me one more time?" Alex asked, and Sarah nodded. Just as I was explaining, Jonathan walked in. I told them everything I could think of. I even told them of the three men who attacked me back home, and how a pack of dogs saved my life. Alex and Jonathan smiled. They must have thought I was crazy. But when I finished, none of them looked surprised. Sarah appeared to be in deep thought, almost annoyed, her thin lips pursed, and her eyebrows furrowed. Alex and Jonathan, though, bolted from the house, furious, leaving Sarah and me staring after them. Sarah's eyes twinkled, and her calculated demeanor slipped for a fraction of a second before she snapped out of her all-knowing trance and resumed her pedigreed look.

I started to clean, but Sarah stopped me. "Leave it. Let us be here for you. You've been through enough for today." She was trying to keep my mind off things. "How was work?"

I told her about the catty girls and Mary. It wasn't distracting me from the mess or break-in, but it helped me distance myself enough to form a list of things to do after the police got here. Alex and Jonathan were gone for about ten minutes, then returned and looked straight at Sarah.

"If they were here, they are long gone now. We made a ten-mile sweep. They covered their tracks well. Not a scent of their whereabouts."

Now I was confused. "Who?" And as if I had said nothing, the three of them went into the other room to discuss what they should do. I could hear every word, so I let them go.

"Well, the only solution I can see is to tell him," Alex said.

"When?" Jonathan sounded like he was planning a military operation. Alex and Jonathan walked back into the living room.

"So, what did you decide?" I asked. Alex looked a little disappointed.

"Well, for starters, you are going to deal with the police." That much I had already figured out, but who was the *him* they needed to tell? "Then, unfortunately, the three of us have business to take care of, and we will be home in a few days."

"A few days? What business?" I asked, angry now. There was more than they were telling me. "Who are you going to tell?"

"We aren't telling anyone anything. At least just yet."

Alex sounded a little upset. Jonathan looked at me, then at Alex.

"We need to leave *now*," he said. "We have been held up long enough. The police can take it from here, and there is nothing else we can do."

Jonathan was not the emotional type, and seemed totally impassive. I, however, was scared to death.

"What happens if they come back? What if they weren't done with—"

Sarah cut me off this time. "Arri, stop! You are getting all worked up over nothing." Her voice took a knowing tone. "No one is coming back and the police are on their way. The house was just ransacked.

Nothing is missing. Just hang tight and we'll be back in a few days."

No way. They were wrong. Whoever had done this *wasn't* finished. I didn't have anything valuable. In fact, the one valuable thing I had they could have wanted was me. And I was still here.

"A few days? How can you be so sure they won't come back for me?"

"You? Why would they want you?" Sarah's voice was edgy now.

"Hey, guys!" I yelled after the men, but they had already disappeared like lightning—here one second, and then gone the next.

After they left, I looked around at my bare and lonely house. A few minutes later, the cops showed up.

"They really did a job on this one," a short, heavy officer said to another as he held up a notepad with notes etched across the paper. His comment was a little bit of a downer, but he was right. Work like this was only done in the movies.

After hundreds of questions and a few dozen strange men rummaging through my things, the police finished their investigation in the early hours of the morning. They gave me their cards and told me if anything else happened, I was to call them immediately.

Their taillights disappeared down my driveway. I dropped my head, let out a sigh of defeat, and headed back into the house. As I closed the door, the waiting mess sprawled around me. I was more convinced than ever that whoever did this was not going to give up until they got what they wanted—me.

I just wish I understood why. I mean, I must have done or seen something, or why would they follow me all the way from Vegas?

I looked at the time on my phone: 2:15 a.m. I was mentally beat and tired, but I needed my mom. I knew that she and dad were in Cairo. The last time she texted, she'd said they would be out of cell phone range for a few days, but I had to try. I pulled up her number and hit send. The phone rang. I prayed she would pick up. With each ring, I felt further away from them. It rang three more times before it went to voice mail.

"Hi, this is Emily. If you've reached this, I am currently unavailable. Please leave a message. *Ciao*."

At the sound of her recorded voice, my chest ached and my resolve to be strong faltered.

Exhausted and drained, my body flooded with numbness. I dropped my phone on the nightstand and crawled onto bed.

Some amount of time later—I didn't know how much—my doorbell rang. The sound echoed in my ears, and a roaring headache protested. All I wanted was to be left alone. I was sure I looked like I'd been through a blender on puree.

I peered through the window. A brand-new, white, pickup truck was parked out front. A few men were sitting in the cab, and a handful stood in the bed of the truck talking. The man at the door had his back to me, but turned when the others nodded to me as I peered through the window. When I opened the front door, a gentleman in painter's overalls was standing there, happy to see me.

"Are ye Arri?" the man asked in a thick Scottish accent. His red hair flamed in the sun, and his pale skin shone, almost iridescent.

"Yes, can I help you?" I began to close the door. I didn't know him, and who was to say that he wasn't the one who broke in? His smile looked friendly enough, but as my parents used to say, looks can be deceiving.

"Aye, I'm Scotty. Gotta wee call from Alex last night. He wanted me to pop by and see if you were okay."

Scotty seemed to be legit. Alex *had* made a few calls last night. I just wish I had paid attention to who he was calling.

"Well I'm here and fine." I opened the door a little.

"Well, lass, if you don't mind, I'd like to come in and check out the damage."

He glanced to the side. Strangers made me nervous in the first place, and after last night, I was a little wary about letting anyone in. I tried to tell him I was fine, but he insisted on going through the house. Scotty gasped when he saw the sight of the catastrophe just inside the door as he pushed past me.

"Aye, a travesty!" he yelled.

"I had the same thought," I said.

"Aye. Sorry, lassie."

"Someone decided they didn't like the way my house was decorated and decided to make a few changes," I joked. "I liked it better the old way." I managed a weak smile.

"We best be gettin' on with the job and cleanin' this place up." He headed for the door.

Confused, I threw my hands up and followed him. I didn't call a cleaning crew. "Wait, what?"

Scotty signaled for the men to come in. Through the window, I glimpsed a half-dozen workers walking to the door.

"Really, I swear, it's okay," I tried to say, but as each man came in, he gave them assignments, and pointed to the room assigned. I was not going to win, and I didn't have the energy to fight.

"Sorry, lass, just followin' orders. Alex said we're to clean the place and watch ya till he returns." Scotty put his arm around my shoulders and led me to my room. "Lassie, why don't you relax, and I will call you when I need ya."

I was too exhausted to argue, so I allowed him to escort me to my room. I went back to bed but couldn't close my eyes. I picked up my iPad and opened my book app to start reading. Even though the curtains were pulled off the rods, and the sun shone in and warmed the cold and uninviting wreckage, the bed and my book made it a place of temporary comfort.

When I awoke, the sun was setting, and the sky was painted a beautiful orange. The clouds were sparse. *I slept? I must have dozed off while reading. Oh no! Scotty and his men!* I went into the living room to see if they were still here, but Scotty was the only one left, sitting at attention on the couch like he was just waiting for something. He looked ready for bear. What time was it? Half-past six already?

"Scotty, are you hungry? I don't think I have anything left, but I can order pizza." I offered. Scotty jerked his head. His movement was rigid and hard.

"No, 'tis not necessary, lass. Alex and the gang are on their way back. I figured you'd be hungry when you woke, so I left some grub for you in the oven. All you need to do is warm it up." He stood up and pointed to the oven. This time his motions were more fluid and gentle.

"Thank you agai—"

He held up his hand and stopped me mid-sentence.

"Lassie, it wasn't a problem, just doing a favor for a friend. Alex and his brother have helped me out of a scrape or two. Any friend of his is a friend of mine." He gave a small bow and headed for the door.

Alone again, I rubbed my arms, uneasy. The house was too quiet. Scotty and his friends had done a lot of work. They cleaned up all the glass, papers, wood chips, covered in the holes in the wall, and fixed and cleaned up the bathroom. I was amazed, and felt maybe a little guilty. I'd slept the day away while they did all the work. Opening the oven. I checked to see what Scotty left me. *Chicken and dumplings?* Well, that was a little excessive, but very welcome. My stomach grumbled. I was starving. After a few days of chaos and heart-wrenching wreckage, with a full, satisfied stomach, I sat on the shredded couch and relaxed.

FIFTEEN

The next day, I woke up at sunrise. I didn't realize that the break-in had taken so much out of me. I must have pretty much slept for twenty-four straight hours. It was really unlike me to be so tired. My curtains were drawn open, and the light from the bright pink clouds and hazy, orange-painted sky lit the living room with a wondrous glow. My neck was a little kinked from falling asleep on the couch. Groaning, I lifted my head to look around and see if the break-in nightmare was real. Sure enough, it was, but what I hadn't expected was to find was Alex in a new recliner, and Sarah in my room placing clothes in my closet. The aroma of eggs filled the air. Jonathan's voice came from the kitchen.

"Will someone wake Sleeping Beauty and tell her that her breakfast is ready?"

At least I was back in good hands. Alex looked at me. "You heard the chef. Breakfast is ready."

We all sat down and ate like a family. Like at home. In the comforting routine, yesterday seemed so far away and forgotten.

I was grateful for the work that Alex and his friends had done, and after we spent a long and relatively stress-free day of friendly conversation and good company, Alex and his family went home, and I headed in for the night.

I was just getting ready to turn out the lights and go to bed when the motion-sensitive light outside blinked on. That thing had had a mind of its own ever since Alex installed it when I first moved in, but maybe after the break-in, it was wise to check it out. Cautiously, I cracked open the door to see what activated it. I was shocked to see a large dog staring at me. Not just large—this dog was huge. It had a pure, flawlessly white coat and stood tall, as if with pride, almost majesty. The lone dog's eyes shone in the light, silver and foreboding. It looked at me almost confidently, like I was the one intruding on *its* territory.

I got some serious chills. Probably best to leave the animal alone. I closed the door and went to my room.

I was hoping tonight would be a little more settling than the last few, and finally, the moment I was waiting for. I collapsed into bed. But no matter how hard I tried to sleep, the constant nagging feeling that I was being watched haunted my thoughts. It was annoying. I was tired of looking over my shoulder. It seemed like just when I thought my paranoia was all in my imagination, something would happen, like an actual break-in. This time, my anxiety was not going away.

It was about one in the morning when something broke my unsettled sleep—an alarmingly loud howling. Angrily, I stomped my way to the backdoor and peered through the window. To my amazement, there was nothing there, just the darkened outline of my large, beaten-up old tree. Grumbling and pounding the doorway with my fist, I cursed the infernal dog. It had to be the one doing this. The howling crescendoed as I made my way through the house to try the front door. Outside, the night was inky, and I searched the bleak and unpopulated scenery for anything. In the moonlit shadows of the old barn across the street, movement flickered.

My breath caught. An unrecognizable shadow crept and snaked its way through the night. I turned on the porch light, hoping to scare whatever it was away, and bolted back to my bedroom, where I climbed back into bed, snuggled under the covers, and ignored the tension that perched on my shoulders.

I wasn't in bed for ten minutes when a grating noise rasped from the tree outside my window. Snapping wide awake, I steadied my sizzling nerves and got up to throw back the curtains.

When I did, my body clamped up in fear. Two frigid eyes stared back at me. My first reaction was to scream and run, but the determined and surprised look on the man's face kept me still. I peered into the eyes of evil that stood only inches from the glass. My mind sputtered. Finally, finding my voice, I ran to the living room, screaming. I grabbed my cell phone from the counter and dialed 911. Behind me, glass shattered and wood splintered as the man barged his way into the house. I screamed again, knowing the intruder was headed toward my panicked yell.

"Hello, 911 emergency." A woman's voice broke through the other end of the line, but my voice faltered as the intruder grabbed my shoulders. The heavy, vice-like grip slammed me to the floor, knocking the phone out of my reach.

"911 emergency," the woman's voice came again from the speaker, but the man kicked the phone away. The stranger stood over me, smirking at my obvious horror. I screamed again, and his rough, massive, cold palm covered my mouth, holding me down without effort. I struggled, throwing my arms at him and kicking, but to no avail. My heart raced. How could I get free? Fighting wasn't working; neither was giving up and hoping his grip would loosen. I could sense his cold, dark, frostbitten soullessness. His humanity was gone, and hatred and worry were the only emotions he had left. That dead, heartless smirk promised pain and suffering. He laughed at my horror.

Suddenly, a loud bang came from the back of the house, sending the back door hurtling across the mudroom. More glass and wood shattered against the wall. The stranger was unfazed, and I was expecting to see his accomplice, but instead, the huge white dog lunged at him and threw him to the floor. When the man's hand was torn from my mouth, I struggled to my feet. Before I got far, a sharp pain crushed my ankle: the stranger's death grip. I cried out in shock.

The white dog tightened its jaws until, with a crack, the man's arm bent back unnaturally. At last, he let go of me, and I hobbled to the corner and cradled my knees.

I was stunned. Since when do men and dogs fight like mortal enemies? Especially in the middle of my house? Was I crazy?

A pure black dog and a tan dog rushed in and took over holding the man down. *Yep, probably crazy.* These dogs were not just working together, they had a strategic plan of attack. Just when I'd thought I'd lost it, the white dog that only a few moments ago was my knight in shining armor blurred and faded until it transformed into Alex.

It was hard to accept what I just saw. Was I hurt so bad that I was hallucinating? Still, Alex stood there, waiting for me to grab his hand. I hesitated. Police sirens wailed in the distance as the sound slowly filled the background, red and blue lights flashing across the living room. Alex looked back to the two other dogs and snapped at them.

"Get him out of here!"

My pain ridden mind fought to stay focused as Alex screamed "NOW!" The two dogs dragged the man out of the house. Just as they cleared the doorway, my attacker yelled back at me.

"Nicholas will have you, one way or another!"

Just seconds before the police ran in the front door, the dogs disappeared.

The cops had their guns drawn. The house was surrounded. They looked and cleared each room before returning to the living room, but there was no one there but Alex and me.

"Where's the intruder?" one of the police asked. Alex pointed to the back door.

"He ran through the back. I tried to stop him, but he was too strong."

"How's the girl? Does she need an ambulance?"

I was so wrapped up in the fact that Alex was a dog, I barely heard the question, but I did recognize the familiar voice that came from behind me.

"I'll take her." Whoever it was was hidden in the shadows. I couldn't tell who it was. I looked at Alex, confused. *Do I know this strange man?*

"It's okay, I promise," Alex said, as the man reached out for me. Alex looked directly at the stranger.

"I'll stay here with the police. You take care of her. I think she's in shock. Watch her ankle. It's been cut open and she's lost a lot of blood. It may be broken."

I looked down, dazed. The bottoms of my pajama pants were soaked in blood and clinging to my legs. As the police left the room to search the grounds, I felt the stranger reach around me.

"Come."

"Why?" I asked. His face was still obscured by shadow, but I felt like I knew him from somewhere.

"No time. Come," he said, in a much softer voice. I was debating the odds of breaking free from his grip when he threw me over his shoulder and ran for the front door. I expected a bumpy ride as we crossed the road and into the fields, but his smooth gait was like floating more than running.

"Where are we going?" I tried to yell, but somehow, he moved me from over his shoulder to cradling me in his arms without missing a beat. *How did he do that?*

I tried to fight and free myself, but my feeble attempts did nothing. He ran for miles through the woods until we entered a large darkened estate. With my head getting fuzzy and my pain worse, all I could make out was the outline of a mansion. We walked through large wooden doors that echoed and crashed as they closed behind us. Light flooded my captor's face. *Michael?* The flawless voice, the unbelievable strength, and the angelic face was none other than Michael?

He set me gently on my feet in the middle of a large antechamber and offered his strong, sturdy frame for support.

"Nana!" he yelled.

"Where am I? Let me go!"

My demand fell on deaf ears. "Nana!" he yelled again, this time more forceful than the last, and just as he opened his mouth, a short, skinny old lady came from behind a door on the right.

"What is it, Michael?" she said in a sweet British accent.

"I don't know. Just clean her up and put her in my office." He shook his head and walked up the stairs, but not without one last look of concern at me.

"What do you mean, *just clean her up and set her in your office*?" I yelled after him. "I have a name!"

The elderly lady gently took my arm. "Come, dear, I'm sure a nice spot of tea will calm your nerves while I call the doctor."

"No, I won't *come*. I'm not a dog!" My voice shook as I rubbed my temples. I grit my teeth and turned on my heel. My stubborn side got the best of me, and I tried to hobble my way to the door. I could only imagine how childish I looked when the excruciating pain in my ankle throbbed. I fell to the floor, overtaken by tears. As soon as I was able to stop the sobbing and gather my strength, I pulled my way to the door. I didn't know where we were, or how far away I was from home, but I was determined to get there.

As I dragged myself along the floor, a familiar touch settled on my shoulder.

"This is an uphill battle. You have no chance of winning." The voice was not Nana's. It was Michael's, the same Michael who made me go weak at the knees, the one I liked. The man I would dream about. He was one of the best parts of moving here. I faced my nemesis, ready to fire at will. But I had nothing. I broke down again, and my strength faded. Closing my eyes, I giggled to myself. *What am I fighting for?* I had to admit, I was enthralled with the thought of being stuck here with him. My emotions churned until a wave of elation and apprehension rushed my heart. The thought that I was unable to leave scared me, but being held here against my will by Michael brought a bittersweet smile to my tear-streaked face. *I must be delusional.*

Michael simply grinned. The emotionless and heartless Michael faded, and a man with gentle admiration shone through.

"Are you going to run?" he asked. There was no winning this battle, even I knew that. I stopped fighting. My strength, now only enough to keep me breathing, let me fall.

"Ahh!" My ankle pounded with pain. Michael carefully picked me up and cradled me. His warmth bled through his clothes and warmed my tired soul. I laid my head against his chest and breathed in his sweet scent.

My leg throbbed as he carried me up the stairs and into a room. Gently, he set me on the bed. Not a moment later, Nana was there, placing towels under my ankle and cutting my bloody, ragged pant leg. Michael sat next to me on the bed and held my hand as I drifted in and out of consciousness. Although I was in pain and scared, I was comforted by his tender touch. The last thing I remembered was a man walking in asking Michael what had happened.

SIXTEEN

My head pounded, my body ached, and I was utterly stiff. I rubbed my cheeks, trying to wake up. I didn't want to face the day. I had the strangest dream and let out a soft laugh. My dream was crazy. Where did it come from? Letting out a reluctant sigh, I finally opened my eyes.

I stared in bewilderment. *Where am I?*

A printed canopy hung above me. Maybe Sarah had taken the liberty to redecorate. But when I looked around, I realized I wasn't home. The memories of last night, and what seemed like a dream, now felt more like a nightmare. Panicking, I sat up and looked at the room around me. A nightstand was next to me, and I searched it—for a phone, a note, or anything that would tell me why, but I found nothing except a small antique lamp and a yellow vase holding a single, red rose. I couldn't lose it. I forced myself to inhale and gain control. I had to think this through. There was something about last night, something about my dream that seemed a little odd. I remembered being attacked and the fight between my attacker and the dog—or Alex? Then I remembered Michael bringing me here. Attending to my injuries.

I pulled back the covers, and sure enough, my ankle was wrapped in bandages. I tried to move my toes. The pain was bad, but bearable.

So my dream *was* real.

Carefully, I pushed myself up and hobbled my way to the door. I placed my ear against it and listened, but there was nothing: no footsteps, mumbling, anything. I tried the door; the old, cast iron handle was stiff, and when I pulled, it was locked. I pulled harder, yanking on it, but the door didn't budge.

Fear surged in me. I didn't like the idea of being locked in a room. Maybe no one knew I was awake. I knocked. No one came. Just hollow silence echoed my pleas.

"Hello, hello?" I yelled. "Please?"

No reply. Panic jumped in my chest. There had to be another way. There had to be something here to help me. But no ideas came to me. Frustrated, I screamed. Hysteria and fear took over, and I fell to my knees.

Time passed. I was running out of ideas—if I'd even had any to begin with. Looking up, I saw the flower in the vase, and a thought came to mind. I pushed myself off the floor, picked up the vase and walked to the window. The grounds beneath me were at least four floors down. Even if I managed to break the window with the vase, there was no way I would walk away from a jump like that.

I folded my arms and muttered. Suddenly furious, I went back to the door and pounded and yelled. My fists hurt, and finally my tired and aching body gave up. Maybe I was forgotten. Defeated, I limped my way back to the chair by the window.

As I waited for both strength and determination to build, I looked around the room. The furniture was extravagant, but ancient. A gilded wooden dresser stood nearby, and ornate tapestries hung from the walls. There were a few little pictures on the walls of trees and flowers in different stages of the season: a large green maple leaf hung next to a maple that was a little older, brown, and with part of its stem and outer shape missing and damaged. It was quite poetic. A few knickknacks were sparsely displayed here and there. The white vaulted ceilings crisscrossed with wooden beams. Three large draped windows framed with the same antique wood as the ceiling above stood tall against one wall. The extended windowsill made a for nice bench—*a beautiful place to read*, I thought. The old stone walls weren't painted. They were original.

I was in a modern Cinderella castle.

This wasn't getting me anywhere. I tried to wrap my brain around it all. I let out an annoyed yell. As soon as I did, my door opened and a white-haired, older lady ran to my side.

"Are you all right, dear?" It was Nana, her voice sweet. She looked me smartly up and down and seemed to conclude that I was fine. I could only stare. Nana repeated the question. "Are you all right, my dear?"

"No," I said. "I'm not okay!" I was trying to keep my voice down and stay calm. Internally, I was screaming, but I wasn't going to yell at Nana.

"What's the matter, dearie? Do you need more pain medicine?" Her innocent expression and her even tone annoyed me. It was like she saw no problem with the situation.

"No. What am I doing here?"

Nana was not listening. She turned her attention to the phone she was holding.

"Excuse me!" I said, slightly louder. Nana stopped her texting and looked at me.

"Yes?"

"What's going *on*?" I didn't hide the attitude this time.

Nana didn't react. Instead, she simply excused herself. But just as she left, she turned back to me.

"The doctor will be in soon to check your ankle. If you want to clean up, there is a bathroom through there, and a clean set of clothes on the bench." Nana smiled at me and indicated the wall next to the bed. I hadn't noticed it before, but there was a hidden door flush with the wall. An idea hit me, and I quickly stood and tried to follow her out, but with my bad ankle, the door closed before I could catch it.

I sighed. I had to admit: if you were going to be held hostage, this was not a bad place to stay. One final time, I banged my fists on the door, but I was alone again.

I walked back to the window and stared at the yard. Light poured through the tall window, the sun's rays scattered in an array of colors as it hit an intricately laced stained glass window with bold hues and bubbly glass. Beyond the window, the lawn was perfectly manicured and trimmed. Pruned trees and bushes outlined the yard with about a dozen men walking around—undoubtedly on some kind of patrol. I knocked on the window, trying to get their attention, but none of them turned. Beyond the expansive yard were trees, trees, and more trees. Beyond the trees, there were mountains in every direction.

If I were to run, I would never know which way to go.

I was lost in the moment when a knock on the door interrupted my thoughts. I smiled.

"Come in," I said, my voice just above a whisper. As I turned, I was a little shocked to see a tall, thin man in a white coat walking toward me. He flipped a chair around, gestured for me to come by, and helped me sit down.

"How are you this morning?" His voice was strong and cordial. I tried to contain my anger as I answered back.

"Fine, I guess. What am I doing—"

I stopped as Michael walked in.

"It's good to hear that. And how about your ankle? Are you in great pain?" The doctor never made eye contact, but kept his attention on my ankle. My own attention was focused on Michael, who leaned stiffly against one of the bedposts.

"No. I'm just a little uncomfortable."

The doctor gently took the wrapping off and carefully palpated my calf and foot before attending to my ankle again. Although I answered the doctor's questions, my attention never left Michael. I didn't know how to act. My heart was caught between the anger of being locked up and my undeniable attraction to him. It was like I was twelve again and had a crush on the guy sitting next to me in homeroom.

The touch at my ankle pulled me back to reality. With all the blood last night, I expected to see scratches, scrapes, or stitches, but my leg was clean. I was astonished.

"So, how is that?" The doctor asked.

Not as bad as I'd thought. "Mostly sore and a little bruised," I said.

"Looks like you're healing rather quickly. If you progress this way, you'll be up and about in two days."

"Two days!"

I couldn't stop myself. The doctor didn't bat an eye at my outburst, but Michael readjusted himself and moved in a smidgen closer. The doctor palpated my ankle one last time before he deftly wrapped it back up. He bowed his head and bid me good day. As he walked away, Michael followed, and the two of them spoke just loudly enough for me to overhear.

"So, what do you think?" Michael sounded skeptical.

"She seems fine, but there are some…"

I lost the thread as the two of them exited the room.

"Excuse me," I yelled after them. "Hey, wait a minute! Hello? Will one of you talk to me? I just want to use the phone!"

No answer. It was as if I didn't exist. I hobbled toward the door, but as soon as it swung shut, I heard it lock.

I pulled again. The cold, hard handle didn't move. I banged and yelled but to no avail. Anger, confusion, and frustration—all toward Michael—swelled in my chest, and I limped, trying my best to pace. Again, I tried the door. My annoyance built until I was no longer myself. The more I thought about last night, the angrier I got, and a fire inside me grew until my control faded and my anger took over. By the bed, I picked up the same yellow vase that held a rose on my nightstand.

"Let me out!" I screamed. With a yell of fury, I threw the vase. It shattered against the door. *That felt good.* I hobbled around the room and picked up an antique wooden clock from the old dresser.

"Let me out!" I cried. "This is ridiculous."

My words were unheard, I knew. I scowled at the door.

I played with the heavy wooden clock for a moment until there was a knock on the door.

I didn't say anything. The door swung slowly open, and before I knew it, I threw the clock, only missing them by inches. The door slammed and locked again.

"You can stay in there all day," Michael called from the other side of the door.

"Oh yes I can," I called back, surprising myself.

I sat in the chair and wandered the room while I waited. Hours later, footsteps padded nearby. I called out for whoever it was, but they never answered. This fueled my fury even more. I didn't know what got into me, but I didn't care. I was always the one that tried to understand and keep my self-control, but now I was able to lose my temper and have no one tell me otherwise.

At last, the day was winding down. The sky was dark, the moon was bright, and though the sterling light tinted the tips of the trees silver, it never quite made it to the ground.

It was beautiful.

I had always lived in the city, and with the urban glare of Las Vegas lights, the stars were nonexistent. I had just learned to live without beauty. But here, it was impossible to ignore. The estate didn't have any outside lights, and with the darkness swallowing the vast expanse, I gazed into nothingness.

I realized it had been a while since anyone had tried the door.

I felt better, knowing I had effectively locked myself in, yet part of me melted as I wanted, and needed, to know someone cared. I glanced around the room. The floor was covered with broken glass, plastic, and some books—I'd demolished the place.

Slowly, I limped around, picking up everything I had thrown. I placed the books back on the shelves and did my best at putting away all the things I had tossed and hurled at the door. I tried to pick up all the glass, but if I was anything, I was at least efficient at shattering glass. After giving it a good effort, the room looked semi-decent, except for the tiny shimmer of powdered glass that still floured the floor.

With nothing left to occupy myself, I stared at the door 'til it blurred into a kind of Picasso painting.

Then I must have fallen asleep.

I woke up stiff. The sun was blinding, as the light bounced off all the broken glass, filling the room with hundreds of little shiny twinkles. The room hadn't changed much—or at all, I thought, until I spied a large breakfast tray on the nightstand: a huge glass of milk, a muffin, a few pastries, and a variety of fruit. *Well, I can still eat.*

After a healthy fill of breakfast, I went to try the door, but as I suspected, it was still locked. But as soon as I let go of the handle, the door flew open, and someone pinned my arms to my sides.

Michael grinned in victory. He scared the life right out of me, but I was happy to see him.

I sucked in air, calming my racing heart. I didn't want to be angry anymore. Being a belligerent hostage wasn't my style—especially if it put me more at risk.

"The doctor had tried to come in earlier, but you were not cooperative." Michael's smile was starting to become familiar. Slowly, he let me go. "Are you going to play nice?" A playful grin teased his lips.

I nodded as Michael helped me to a chair. "If I could just use the phone…I'm sure my parents are worried sick."

The doctor followed Michael in and removing the wrapping.

"Does this hurt?" He poked and turned my ankle in different directions.

"No, just a little stiff." I felt a pang of panic. "Why? What's wrong?"

"Nothing. Can you put some weight on it?"

I slowly stood and placed my bare foot on the cold wooden floor, bracing myself for the pain. But none came. I moved my weight on it, little by little, 'til finally I was distributing my weight evenly. I took a brave step. Still—no pain. I grinned at the doctor, then at Michael. Despite everything, I wanted to jump up and down with my sense of relief.

"Wasn't that supposed to take longer?" I asked the doctor. I was no physician, but whenever a cheerleader at school twisted or sprained her ankle, she was on crutches for at least a few weeks. With a glance at the doctor, Michael answered for him.

"He might have misdiagnosed it." Michael offered his hand to support me as I tested out my healed ankle. When he was satisfied I was stable, Michael escorted the doctor to the door and glanced at me.

"I'll be right back. Please, no more temper tantrums." He raised his eyebrows at me and closed the door. I was tempted to try it one more time, but I knew it was fruitless, and I wasn't going to cause any problems. Because maybe, if I *played nice*, as Michael put it, he would tell me why I was here and what was going on. *You get more flies with honey than you do with vinegar*, I reminded myself,

I took Nana up on the offer to get cleaned up. My aching muscles melted as the warm water from the shower washed away my stress. The towel was soft, and the bathroom was better than any five-star hotel. I wrapped the towel around me and went to the dresser in the bedroom. Nana had cleaned up while I was in the shower. After dressing in the clothes Nana mentioned yesterday, I sat on the bed waiting for someone to come in, but no one did. The minutes turned into hours, and Michael still hadn't come back. This whole damsel-in-distress thing was way overrated. I positioned the chair to face the window and noticed motion outside. I was excited to hear voices outside my bedroom door, even as they grew aggravated. I moved closer to the door to listen.

"I pray thee, why didst thou call me? Why wouldst thou have me bring her here? The problem is hers. Furthermore, she is human and thus she does not belong here. Is the reason thou callest upon me because thou findest her to thy fancy?" The voice was definitely Michael's, and he was definitely angry. A slight English curve wrapped his words, the acid pouring out with every syllable.

"*No!* I feel nothing for her. I am her guardian and nothing more. Her mother contracted me to safeguard her."

Alex?

"Alex, thou hast no thought. I am not a safe house for thy charges, and I am not a babysitter. What danger precedes her for thee to bring her here?"

"This situation is different," Alex said. "Arri was assigned to me by..."

The conversation paused. I was so captivated, I almost shouted "who?" but caught myself just in time.

"Alex, I beg thee, tell me who is after thee."

Michael was not like I thought he would be. Not just by the way he spoke—this was someone who was well brought-up, carried himself with pride, and treated everyone with respect. But he hated having me here, and was mad at Alex for it. I thought he liked me.

"I'm afraid she might have seen more than I intended her to." Alex sucked in a breath as if he were bracing himself for impact.

Michael spoke again, that angelic and harmonious voice now sharp with annoyance.

"How much does she know?" he gritted out.

"Well," Alex said, "she saw me change from a wolf to man?" His tone was nervous, tentative.

"What!" Michael cried. "She saw thee change? Thou shouldst be more careful. And what if she remembers?"

"Look, she was being attacked by one of Nicholas' men. I didn't have much of an option." Alex's voice was harsh and stern, no matter his nervousness. His tension radiated all the way through the door.

"What dost thou mean, *Nicholas*? What would he want with this particular child?"

Alex answered so quietly, I found myself pressing my ear against the door to hear.

"There is a lot about this child I hadn't told you. She is Steven's daughter."

A growl came from the other side of the door.

"I thought him to be dead!" Michael said through his teeth. "No word for centuries and thou tellest me thou knew? Alex! Speak to me!"

"I'm sorry, but I was sworn to secrecy. It was life-threatening, which is why I sought you out."

"And what of her? When the other guests return?" With that, Michael ended the conversation and opened the door. As the door swung open, I tumbled out and fell to the floor. Above me were the faces of Alex, my ex-friend, and Michael, the key-keeper to my prison.

Hurt, I glared at them. Alex had deceived me—claiming to be my friend, then saying to Michael that he felt nothing for me. Not just as friends or anything, just nothing. My eyes welled up with tears. Alex's face fell as he realized I had heard the whole conversation. I scrambled to my feet, ran to the bathroom, and locked myself inside.

"Arri, please be reasonable," Michael said, obviously upset with my behavior.

"Arri?" Alex sounded genuinely concerned. "Why don't you come out and let us explain?"

I didn't care what he had to say. I didn't want to hear it. I had heard enough. "*No*!" I yelled back. "You lied to me." I was crying, and my words were muffled.

Silence. The door closed.

I slowly peeked outside. I was alone again. The intense anger from earlier faded, and the real severity of my situation took its place. I had been attacked and kidnapped. I was being held hostage. My parents had no idea where I was.

But more than that, I had been lied to by the only friends I had.

I barely made it from the bathroom before I fell to the floor, cradling my knees in my arms.

What was going to happen to me?

SEVENTEEN

Loud claps of thunder rumbled and rolled as rain pounded against the window. Yet I found the deafening roar quite tranquil.

Warily, I opened my eyes. I stretched my arms and let out a soft moan. I remembered curling up in the corner and feeling sorry for myself, but here I was awake, and lying in bed staring up at the soft white silk that draped my canopy. I noticed the vague memory of Michael's cologne clung to my clothes, but wouldn't I have remembered if he'd been by? How could anyone miss his presence awake or asleep?

Yawning, I flung the blankets off. A sliver of light softly illuminated my room as it peeked through the slit in the thick curtains. I pulled back the window coverings to see that the clouds were concealing the sun from shining through. I stared out of the window mindlessly and looked at the rain-soaked ground and the puddles below.

I didn't know what to think anymore.

After showering and dressing, I returned to the window and watched the storm. I tried to figure out what my next step would be—or, even more importantly, what their next step might be. Was I to stay here forever in this room? Would they ever let me out, or would I have to devise another plan to escape on my own? The thoughts drowned my mind. What did they want me for? What did I have to offer them, and who were they really?

I knew I wouldn't be able to get far if I did escape, and who knew if they would ever let me go. I couldn't help but think about my parents, and how worried they must be. I missed them. I had been so anxious to leave my parents, and now I would do anything to be with them again.

A hard knock rapped on the door. I squared my shoulders. Gradually, the doorknob turned, and Alex slowly stepped in. My heart jolted.

"Good morning, Arri," Alex said in a smooth voice. He walked toward me so gradually he seemed almost slow-motion. "How do you feel?"

After last night, I didn't know who Alex was. I was nervous. I overheard him say he was a…a…a *werewolf*? Even my mind couldn't say it. Possibly he was crazy or confused. Either way, I didn't want to be near him.

Alex closed the gap between us, and instinctively I backed up into the corner between the wall and my bed. Not the best move, but it was the only place to get away from him. He stopped dead in his tracks. Taking a few steps back, he sat in the chair by the window. Calmly, he looked at me and waited for me to come around.

"Have you come to let me go?" My voice was helpless and faint, since I knew the answer was no.

"No, I'm afraid not." Alex sighed.

"Then, can I call my parents?" I asked. "Please. I know they're worried."

"I'm sorry." Alex looked truly repentant. "There is no safe way for you to contact them right now. The phone lines are too risky, and leaving would be far too dangerous. But I've sent word about where you are."

"And I'm just supposed to take your word for it?"

Alex smiled at my sneer, but I folded my arms and pushed myself further into the corner.

"How about my job? Can I call them?"

"No. Because of your situation, I took the liberty of relieving you from your position at the credit union. You resigned yesterday. I'm afraid Mary was rather upset. She may make it difficult for you to get a position in the credit union later, but maybe your mom can smooth things over." Alex frowned and braced himself for my reaction.

"You what?!"

Alex flinched but remained seated.

"I worked hard for that job," I said.

"I know, but if you went back…" He didn't finish. Alex readjusted himself. His unease scared me. I hugged myself, not feeling angry so much as afraid of the unknown: why I was here of all places, and why Alex seemed different—less friendly, more businesslike.

"Arri, maybe if I knew what you were thinking, I might be able to help you in your decision."

"Who *are* you?" I asked.

"Alex," he said. "Why are you afraid?"

"A stranger abducts me, and then I hear you tell Michael you are a werewolf. What am I supposed to feel?" I was hoping at this point that I was wrong, that I was just delusional.

"I am," Alex said without hesitation. "A werewolf, I mean."

"Awesome. Not only am I stuck here as a prisoner, but my best friend is also totally certifiable. Perfect. Is there anything else I should know? Are there wood sprites and trolls too?" I couldn't stop the sarcasm.

"You don't believe me?" Alex looked amused even as I scoffed. "I would have thought that after the attack at your house, you would be a little more understanding."

"The man who broke in didn't think he was more than a man, Alex. He knew he was human."

"Are you sure?"

He was right. I didn't know for sure.

"Okay, just a hypothetical question, if I did believe you," I started. "Then could I go?"

"I'm not crazy, Arri. Humans tend not to believe in things they don't understand." Alex chuckled tentatively. "But this is real."

"Fine. You can believe anything you want to believe. Can I go now?"

"You're not going to make this easy, are you?" He cocked his head. "All right then." Carefully, he stood, put his hands up in surrender, and grinned. "I'm sorry, Arri."

I sensed his fear. He looked down at his shoes and shuffled his feet, then squared his shoulders and steadied himself. I thought he was going to turn to the door and leave. The pain in his piercing eyes was too much, so I looked away.

Suddenly, I shuddered. My neck prickled, my hair stood on end, and the room went cold. His body blurred and slowly faded, then disappeared into the background entirely as a large white wolf gradually appeared out of the void. The air had turned wavy, like looking through a campfire.

The thunder sounding outside and the lightning flashing in the background made it all the more terrifying. I couldn't believe it. The blood drained from my face. *Do I run? Do I dare move at all?* I was scared to death. *Things like this don't exist.* I found it hard to breathe—I was hyperventilating. Slowly, I moved to the bed and sat down and I laughed nervously. Alex was turning back to himself. He tried to speak, but I raised my hand to stop him.

"For my own sanity…" I said, voice quivering, but I couldn't finish. There were no words.

"I'm sorry, Arri." Alex sat back down.

All I could do was nod. There were no words, just total betrayal and fear. What could I say, to a werewolf, a man who changed into a dog, a friend who had deceived me?

"Why didn't you tell me?" I said in shock.

"You weren't ready. You had no clue you were in danger. Your parents and I wanted to keep you away from everything as long as we could. I was lucky enough to have Michael keep you here 'til I was able to interrogate and dispose of the intruder."

I sat and thought for a moment. I stared at him, desperate to find something I might have missed, like an elongated nose, or furry arms, that would have indicated he was different, but there was nothing. He still looked like the same old Alex.

Alex sat there calmly, unaffected.

"Are you going to kill me?"

"No."

"Are you in control when you turn?" I bit my bottom lip.

Alex smirked. "I won't hurt you, if that is what you are asking."

"No, I..." I couldn't finish.

"Arri, your parents entrusted me with your life. If they thought I wasn't able to handle myself, you would be with someone else right now. But you're not. You're with me. It's not a matter of losing my temper or turning while I am angry. It is more...I only turn when I tell myself to. It's not involuntary, and we don't have the drive for the kill; we are still in full control of our actions."

"Wait, how do you know my parents? Where do they fit into all this?"

Alex let out a chuckle. "I'm afraid I know your parents better than you do. Who do you think assigned me to you as your guardian?"

"What *is* a guardian?" I thought back to the man who pinned me to the wall. He mentioned my guardian. How did he know I had one?

"A guardian is like an overly trained bodyguard."

"I'd ask you why I need one, but I guess it's obvious now. Who was that guy?"

"I'm afraid it's not my place to tell you." Alex relaxed his rigid posture, slouching back in the chair. His softened demeanor and the carefree way he spoke calmed me a bit.

Was I relaxed, though?

I found myself moving to the foot of the bed, carefully, just feet from him.

Alex being a werewolf was a shock in itself, but I was far more hurt by all the deception. The only friend I had had been assigned to me by my parents.

"Are you okay, Arri?"

I didn't have the heart to tell him my real feelings.

"Oh, it's nothing," I lied. "I just remembered how hungry I was."

Alex looked down at me. His expression was sullen.

"Arri, exactly how much did you hear yesterday?"

I twiddled my thumbs. After a moment of shared silence, I glanced up to see Alex staring out the window, as if hiding the pain or guilt.

"Well, Michael doesn't want me here. He made it very clear. And the only friend I have lied to me." I let out a small laugh, more embarrassed than anything.

Alex's look of distress mirrored my feelings.

I thought for a moment. "Were you ever really my friend, or was it all just an act?"

"I was a friend from the start. Being your guardian was just a perk." Alex smiled at me, and gestured to the door. But did I trust him?

"Are you ready to eat? I thought I heard you say you were hungry."

As I took his outstretched hand, I found myself examining it for freakishly long fingers, claws, and even fur.

Alex noticed. Shaking his head and letting out a hearty laugh, he pulled me along behind him. Like a gentleman, he opened the door for me.

As soon as we cleared the doorway, the size of my prison—or castle, more like—took me aback. Cool, gray stones lined the walls, and the smell of damp air, rich wood, and citrus furniture polish gently drifted over me.

I was speechless. Alex laughed.

Over the banister, looking down onto the room below, I could see the large castle-like doors Michael had brought me through, and the rug I'd tried so hard to make a stand on. There were high ceilings with square, plaster moldings painted in ivory and inlaid with gold. All sorts of designs filled the open cavities. A large chandelier hung in the center of the open space, breathtaking in its intricate design and delicate shapes. Several hundred prisms hung around the enormous work of art—a crown for a king. Tastefully placed works of art hung on the walls: Some were modern, and some were old, each basking in individual illumination. All the grandeur took my breath away.

Large windows divided the walls such that the already grand mansion felt even more massive. Enormous and thick red velvet curtains covered them. The only light in the room danced playfully from the hanging candelabrum. The flickering reflections from the lit sconces bounced off the polished hardwood floors, and after a minute or two, I became acquainted with my surroundings.

"Yeah, yeah, I know. Cool, huh?" Alex laughed. "Michael had this place brought over from Europe. Apparently, it belonged to his parents."

Impatiently, he dragged me down the hall. A simple but detailed banister divided me from the floors below. A small engraved coat of arms marked the top and bottom of each newel post.

Allowing Alex to guide me toward a grand staircase, I felt like I was in *My Fair Lady*. A thin blue Oriental runner carpeted the large staircases on each side of the room. Its florals and fleur-de-lis patterns beckoned with an old-fashioned look like you would see in the movies. Alex walked me down the left staircase and we walked briskly through the palatial room and into a hallway.

Strangely, except for the décor, the mansion seemed empty—deserted.

Eventually, we found the kitchen. Industrial-style, the kitchen had stainless-steel cupboards that lined the walls and two large islands in the center of the room. Marble countertops sparkled in the beams of the many inset can-lights. It was a little odd to see a castle that kept some old, elegant charm but had a kitchen right out of HGTV. As soon as I walked in, I stopped in my tracks.

"Who even *needs* a kitchen this size?" I asked.

Alex laughed. "Well, if you entertain as many people as Michael does, you need a large kitchen. Actually, during his meetings with dignitaries, royalty, and nobility, this place gets really crowded. Feels kinda cramped."

I found that hard to believe. How a place this size could seem small was beyond me. We walked up to a bar and sat down. I was still getting my bearings when a man came up from behind me.

"May I take your order?"

I flinched. He was well-spoken, but I couldn't place his accent. His slick ebony hair and taut alabaster skin stretched over bold and square features. For his height, he was a bit scrawny, and his hard, narrowed eyes were not welcoming.

"Sorry?" I said.

Chuckling, Alex went ahead and ordered for me.

"Yes, the lady will have spaghetti topped with parmesan cheese and garlic bread. For dessert, she will have the raspberry-wine cheesecake. I will have the same, but instead of the cheesecake, I will have an angel food cake with extra cream."

I looked at Alex. He knew me well, but after the chef left to prepare our meals, I scolded him.

"It's not like we are ordering at a restaurant, Alex. This is someone's home. I would have settled for a PB&J."

Alex laughed. "Michael would have my neck if I allowed you to order a sandwich when he has a chef on retainer."

To be fair, I was *so* hungry. The wait was agony as the aroma of baked delicacies, strawberries, and pasta got stronger. Alex and I sat at a wall facing bar talking about the relationship between Jonathan and him. After the chef brought my food, the savory scent of homemade spaghetti sauce had my mouth watering. The food was great. The creamy texture of the tomato sauce, the *al dente* noodles, even the lightly browned and crisp garlic bread danced on my tongue. It topped any of the gourmet meals my parents and I had. Finally, when I had eaten enough to feed fifty people, I was ready to leave with Alex, feeling full and a little potbellieish.

Alex was amazed at how much I ate.

"Did you leave any food left for the rest of the planet?" he teased.

"Hey, I was hungry." I felt my cheeks warm.

"I would hope so. You have been holed up in your room for a few days."

Alex looked away and appeared to be studying his watch before slowly standing and brushing out the wrinkles in his shirt and jeans.

"Shall we?" Alex gestured to the kitchen door. Leaving the dishes where they were, Alex and I left the kitchen. The chef was nowhere to be seen, so I whispered "thank you" into the empty room.

We slowly sauntered toward the front door, and after he'd finished teasing me about my wolfish appetite, we walked the grounds. Michael's immediate yard was well cared-for—manicured lawns, trimmed topiaries, a few benches scattered around—but somehow it looked abandoned and lonely. Alex and I never left the fenced in grounds as we walked. I asked him question after question about Michael, his house, and the trouble that followed me from Utah to here, but he avoided and skirted around my questions like a pro.

"Alex?"

"Arri?"

"Ha ha, very funny. Seriously, I know it's like a lamb asking a lion if it's safe, but am I? Safe, I mean."

"Arri, right here, right now, you are safe. There is no safer place. Michael has opened his home to you to make sure of that."

Michael? How was *he* going to make me safe?

The yard lights came on as the sun fell below the mountains. Pinks and oranges tinted the clouds like watercolors and Alex brought me back to the house.

"I have to go for tonight and fulfill some of my wolfish duties. I'll be back tomorrow. Promise you won't throw anything?" He folded his arms over his chest, his eyes sparkling with mischief.

"I make *no* promises." I sing-songed back as I walked back into my room. The door closed just after I saw his wide eyes and shocked expression. I giggled.

Nana must have been in my room while Alex and I were out. It was like having room service, only instead of once a day, it was every time you left. The bed was made, the covers were turned down, and pajamas were laid out at the end of the bed. Even though it was only eight o'clock in the evening, I climbed into bed. With nothing to do—no television, books, or entertainment in my room—I had little else to do besides sleep.

The next few days got better. I was no longer locked in my room. I never did see Michael again. I would hear his voice as he spoke to Alex and some of the staff, but never the physical presence. Alex would come and greet me every morning, and we would take our daily walk around the grounds. I learned how different we were—human versus werewolf. He told me all about his pack, and who he was. He was born a wolf cub, and he turned into a human for the first time when he was weaned. Not all cubs turned into werewolves; only a select few inherited the werewolf gene.

"My mom and dad were two of the last twelve remaining werewolves," Alex explained.

"After Nicholas ordered them dead, they fled, and I was born here. Out of all the litters my mother had in two hundred years, I was the first to turn. Jonathan and I are not from the same litter, but we were the first two to turn, making our bond stronger. I am the pack leader, the alpha, and Jonathan is second-in-command, my beta."

My mind wandered as he spoke. *Nicholas had ordered the death of an entire species.* He had ordered my death as well.

This was not comforting to learn, especially remembering the psychopath who'd attacked me almost a week ago, the one who'd said Nicholas would get me. Now those cold, callous words haunted me.

To distract me from my circumstances, Alex would tell me a new story every day. In the meantime, we talked, watched movies, and hung out like normal friends.

Yet although Alex and I were renewing our friendship, I was still furious with Michael for keeping me here.

When Alex wasn't around, I ate alone in the cold, empty kitchen, and kept to myself, isolated in my room. The castle wasn't mine, so exploring was out of the question. Time passed slowly, and I realized that I missed the strict and structured life my parents had provided for me. With that thought, I found that I cried myself to sleep several nights.

Because even though I missed my parents, I needed more than just my normal life back. I needed to understand the reason for my imprisonment.

EIGHTEEN

I hung my head over the side of the bed and watched the clouds roll by as I waited for Alex. Over the last few weeks, he came and kept me company, but when I asked him questions, he delicately avoided them. I was getting light-headed from being upside down when a knock at the door finally startled me.

"Come in," I said, sitting up to regain my balance. Flushed, I planted my hands on the bed to steady myself.

"Are you okay?" Alex asked. Today, his demeanor was different. The tips of his fingers drumming on his leg seemed nervous rather than assured and confident.

I ignored his question. "Is something on your mind?" His distressed look worried me. "Tell me. What is it?"

"It's a good thing you are sitting down." He chuckled and exhaled hard. *How bad is this news?* "Michael has asked you to dinner tonight." Alex took a breath.

"Is that all?" I let out a small laugh. "I thought it was something much more serious than—"

"Arri, focus!" Alex snapped. "It *is* serious, but I need you to stop and listen until I finish. Okay? A simple nod will do," he added when I opened my mouth.

I nodded, my eyes wide.

"Here goes nothing." Alex sighed. "Michael approached me yesterday. He's under the impression you are upset with him. I guess I could see where that would come from, but I am afraid your anger is misplaced." As Alex spoke, I kept nodding until the last part, when I cocked my head.

"Misplaced? How so?"

Alex looked out the window. "Michael didn't kidnap you." His gaze fell on me, and his fingers resumed their tapping as he waited for my response.

"I beg your pardon? How can you be serious?" My voice rose, my fear turning into a twinge of anger. "I was there when he picked me up and brought me here. He is the reason I am still a prisoner. How can you claim it wasn't him?"

Alex let me finish and then slowly furrowed his brows.

"Do you remember that night?"

I frowned. The hair comb and the music box my parents gave me were gone. I didn't own much, but what I did, I treasured with all my heart. My chest ached as I remembered the things I loved being destroyed by a monster.

"Yes, I remember." I hung my head, and a single tear fell from my cheek and landed on my charcoal slacks. My pink blouse caught the next few that fell. And Alex's pain only added to mine as I sensed it flooding from him.

"After I changed back into my human form, and when the police asked how you were, a man said he would take you." Alex began to pace.

"You mean Michael? Before he told me to come like I was a dog."

Alex glowered at me as he paced, and I searched the back of my mind for the detail that he insisted I missed. "Yes, but—"

"No, Alex. There is no *but.* I remember perfectly. I was there. Have you forgotten?"

Alex steadied himself. I could feel his anger rising, and his desperate attempt to keep it under control.

"No! I haven't forgotten." Alex raised his voice anyway. "I was the one who told Michael to take you. Michael was only there because I asked him to be!" He was yelling now, and the more he shouted, the quicker he paced the floor.

"Wait, what?" The belated realization shocked me.

"Arri—"

I raised a hand. "It was you? This whole time, you've been acting like a friend, to comfort me, when *you* were behind it all?" Then it hit me. "Michael never wanted me here." My voice quivered, and my chest hurt. I buried my face in my hands.

"No, he didn't. But it's not that simple."

"You lied to me again?" I folded my arms and glared at Alex. "You are my best friend. I trusted you." He looked regretful. But that didn't change the fact that he'd hurt me, twice, and both times, he betrayed my trust. "I never want to see you again." I whispered.

Alex just sat there and stared, his mouth wide open, his eyes confused and hurt.

"Is everything you told me a lie?" I waited for a response, but Alex said nothing. "Wow." I looked away and laughed without humor. "Then I have no reason to stay." I didn't know what was stronger: the pain, the anger, or the frustration.

I yanked a small duffel bag from the closet and started throwing in a few things from the dresser.

"Arri?"

I paid no attention. Grabbed a few things from the bathroom. A final sweep of the room.

"Arri!" Alex's voice was growing louder. "Let's talk. Where do you think you are going?" He spun me around to face him.

"Home?!" My voice cracked, and my eyes filled with tears. Alex's grimace was full of pain and disappointment. He grabbed my hands.

"Arri, wait. Please be reasonable. Let's just sit down and talk about this. Besides, you are in the middle of nowhere. You don't even know your way home."

His words were there, but I heard nothing.

I hoisted the duffel bag onto my shoulder and stepped away. "I don't know where home is, but I will find it without you."

I was actually sad to leave, and a part of me wanted to stay. But I took a mental snapshot, then left. As I cleared the door, I saw Michael leaning casually against the wall. He looked emotionless, but then, as if by magic, his lips turned into a sweet, amused smile. I waited for him to stop me, but he pushed off the wall, stood straight, and bowed.

Guilt washed over me. I couldn't help but grin.

"I'm sorry for the way I've acted. Thank you for everything. I don't believe I will be taking up any more of your time or space."

I tried to keep my emotions at bay, but my bottom lip quivered. I knew it wasn't his fault. Swallowing hard, I turned down the open hall. Behind me, I heard Alex yell, his roar resounding off the ceiling and open cavern below.

"Argh, Arri, wait! Doggone it, Michael. Why did you let her go?"

When I got to the end of the railing, I saw Michael holding Alex back as he watched me go.

"Let her go. I promise that no harm will come to her." Michael's voice was calm and confident.

"Michael!" Alex, meanwhile, sounded angry. I walked down the stairs.

"You know, she might have been a little more understanding if you had told her the truth," Michael said behind me. "If she knew the attackers were out to kill her, she would have been more willing to stay. You underestimated her."

I stared at the giant castle doors, feeling small and insignificant. Just as the cold and uninviting metal of the handle brushed my fingers, I yanked my hand back.

I didn't know if I wanted to go. That was the truth.

Is this what I wanted—to sacrifice safety for freedom?

A part of me knew what Michael said was right. The man in the window would have most likely killed me, or worse. I shuddered.

The longer I stood there, the more my chest tightened. I snaked my arms around my waist and hugged myself, trembling. Somewhere above me, I could hear Alex and Michael still discussing my not-so-graceful exit.

Their voices faded out as I took a few reassuring breaths. I thought of everything that I had gone through in the last few months. I wished so badly I had my mom here to be my voice of reason. She was always the one I went to for advice, a simple chat, or even silent comfort: her sweet smile as she laughed at my naïve, childish fantasies, her voice as she told me I was acting foolish, or telling me to follow my heart and see where it leads….

But somehow, tonight, her words weren't what I needed. The memory of her encouraging smile offered me comfort enough.

"Where are you going?"

I let out a surprised shriek. Michael's voice had snatched me from my hypnotizing thoughts. He stood just feet from me, his green eyes glittering with understanding and concern. With another jolt, I shrugged.

"Nowhere, I guess. Wherever my feet lead me." Reality materialized around me. Somehow, through all my thoughts, I had managed to make it out of the front door and all the way to the tree line just outside the fenced yard. I looked at Michael, expecting him to stop me. I turned and walked the other way, but he stepped in front of me.

"I am not letting you leave until you hear me out." He smirked. "Please."

I swallowed hard; I was only holding it together by a thread. I turned, but yet again, Michael blocked my way. I sucked in air, ready to yell, but instead, unexpectedly, I fell into him. I knew I didn't have a chance if I fought him, nor did I really want to. Michael was not the one at fault. Alex was. I trembled as Michael's supportive and gentle embrace held me softly. I knew I was childish for running and foolish for crying, but I had no other choice. Michael kissed the top of my head.

"Hey, it's okay." He ran his fingers through my hair, pulling strands away from my face. "Why are you crying?" His words were kind and soft. Comforting. I pushed myself off his chest and looked at the endless forest surrounding me.

"I guess there is nowhere to go, is there?" I asked, watching his wavy, brown hair fall forward as he looked down at me. "I don't have a chance, do I?"

He grabbed my hands. "My dear Arri, my meeting you was fortuitous, but my feelings are not. If you are willing, I desire you to stay as my personal guest." His gaze penetrated my very soul.

"After the last few weeks, how could I trust either of you?" It hurt to look at him.

"Alex has lost your trust, but I have the chance to earn it yet. I promise that you will be treated with dignity and respect. I don't know if you will learn to fully trust either of us, but I welcome the challenge." We stayed silent for what seemed like a lifetime. We held each other's gaze. I thought about what I wanted. Did I want to stay? If I went home, what would I go back to? An empty life? A boring job? People chasing me?

"The rest of my staff will be here tomorrow," he went on, "and I would be furious if anything happened to you." I looked into Michael's eyes. The connection was deep. The butterflies in my stomach flittered, and I tried to pull away, but there was something about him that made me want him more. I wanted to be close to him, feel his skin against mine. Whether it was for comfort or other reasons, the need engulfed me. He tightened his hold on my hands as if he read my thoughts. I tried to break free so I could gather myself, but Michael wouldn't let go.

"Do I have a choice, or is the offer false?" My breathing quivered as I waited for the answer. Michael nodded.

"Yes, you have a choice. I will be more than thrilled if you'd stay, but if your desire is to leave, then I will make the arrangements to ensure your safety."

I searched his features. Was he lying?

Suddenly, his lips turned into a mischievous smile, his eyes bright and curious. Cautiously, he leaned in. Excitement churned in my chest, and my rapid heartbeat was unbridled. He ran his hand through my hair, coming closer and closer, his breath against my face, his body against mine. With one hand behind my neck and the other on my waist, he pulled me flush against him.

I closed my eyes, trembling.

His breath teased my mouth, irresistible, but just as I felt the warmth of his skin and the touch of his lips, he pulled back.

Why did you stop?

Snapping my eyes open, I expected to see danger, something dire, but all I saw was Alex, staring at us in shock.

"Alex?" Michael wanted to say more, but Alex put up his hand.

"I'm not interested in your story, Michael. I came to see if you'd found Arri, and I see you have." He stalked away, and his figure changed from man to wolf just before he disappeared from sight. I stared after him.

"What just happened?"

Michael grabbed my hand, and we walked toward the house. I yanked away. "What just happened?" I repeated. Michael sighed.

"Alex just realized why I wanted you to stay." He fixed me with a stare. "Arri, I am not like you. There are several scary things about me that you may not want to know. Alex knows who I am."

I looked at Michael's vibrant green eyes. "What would scare m—"

Michael picked me up, cradling me in his arms, and ran to the house.

"I need to find Alex," he said. "When I come back, will you be here?"

I didn't answer. I didn't know myself.

"I want you to stay." He set me down on the lawn. "I need you to stay." He leaned over ever so gently and kissed me on the cheek. His lips were perfect—warm and soft.

NINETEEN

Waiting for Michael felt like it took hours. Finally, as I paced the room, I heard a soft knock on the door.

"My apologies for your wait. Alex proved to be harder to track than I had expected." He took my hand and led me to the bed. My foot hit the unpacked suitcase still sitting next to the door.

Michael's disappointment was beyond visible; it was almost tangible. "You haven't unpacked?" His breath and his gait went taut with unease.

"No." How could I tell him how I felt without hurting him?

"Do you require assistance?" His voice was lighter now, but the look in his eyes said he wasn't fooled. He knew.

"It's not that. I just don't feel I belong here." I plopped down on the bed and stared up at him. Michael stiffened. I tried to explain. "I am a peasant in your world of royalty and castles. You're obviously someone of importance, and I'm a nobody. Maybe if I left, then things could go back to normal: me to work, and you to your lavish parties." I laughed. Michael stayed serious and never took his eyes off of me as he sat down.

"If it pleases, maybe explanations are necessary. Thereafter, if you choose to leave, then so be it." He was offering me something more than excuses and reasoning; he offered honesty.

"Thanks, but what about Alex? He's really not happy."

Michael smiled. "Let me deal with my friend. Our arguing needn't upset you."

"I don't want to make you guys fight." I fell back on the bed.

"We fight over you for different reasons." Curiosity flashed across his face.

"What reasons?"

"Well, as your guardian, Alex is bound to you. His feelings for you are purely platonic."

"What do you mean *bound*?"

He smiled broader. "I forget. There is much for you to learn." He took my left hand and pointed to two tiny and almost invisible scars on my wrist.

"Those?" I said. "I've had them from birth."

His thumb made tiny circles around the marks, and his warm and comforting touch relaxed me. "My mom said it was from an IV when I was an infant."

He traced his fingers over the two tiny pin dots one last time. "These marks are not just any marks. They are the marking of a werewolf." His stare was intense—understandably. It was more than a little heart-wrenching to think of. "They were put there by Alex. When your father hired him, he needed the two of you to be bound. Alex bit your wrist for a taste of your blood, and to seal the binding. When you are in trouble, real trouble, Alex can feel it." Michael interlaced his fingers with mine.

"Can he feel everything I feel?" I asked. Michael looked amused. It was odd, really: Every time he was near, and every time he touched me, the air around us was charged.

"No, just fear. He will forever be bound to you unless you, or your father, release him."

"How do you know all this?"

"Alex and I have been friends for a long time. I hadn't realized Alex was so good at keeping secrets." Michael nudged me with his shoulder. "But I am happy to finally meet you."

"Okay, so Alex is bound to me by some mystical blood thingy. What about you? What's your reason?"

Michael sat up and looked straight ahead. He even blushed, a slight shade of pink touching his ears.

Finally, we were even. Well, sort of.

"Well, I…I…" He withdrew his hand from mine and rubbed his face. "I adore you," he said quickly. "Alex feels that I am not properly suited for you, hence our quarrel." Michael still didn't meet my eyes.

I looked around the room. I was out of place here. I wasn't wearing rags like Cinderella, but I was talking to a man who lived in a mansion in the middle of a forest surrounded by guards and I worked for a living, with no savings account. I guess I could see what Alex did, but it still hurt to think even Alex thought Michael was beyond me.

"Does he think I am below you?" I said in a slight voice, confirming my thoughts.

"No!" Michael said sharply. "The other way around. He thinks that with my past, and with who I am, you are suited for someone better than me."

"How could anyone get better than you?" Even though I barely whispered, Michael heard. Silently, he grabbed my hand and kissed it twice.

"Once, for the kind words, and once, for how I feel." Michael turned his gaze to meet mine. "Your suitcase is by the door. I'm afraid I have some neglected business to attend, but I will see you in the morning."

I sat alone at the edge of the bed. My pajamas were folded on the bench. The sheets had been changed, and my clothes were pressed and hung in the closet. With the exception of my duffel, it was as if I had never left. Michael had never planned on letting me go. I'd have liked to think I'd had a choice, but I didn't think I really ever did.

I lay back, and, staring at the canopy above me, exhaustion overcame me. I hadn't done anything yet, and still, all my energy had been depleted, my mind and body begging to rest. My eyes fluttered closed. The next thing I knew, darkness took over.

Then I woke up.

As I stretched my arms and legs, uneasiness washed over me. Sitting up, I squinted in the darkness. Somehow, I was in my old house, on my comfy bed. There was no sign of a break-in or an attack. The window was as it was before, stable and undisturbed. The bright, full moon pushed beckoning rays of light through the thin gap in the curtains. The clock on my dresser said two a.m.

Were the last few weeks nothing more than a silly nightmare? I switched on the lamp.

The air chilled and I gasped. A man with white hair sat in the chair next to the bed. His well-fitted white Gucci suit shone in the light, almost glowing. His translucent skin looked delicate; I could see his veins move as he rapped his fingers on the arm of the chair. But as the cold, icy air bit into me, I knew he was far from weak.

Stale sweat and the deep musk of age assaulted my nose. My breath halted.

Cautiously, I adjusted my position, readying myself to run. But the man spoke up.

"I have to admit, you have proved to be much harder to kill than I thought. You have a skill for self-preservation. Or maybe it is just plain dumb luck." His voice was raspy and deep, but the cold, soulless look in his eyes told me he was full of malice.

"Who are you? What do you want?"

"Oh, my sweet, you know who I am, and I would think it is obvious. I mean to kill you." He sneered.

It was Nicholas.

"Why? Why me?" I slipped my foot from under the covers onto the hard wooden floor, sending a chill up my body.

"Oh, my sweet." Dread filled my soul as he repeated the pet name he gave me. "It is because of your existence I seek your death. I can't allow you to threaten what I have made."

The man spoke in riddles. As I struggled to keep eye contact, refusing to show the fear pooling within me, I squared my shoulders and lowered my other foot to the floor.

"What makes you think you'll win?" I asked, the thunder of my rising fear and the quivering of my voice giving away my fear with neon lights.

His laugh broke the eerie silence. "Oh, I'll win, and your death will seal my fate."

Something happened in that moment. My fear fled, and courage staked its claim within me.

"Tsk, tsk, tsk. You are powerless against me." The man stood, revealing his deceptively feeble form. Keeping close watch, I stood too. Mentally, I calculated the distance between me and the door, but it was useless—I'd never get there first.

"You'll never win." My outward appearance might show courage, but the whimper in my voice gave me away. But I had to stand my ground. "You've already tried and lost. Can't you just leave me alone?"

The feral look in his eyes deepened. "Careful, my sweet, I have been waiting a long, long time to kill you. You may meet your fate before time, and I was hoping to show you off first."

"Don't call me your sweet." My skin prickled at the word.

"Oh, but you *are* my sweet. There will be nothing sweeter than the vision of your tormented body as I watch your demise."

He smoothed his hands over his suit, never letting me out of his sight.

"I was hoping you'd run."

The idea was tempting, but as I readjusted my footing, his attention snapped back up at me with excitement .

"Great. Now he's threatening me," I whispered. I wrapped my arms around myself to push away the biting air.

Nicholas's eyes burned as the lines in his face hardened. He cracked his neck, his control slipping for a second, before he forcibly calmed himself.

"My sweet, you're so young and innocent. You ought to know by now the difference between a threat and a promise. That…was a promise."

"What do you want?"

"I've already told you. Your death."

"No."

With a slick smile, Nicholas closed the gap between us and ran a finger down my cheek. Then he squeezed my neck and whispered.

"But can you live with the consequences?"

His words hit me like a freight train.

"No!" I yelled as I shot up, panting, sweating. The sense of a promised death still spun in my head. The smell of bar soap and cologne drifted through the air. I was back at Michael's.

"Arri, are you well?"

Adrenaline raced through me once again, but calmed at the sight of Michael. As if sensing my panic, he carefully pulled me in for an embrace.

"Yeah," I stuttered. "I'm fine, I think. How long was I out?"

Michael regarded me. "Only a few hours?"

I absently touched my neck. The feel of Nicholas's cold fingers still haunted me. "It was just another nightmare." I rested against Michael's shoulder. This nightmare was no ordinary nightmare. It was a warning. "This one felt so real, like I could actually feel his touch, smell his presence. How can I sense his desire to kill me without him being here?"

It was then I noticed Alex leaning against the open door, his exterior calm and emotionless. Still, I could feel his emotions were tight with concern.

"What is it?" he asked.

He and Michael shared a silent look as he pushed off the doorframe with ease. I knew Alex well enough to know it was more than just a shared sense of worry; the silent glance was a conversation of sorts. He sat at the foot of the bed. I sat up, and Michael's grip loosened slightly. I fidgeted with the blanket, twisting the corner.

"It was the white-haired man who's been haunting my dreams for months. I think it was Nicholas." I gave an involuntary shiver. "Usually it is just the slight sight of him or his creepy laugh, but this time he was threatening to kill me. I know they are just nightmares, but wow." I folded my arms. "I guess that is why they are called *nightmares* and not *warm and fluffies*." I felt anything but relaxed. Honestly, a lack of emotions would be a plus right now.

"You shan't worry. You're safe with us." Michael's embrace was tight but consoling.

"I feel like such a child," I said, looking back and forth between the two of them. .

"Nightmares would scare even the toughest of men," Alex said, but I knew he was lying. I knew it was just a dream, but it still felt like the stench of Nicholas clung to me. Trying to shake off the unease that had settled over me like a wet cloak, I gently shrugged out of Michael's arms.

Michael grabbed my hand. "Are you okay?" Concern was etched in his face as his warm eyes perused me.

"Yeah, it just feels like I'm in way over my head. There's still so much I don't know, yet Nicholas still threatens me." I shuddered as Nicholas's last words echoed in my mind. But can you live with the consequences? "I'll be fine. I just need to shower and rinse this nightmare off."

With a reassuring squeeze, Michael let go of my hand.

Grabbing my clothes, I headed to the bathroom, where I leaned against the wall, then sank to the ground. I cradled my knees, wallowing.

Michael's and Alex's conversation was still audible.

"What do you think? Are they connected?" Alex asked in a hushed tone.

"It's unlikely. No one carries the power of foresight, even telepathy. The ancient powers were lost many millennia ago, but her description sounds right. Maybe she has seen him before, maybe in passing?"

"I doubt it. Besides, do you think he would have let her just walk away if he had?" There was a long pause until Alex broke the silence, reluctance in his voice. "You seem very protective of her. Have you decided to make her your mate?"

"And how would this matter concern you?"

"It doesn't, but if you have, then you may want to tell her. She has the right to know. She is bound to find out eventually, and I think it would be better if she found out from you. I speak from experience." Then Alex pivoted. "Your family will be here tomorrow. I think they will find it a little odd to have her here. Besides, being involved will raise some questions."

"Are you challenging me? You may be her guardian, but you are in my house and on my land. You would be wise to watch your place, or I shall have to put you in it." Michael's voice lowered to a growl.

"My apologies, my lord. I'm not trying to challenge your position. I am speaking on behalf of Arri, and I know her. She is human, and it has been a while, my lord."

Silence. The bedroom door slammed with a clang.

TWENTY

An hour later after rinsing and getting dressed, I cracked the door to let the steam out.

After the last few touches of makeup, I looked to the door and saw Michael staring back at me. The relaxed lean of his perfectly toned body suggested he had been there for a while.

"Are you ready?" His voice was seductive.

"For?"

"I did promise thee an explanation." He shoved himself off the door frame. With a gentle hand, he tucked in the tag of my shirt, his touch sending tingles and a wave of pink to my cheeks. Every time he was in the vicinity I knew it: the hair on my arms stood up, and my heart danced the rumba.

Silence filled the hallway as we walked to the garage, nothing but the padding of my feet on the polished wooden floors.

Opening an ordinary-looking door, Michael flipped on the lights, revealing rows and rows of cars of every shape and size, from a Model T to a Rolls-Royce. Michael, looking rather pleased, gestured for me to pass. The smell of oil, gas, and rubber permeated the massive room.

"So?" he asked, sounding proud.

"This is definitely… something." Passing through the vehicles, I saw my old SUV parked between two expensive-looking cars.

I looked at Michael as a smile lit his face.

My old car was polished and looked better than it had when I got it from the dealership. Michael jingled the keys in his hand, but playfully pulled them out of reach when I grabbed for them.

"Really?" I asked.

"I'll drive. I've seen you in action, and I fear for the pedestrians on the sidewalk."

"Hey, not fair! I will have you know I am a *great* driver." Still, I grudgingly crawled into the passenger seat. Michael flashed a grin and started the engine. It sounded different, quieter, and smoother.

"I had the engine redone." Turning the car off, he gracefully hopped down, then wandered his way to my side.

"But we will not be taking this. If we are going to town, it will be in style—my style." He picked me up; then smoothly placed me in a sleek and stylish silver and red car.

My knowledge of motor vehicles was that there were three kinds: cars, SUVs, and trucks, and I was pretty sure they all had four black wheels. That was about it. But even though I was usually oblivious about vehicles, this one I knew. The name on the car confirmed it.

"A Mercedes-Benz?" I was afraid to touch the interior. I placed my hands on my lap to keep them carefully to myself.

"A Mercedes-Benz AMG Vision Gran Turismo," Michael corrected. "I arranged and supervised its build based off a concept. It's one of my crowning achievements. I've made some improvements since I purchased it as well." He climbed into the driver side and started the engine. The car rumbled everything around us as it roared into action. Michael closed his eyes and listened to the engine's melodic sound.

As he pressed a black button in the glove box, the garage door opened, the sound masked by the engine.

"Ready?" he asked.

Smiling calmly, but internally jumping out of my skin, I nodded, and he slammed on the gas. We tore out of the drive onto the gravel, rocks spitting in every direction. I didn't think these cars were designed for off-road, but it seemed to handle just fine. As we followed the winding road, weaving in and out of the trees, my body relaxed against the seat and the rhythmic hum of the engine pulsed through me. Michael was definitely an experienced driver. We drove for about two hours or so at top speed until we finally met the paved road. Entering the freeway, Michael made no attempt to slow down. He kept the speedometer steady.

Richfield was not the largest city, but it definitely had its charm. Several brick buildings lined Main Street; the small-town look complimented by the older houses. I could feel the eyes of the townspeople staring at the high-profile car. Passing through town to my old home in Elsinore, a sinking feeling filled me at the core. The closer we got to the house, the more I feared what I would see. My heart was still raw from the last time I had been here. I didn't know what to expect.

We turned the corner. A dilapidated pile that only barely resembled my home came into view.

"I remembered leaving it a little less...eerie." My voice came out in a whisper. Michael slowed down but did not stop. I could feel sympathy and anger brewing behind the placid and calm exterior Michael put on.

"After you were secure in my home, Alex and I came back to salvage what was left. Apparently, the men assigned to retrieve you took everything they thought would lead them to you. The house was left in ruins. There was not much left to reclaim." His voice was heavy, and I could sense his empathy. He turned the corner, heading for the convenience store less than two blocks away.

He pulled into the parking lot and stopped. "Do you know why they are after you?"

"No. I mean, I had trouble in Vegas, but I never imagined it would follow me here. I thought it was just a random break-in."

"Unfortunately, it was not a random break-in. It was planned. Their goal was to find and retrieve you. Apparently, you are far more valuable than you thought." Michael smiled and got out of the car. "Here, get yourself a drink." Handing me some money, he left me to go into the store. I got my drink as I always did, on autopilot. My mind was elsewhere, wondering why anyone would go through all this trouble for me. It's not like I had enough money for a ransom, or had secret information of any value.

As I left, I noticed that everyone was staring at me.

When I got back into the car, I placed my drink in the holder and folded my arms.

"Is there anything else I should know?" I asked.

"Yes. I have something else to show you. Do you feel up to it?"

I nodded. We rode back to Richfield in silence.

"Was anything recovered?" I asked. "From my house?"

"Just one thing. We retrieved it after the…" His voice broke off as he pulled in front of the diner. Looking regretful, Michael handed me a newspaper. The date was three days ago. The front page jumped out at me: a picture of a woman blanketed by a sheet on a stretcher that two men carried from the credit union doors. Everything was hidden except her arm, bruised Technicolor, and brown hair. But what caught my attention was the thin, almost unnoticeable cut that ran down the outside of her arm, and a small pearl comb that was unnaturally placed in her right hand. A comb cut from buffalo bone with ten little pearls set with a blue abalone daisy in the center.

My heart clenched. By the way she held it, she couldn't have had it before the incident. I knew she couldn't have, because it was mine. It was a sweet-sixteen gift given to me by my parents, along with a gold ring with two diamonds in the middle of two hearts. Tears streaked my cheeks. I looked up at Michael, but he had already read my face.

"Maggie Cartmen lies beneath that sheet." With a gentle stroke, he swiped a tear off my cheek. He grabbed my trembling hand.

"Maggie? From the bank?" My heart clenched again.

"There is one more thing." Michael produced a taped-together piece of paper from his pocket. "I have a few friends on the squad, and this was found in her pocket. No one has seen it except Alex and me. My friend Ryan from the police department saw that it was addressed to you and gave it to Alex. Alex and I were in disagreement whether or not you should see this, but I didn't want you to be misled. I want you to understand why it is you need to stay in my home. You are not safe out here."

He gingerly placed the piece of worn paper on my lap. I picked it up. It was thick and coarse, and a wax coat of arms had once sealed the letter: a shield with a Viking helmet set slightly askew and a bear hovering above it. The writing looked familiar, and purposefully so: It was the same writing as the card I received with the flowers before moving here. I opened the letter and read.

Arri,

You have eluded me thus far, but I have yet to give up. You are close, and I can taste it. Your existence here was not meant to last, and already you have lived longer than I feel necessary. I will have you, and I will stop at nothing. Let this be my proof.

Nicholas

I froze, the letter stuck in my hands.

"Why?" My mind raced. Why would anyone want to kill me? I was a nobody, an insignificant person that meant nothing to anyone. The letter fluttered to my lap as I stared out of the window. I wanted to crawl in a hole and cry. Now I knew what Nicholas meant when he asked if I could live with the consequences.

"I'm afraid only your father can answer that. Alex and I are only here to protect you." I looked into Michael's eyes, and I could feel his sorrow and regret. He knew I was not prepared to handle any of this—he was trying to help. Still, he smiled.

"Are you hungry?" His voice was soft. I shook my head.

"No, just take me home."

"Do you want to come home with me?"

"Yes. I think it's the only home I have." I folded my arms and sank into the seat of the car, pulling my knees up to my chest. Michael tore out of the parking lot, and we sped off for home.

TWENTY-ONE

As we pulled into the driveway, my heart froze in fear.

Someone is trying to kill me.

I was glad to see the castle as it came into view, but my nerves hiccupped when my eyes landed on a young dark-headed man at the front door.

"*Quis advenit?*" Michael's voice was frustrated. I had no idea what he said, but his fidgeting and nervousness showed. He was afraid as well as annoyed as we approached the house.

The unexpected visitor was tall, with short, spiky hair. He wore a black, floor-length cape with a hood and red satin lining. His fingers were loosely intertwined and placed gently in front of him, and the bottoms of his jeans were soaked from the snow. Confusion sparked in his eyes when he saw me. Cocking his head, he followed us to the garage. Before the car was even in park, the man swiftly opened the door to help me out. Cautiously, I took his hand and allowed him to pull me up. His grip was gentle, but his eyes were dark and hard, and his jaw was clenched as though restraining himself.

Let go. Step away, warned a voice in my head. But the anger and frustration directed at me knotted my stomach and froze me. His dislike was palpable.

Michael got out of the car and quickly ran to my side.

"Michael, I thought that outside food was..." The man's Italian-accented words broke off at Michael's interruption.

"Ransom?" Michael's deep voice was coated in ice. "May we continue our meeting inside?"

"Yes, my lord," Ransom said. He offered Michael a gracious bow as he let go of my hand and took a cautious step back so Michael could place his hand protectively around my waist.

Michael ushered me to the house.

The mansion was quiet as a crypt. Ransom followed us silently as Michael led us to the library. Careful to keep a reasonable distance, he stopped at the door and awaited instructions from Michael.

"My good friend, have a seat." Although the words would sound friendly, Michael's tone was biting.

The smell of dust, polish, and paper filled my nose. "Achoo!"

In a half second, Ransom was in full alert and back on his feet. Swiftly, Michael flew between me and Ransom before I'd even opened my eyes. Ransom glanced back to me, and then to Michael.

"I said *sit*!" Michael's words echoed through the small room and into the entryway. Ransom took a few hasty steps back, then, as if physically forced to sit, he heaved awkwardly into the chair. A touch of satisfaction touched Michael's lips.

"Arri, this is Ransom. He is one of my family members. His job is to secure the northern territory. The Canadian border, to be specific. Ransom, this is Arri. She is my personal guest." Although Michael's voice was matter-of-fact, there was an undercurrent between them like a second, silent conversation. "So, you have news. What, pray tell, is so urgent as to arrive early?"

"Sorry for the intrusion, my lord." Ransom reverted his gaze to Michael, concentrating on keeping his attention diverted away from me. "I know I am early, but there has been a breach in the northern territory, and I am afraid that some of the men made it through our defenses." He paused and studied Michael.

"Yes, well, that is unfortunate." Michael was irritated and vexed. Ransom grimaced, unable to hide the fear. With a simple wave of his hand, Michael dismissed his friend, who left.

As soon as he was sure we were alone, he turned to me. "Now for you." His expression softened and his stiffened posture relaxed. "How are you?"

His voice was soft with concern.

"I'll be okay, I think. Besides the fact that I'm being hunted by people who are trying to kill me, and my friend is an oversized dog, I should be fine as long as there are no more surprises." I laughed, a bit nervously. "The only good thing I can think of so far is you."

I blushed and looked away. Michael put his finger under my chin and turned my face back to him.

"If you ask me, the last part is the best part." When he smiled, I giggled. He chuckled. "My family will be arriving tomorrow. As you may have guessed, Ransom is the first to arrive. Although it is only a small fraction of them, a group of eighty or so relative's will be here." He paused.

I gasped in spite of myself. "*Eighty*? That is *not* small. How many family members do you have?".

Michael paced. "I have a very unique family," he said, raking his hands through his hair. "We sort of...go beyond marriage and blood."

Striding back to me, he took my face in his hands and traced my bottom lip with his thumb. "But the important thing is that you feel safe. My family does not have the same self-control as I do."

"Self-control?"

"Yes, well, they are not used to visitors, especially ones as unique as you." He kissed my forehead and held me in a gentle silence. "Well now," he said at last. "I'm sure Alex is gnawing at the leash to see you. It was my thought that if I told you the truth, then you would understand a little more about why you are here. Give him a chance."

I nodded. Michael was referring to my little bout with Alex yesterday. He gave me a teasing wink and led me from the library.

When we got to my room, Michael opened the door and kissed me on the cheek to bid me good night. With my hands in his, he took a nervous breath. "I must say that you are a pretty understanding person to be taking things so well. I could only imagine what you feel."

I sensed a pang of regret and sorrow. Fear crossed his features before he rearranged them. "I am afraid to say that there is one more thing for you to learn today."

I didn't think I could take any more. I had maxed out my crap-o-meter. Sensing my alarm, Michael hesitated. His confident look faltered, and his shoulders fell. I had been strong so far, but I didn't know how much longer I can keep it up.

"Alex suggested that I tell you who I really am." His expression relaxed somewhat. "The person I am all the time, not just when I am with you."

Fear welled up in my heart. I didn't think I could take anything else, especially Michael.

"Alex is right. You should know. I have not lied to you, but I may have masked the truth." He paused. "I am not like most people."

I had to laugh. That had been obvious from the first time I saw he lived in a castle.

"I am different in more ways than one. I don't want you to think I am someone I'm not."

"Michael?"

It was Nana, calling for him. He gave me a regretful smile. "I suppose I will tell you more tomorrow. Get some sleep, and I promise tomorrow will be better." His voice seemed genuine, but with a hint of worry.

The sky was dark. Only a few stars were visible through the clouded night. I moved the chair to face the window. Something about the night gave me comfort. I pulled the blanket up to my chin, slouched down, and watched the stars come and go as the clouds glided through the night sky. Muffled voices echoed against the hall walls. I'd almost bet that Michael was yelling at his new arrival. The sound of loud footsteps was heard stomping down the stairs, followed by the slamming of the sizable heavy castle doors.

"Why now? What is my old friend up to? What game of chess is this?" Michael mumbled to himself. After a few moments, his footsteps and the mumbling quieted as it faded in the distance. I looked out the window and felt tears run down my cheeks.

Walking echoed in the distance, and a growl reflected back. Wiping the tears from my face, on the off chance they paid me a little visit, I brought the blanket to my chin and nestled further into the chair.

"What now?" Michael yelled. "Art thou not yet tired of flexing thine authority, or art thou purposefully trying to irritate me?" The yelling was not far outside my door. I could hear the shifting of weight on the wood floors. Small creaks sounded as the teetering weight moved back and forth.

"You do understand that I cannot be here all the time." Alex's voice was upset.

"If thou mistrusted me, then why didst thou entrust her to me?" Michael said.

"It isn't you I am concerned about. It is them. What if one of them is working for Nicholas? What happens then? Your guests are unlikely to welcome Steven's daughter." Alex sounded concerned, and his voice was on the verge of yelling.

"Even thou wouldst admit that tomorrow's events are unknown. What will come, will come! We can do nothing to stop it. I cannot guarantee anything, but neither canst thou. I have offered her a room here as a guest, and I plan on keeping it that way. If for any reason she wishes to leave, then I will rightfully grant her wish, but until then, she stays. I think thy affections for Arri are clear, and I hope that she can accept me for who I am."

I heard a sigh. Then, as if Alex had conceded, Michael went on. "Now, with that said, thou and I both know that my family will be arriving tomorrow. They all know that hunting within town limits is forbidden, but just in case, I would like thee to post thy pack in town." There was a pause, and then, Alex spoke again.

"I don't like it. She doesn't know who you are. She has the right to know, and make that decision for herself." There was a little bit of a challenge in his voice. I waited impatiently for Michael's response.

"I know, and she will, but for now, some last minute details need my attention, so if thou wouldst excuse me." The conversation went silent. I listened carefully, but there was nothing. No footsteps approaching or retreating. Shaking my head, I returned my attention to the view outside.

"Why me?" I asked myself. *What do I have to offer, and what does this Steven have to do with anything?* I huddled into the blanket. *My life was boring. Now all of a sudden, I seem to be popular for all the wrong reasons.*

"Maybe I can answer that." Alex was standing at the door.

"Hey, how's it going? Come in." I waited for him to take the chair next to me.

"What are we looking at?" he asked, squinting through the darkened window.

"Nothing, I was just trying to keep it together."

"Upset?"

"Yeah, a little. Did you see the way Ransom acted around me? It was like I had the plague. His piercing eyes and his gun-shot reactions to a sneeze. I mean, I was supposed to be an assistant branch manager, not being chased by crazy people." I huffed as I sunk further into the chair. "I mean, really? Who is this guy?"

"You know of him," Alex said, staring straight forward as if looking at me would halt his words. "You just don't know anything about him. You've heard his name before, Nicholas. He is a ruthless tyrant. He..." Alex sighed. "He lives without compassion or mercy. He makes many evils in your world look like child's play."

"Why would you tell me this? It doesn't exactly make my heart all warm and fuzzy."

"I don't tell you this to scare you, but I wanted you to know. I need you to know what you are facing. He is not to be underestimated. He will kill you for whatever it is he is after."

"So you don't know what he wants?"

The question stumped Alex for a moment, but after thinking it over, he shrugged. "I didn't say that." He looked back outside and followed a rain droplet that fell on the window.

"Did you and Michael get together this morning and have a little meeting of the minds to see who could scare me the most? First, Michael shows me the house and Maggie, and now you are saying that the man is evil. Wow, this day just keeps getting better and better. The next thing I know, you're going to tell me that I'm some kind of elf, and he wants me for my immortality, right?" I stopped and took a shaking breath. I looked at him through watery eyes. My hands shook and the breakdown I had been hiding from finally found me. I let out a mocking laugh. "When Michael left here earlier, he said he was surprised how well I had taken everything, given the circumstances.

In reality, I was just waiting until I was alone. When I woke this morning, I didn't expect you two to tell me all this." Averting my eyes, I took a few shaky breaths. "Alex, I think I just want to be alone. Can I see you tomorrow?"

I didn't want any arguments or questions, so I was relieved when he left peaceably.

Thoughts of the man tearing me limb from limb, and being executed in front of a rioting group of people filled my thoughts. I broke into uncontrollable sobs and I curled into a ball. Eventually, I cried myself to sleep.

The brightly lit marble room shone in its entire splendor. The windowless cavern reeked with death as blood dripping vampires yelled and hollered in agreement. I was bound and chained as a man's cackle echoed through the halls.

I was doomed. I knew it.

I tried to free myself, but the relentless restraints prevented any movement. Just as the cackling stopped, soft thudding stirred behind me.

I was jarred awake.

Footsteps paced in front of my bedroom door. Shadows stretched and danced across the walls like my room was taunting me. I sat up and attempted to stretch my aching body. *Apparently, sleeping in a chair isn't the best idea.* My head throbbed. Every heartbeat pounded above my eyes. 3:21 a.m. I squinted at the clock's bright blue light. Slowly, trying not to joggle too much as I walked, I opened the door. A few candles burned just outside my room, illuminating the hallway. The change in light pushed my pounding headache to a rumbling roar. I leaned against the ajar door and watched Michael.

"Did I wake you?" His voice was soft.

"No, a headache did," I lied.

The pain in his features told me he was worried.

"I heard you crying. Are you okay?" He looked down at his shoes and rocked back and forth.

"Yes, thank you."

"Sorry, Arri. I wish there was something I could do." He kissed the back of my hand, then bid me goodnight.

"Michael." He slowly turned but didn't look at me. "Would you like to come in?"

"You're sure?" His curious tone stunned me, as did the uncertainty that danced behind the surface.

Michael, unsure?

"Well, I'm not going to throw anything at you." I did the Boy Scout salute. "This way, you can watch over me without pacing in front of my room."

Michael grimaced. "Sorry, I just, I mean…I worry about you." He pulled the chairs together, then waited for me to seat myself before easing into the chair. The stern contours of his jaw softened as he stared out the window. I leaned my head against his shoulder and snuggled as close as I could through the hurdle of the armchairs. It wasn't long before he relaxed into the chair, and we watched the clear night sky through the arched window. With ease, the natural silence stretched into commonplace. The blackened sky was flawless and spellbinding as a shooting star shot among the dark winter sky.

I closed my eyes and made a wish. The desire for normalcy was replaced with dreams of adventure, excitement, and love. When I opened my eyes, the sheer intensity of Michael's amused gaze caught my attention.

"Staring is becoming a habit of yours," I said, surprised to find I was more than a little shy. It seemed that when Michael was around, I was strangely aware of myself, Michael, the movements we made, and even the very breath I took. Ever so sweetly, Michael pulled me close and brought my palm to rest against his face, his cheek warm beneath my fingers.

"I am fascinated by you. I can't help it. It is like you are still innocent in many ways. Wishing among stars, blushing, even the way you fidget when you are nervous, I adore that side of you." He interlaced our fingers. I gave a little shiver. "Are you comfortable?"

I yawned and snuggled into the warmth.

"Yes, thank you." Somehow, I knew I belonged with him.

I was awakened by a slight jostling as Michael picked me up and placed me in bed. He covered me with the comforter and tucked me in.

"Don't go. Stay with me," I said sleepily. Michael didn't move.

"I thought you were asleep." Walking back to the bed, he laid down next to me as I pulled myself closer to him. It was the one place through all the chaos I felt safe and secure. I dreaded the morning when this would all change. I wanted it to be just Michael and me, alone forever. I thought of all the ways I didn't want this moment to end. Finally, I managed to fall asleep.

But the next day, something had happened. I could feel it.

Whatever the small uproar was, Michael didn't want me mixed up in the upheaval, so he decided to take me camping. The ambiance of the winter silence and the quiet whisper of wind through the trees in hushed tones filled the otherwise still forest. A thick, white layer of snow blanketed the forest floor and crunched and pressed beneath our shoes. It was perfection. Nothing stirred in the distance, and the silence enveloped the vast forest in a spell of peace and tranquility. I was so involved in the beauty that I nearly jumped out of my skin as Alex approached. Standing next to me, he was on constant alert. He had been following nearby, along with Jonathan, as we explored the vastness of Michaels' extended grounds. Jonathan had taken the protection thing seriously. Apparently, he had been pacing the perimeter of the mansion ever since I got here. I was completely unaware of his presence, but I was coming to see that he was all work and no play.

As we cleared the forest line and wandered into a small meadow, the sun was setting. The chilly temperature plummeted further, and the rising moon erased any trace of day, including what little heat there was.

In the center of the clearing, Michael had pitched two tents, one for me and one for him. Between the two, a warm and inviting heat radiated from the small fire pit. As it got dark, eerie sounds reverberated from the woods close by. Leaving the comfort of Michael's and Alex's company, I decided to turn in early. The weird and creepy noises made me think of things that go bump in the night and had me on edge.

I slipped between the layers of the sleeping bag, pulled it to my chin, and closed my eyes. I tried to sleep, but there was no way I could after learning werewolves were real. I mean, if they were, then what else was?

I heard owls hooting and branches breaking under the weight of a heavy foot. I sat up in the sleeping bag and tried to calm myself. Then I heard the footsteps again. A large and unnatural shadow haunted the thin fabric of the tent. Panic rising, I screamed. I couldn't stop it. I had never been the outdoorsy type, mostly because I was never allowed, but now I was in a tent by myself. I let out another loud shriek and covered and pulled the blankets over my head as Michael threw open the tent to find me huddled under my sleeping bag in the corner. Kneeling beside me, he cupped my cheek, pulling back the fabric of the sleeping bag.

"Are you all right?" His eyebrows arched with curiosity.

I looked at him like the word *duh* was plastered across my forehead.

"I don't like the outdoors." I buried my face in his shoulder.

"Look, Alex and Jonathan are scouting the perimeter, no doubt, so there is nothing to worry about." I didn't care. Sensing my hesitation, Michael chuckled. "All right, then, why don't you come and stay with me?"

It didn't take me long to come to the conclusion that if I didn't want to be scared to death, I'd better chance it. With a wry smile, Michael grabbed my sleeping bag and led me to his tent, where he opened both bags up and spread them one over the other.

"There. Now we have a real bed," he joked. He helped me in and slid in next to me. Careful not to touch me, he turned on his side. "Good night, Arri," he said with humor in his voice, and then I faded away.

I was vaguely aware of my position when I woke up. At some point in the night, I had turned over and settled on Michael's chest. He smelled so good, a mixture of soap and cologne. I inhaled deeply, holding on to his scent as long as I could. It was then that I realized where I was, and the embarrassing position I found myself in.

Quickly, I pulled the sleeping bag over my head.

"Michael, I am so sorry," I said, I always found myself in these predicaments. Michael gave one quick tug of the sleeping bag, and I was there in the open for him to see.

Giving me a knee-melting smile, he leaned over the small space and kissed me on the cheek. "It didn't bother me. I rather enjoyed it, to be honest." With a jerk of the fabric doors, he headed outside into the cold winter air. "I will make breakfast. You get ready, my sleeping beauty." He shot back over his shoulder as the tent closed behind him.

Belatedly, I realized how bad I must have looked. My hair had its own personality and had a habit of making a fool of me. If I was lucky, my face wasn't on backward. After brushing my teeth, I pulled my hair into a ponytail and dressed as fast as I could. As I stepped out of the tent, Michael just walked by with a glass of juice and a large silver canister. It wasn't fair. He looked like he had just stepped out of the shower with damp styled hair, faded jeans, and a nicely fit T-shirt. I, on the other hand, wore wrinkled clothes and had hair that would rival Medusa's.

"Breakfast is ready," Michael shouted without looking up.

After taking a seat on the closest log, Michael handed me a plate. The ham and cheese omelet smelled delicious, as did the seasoned baby red potatoes.

"Are you two ready?" Alex and Jonathan seemed to be coming back from their morning hunt.

"Yep, just eating breakfast," Michael answered, looking down at the plate in front of him. I almost missed the slight grimace that touched his face.

Alex laughed. "Why don't you scout the area while the two of us sit here with Arri?"

"Thanks." Michael sighed. "I think I will. I should only be but a moment." With graceful speed, Michael disappeared into the thicket of the trees.

While I finished eating, Jonathan and Alex broke down camp and packed the bags.

After returning with added color in his cheeks only an hour after leaving, Michael decided to show me his property and took me on a hike. Well, he called it a hike, but it would have been easier to climb the Andes. The ups and downs, gorges, and rivers killed me, but didn't seem to affect the other three. Cursing their athletics, I kept up as we passed a small dip in the terrain the size of Rhode Island. I almost ate it twice, but Michael came to my aid and rescued me from total humiliation.

After my demanding we stop, we took a rest at a small waterfall next to a river. As Michael and Alex talked about meeting up after they hunted and scouted up ahead, I decided to take a closer look at the beauty of the frozen water. Just below the arctic surface, I could see babbling water following the current. The dance of the water rushing through the icy climate hypnotized me. For a moment, I allowed myself to be swept away in the serene scene before the growing voices of Alex and Michael's constant bickering pulled me from my trance. Glancing up at the two of them, I noticed a small waterfall and icicles that formed as the water gradually froze, creating hanging crystals. As I reached for one, I got the sensation of icy fingers grabbing my ankle. Before I could look, the fingers tugged, and I lost my footing. The ice shuddered as I plunged into the frigid water. My breath stalled as the water splashed against my face and neck. The deceptively deep river pulled me down as the strong undercurrent fought its way down the ravine. The sound of water gurgled in my ears as I tried to keep my head above water.

It seemed like a lifetime as I fought and thrashed about trying to find the surface. As the current pulled me, the solid ice above me kept me from breaking through. Just as I thought I was going to die, I felt a comforting touch. Michael's arms wrapped around me like a warm blanket. My fighting ceased, and Michael turned me around to face him. I looked at him in panic. I wanted him to save me.

The icy water bit at me and I shook uncontrollably. Michael's bright green eyes were sad and hopeless. He knew there was no way to save me, but he was there to be with me, so I didn't have to die alone. I thought of the many things I still wanted to tell him. I wanted to tell him I was falling in love with him. I thought of how I would never be able to feel his lips on my own, and all the time we would no longer be able to spend together. My head hurt as my chest begged for air.

Michael and I stared at each other. As I slipped away, my grip weakened. I was losing consciousness. In the darkness, before I died, a haunting face appeared before me, taunting my death. His white hair floated around him as his grim and menacing cackle mocked me. "You can never run from me. I am everywhere." His wicked and hypnotic voice made me shudder, and then total darkness overcame me.

I had given up. It felt like invisible bindings were wrapped around me, squeezing me tight. I couldn't move, my mind became foggy, and my will had vanished. All that remained was the constant whispering voice in the back of my mind.

"Arri, Arri!" In all the darkness, I heard my name. It was Michael's voice begging me to come back.

With a jerking shake, I awoke. I took a sigh of relief when I saw and his alarmed look.

I was still in bed.

"Are you okay?" He asked, in a worried voice.

"Michael!" I yelled, and threw my arms around him.

Michael pried himself out of my grip and held me by the shoulders.

"Are you okay?" he asked again.

"Yes, I'm fine." I threw myself at him; this time, he didn't fight. Instead, he placed his arms around me. "It started out so normal, then just as we drowned, I saw Nicholas's face." The haunting memory and his words scared me.

"Don't leave me," I said, shaking beneath his grip.

"Never." Without having to look at Michael, I felt the certainty and promise in his words.

Even though I was safe, and far away from water, I drifted in and out of sleep, waking every now and then, making sure Michael was still next to me. I was happy when I saw we were still wrapped in each other's arms. His warm, smooth skin felt like silk, and I couldn't get enough of him. He looked so peaceful and perfect, his face serene and angelic. It was hard to believe that just a few weeks ago this was the face of a man I thought kidnapped me. Now, it was the face of the man I had fallen in love with. I took a few heartwarming breaths and drifted back to sleep.

TWENTY-TWO

When I woke, Michael was already up and changed.

"Arri? Arri? Are you awake?" He shook my shoulder gently.

"No," I said, rolling over and pulling the covers up to my chin. The soft satin brushed against my skin.

"Come on, Arri, I need you to get up." Michael's chuckle reverberated through the room.

"What time is it?" I squinted at the darkness that still consumed the night sky. "What happened to the sun?" I asked, sitting up and pointing to the window.

"The sun will be up in a moment, but first, I thought I would give you enough time to get ready before my company arrives." That woke me up. My eyes shot open, and I stared at Michael in a panic.

"That's today?" I threw off the covers and bolted to the bathroom door. As I brushed my teeth, I turned on the shower, and ran out of the bathroom and gathered a few outfits. I was sure one of the six would work. After rinsing my mouth out and jumping in the shower, I was washed, dried, and moisturized in record time.

With the towel still wrapped around me, I peeked out, and Michael was gazing out of the window. It was just light enough to see the outline of the yard and trees.

"Which one?" I asked, throwing all my pre-selected outfits at him. Laughing, he threw me a thin, dusty-orange, scoop neck shirt and well-fitted jeans. Slipping into the outfit and exiting the bathroom, I was caught off guard when Michael grabbed me by the waist and pulled me close to him.

"Have I ever told you I adore you?" His smile was priceless, and his eyes had a sparkle.

"Maybe once," I said, remembering just a day or two ago when he so nervously admitted to his liking me.

"Yes, well, I meant it." My heart giggled. With a warm touch, his mouth pressed gently against mine. I closed my eyes. His breath caressed my lips, and his hands ran through my hair. This was perfection.

"Ahem?" A small voice came from behind us. Slowly and reluctantly, Michael pulled away. With the usual impassive expression on her face, Nana stood at the door. Her behavior was detached, devoid of all emotion. "Sorry to interrupt, but your guests will be here soon, my lord. They will be anxious to speak with you." My stomach turned, and my heart sank. If Ransom was any indication of how the rest of his family was going to be, then today was going to suck.

Michael studied me for a moment as if he could read my thoughts. Placing a light kiss on my forehead, he pulled back and looked at me with a rueful smile.

"I need to meet with my family and brief them on your arrival. After our meeting, I would love it if you would accompany me for lunch." After a short pause, I gathered myself and agreed.

"I will send for Alex. I'm sure he could keep you company for the time being." He kissed me on the cheek, and then left with Nana on his heels.

The small break gave me a chance to think. Pacing, I let out a frustrated sigh. Ever since arriving in Utah, maybe a little before, I'd had a chilling thought that all these nightmares were somehow connected. Somehow, they felt like more of a promised dream, like a glimpse or vague peek into the future, each one growing more lucid and vivid. If that were true…I shuddered. That meant that eventually, Nicholas was going to… "*No,*" I said aloud as I rubbed my arms and tried to shake off the unwelcome thoughts.

I leaned against the cold window. A small, foggy outline of my warm body appeared against the chilled glass. From atop the promontory, the still and calm winter scene was peaceful and serene. A pale blue glow from the dawning sun washed over the valley below. Last night's snow was undisturbed; a continuous blanket covered the entire yard.

Everything seemed to be in perfect harmony. The still winter's day promised pastoral beauty. The trees, unyielding to the weight of the newly fallen snow, showed strength and might. But even as the peaceful winter tide claimed the serene scene before me, a sturdy and stout white gypsy horse pulling a simple but elegant white carriage, flew down the driveway. Billowing clouds of snow followed in the wake of the carriage, showering the countryside. When it reached its destination in front of the castle doors, it came to a startling halt.

I watched in amazement as a single figure stepped out of the carriage. The passenger wore knee-high black boots under a heavy maroon-hooded cloak. The hood was drawn, and the person stood for only a moment, waiting for the driver to produce their bags. A single large suitcase was handed to the passenger.

I'd heard of showing up in a limo, an SUV, or even an expensive car, but to arrive at someone's house in a horse-drawn carriage was just over the top.

As the hooded figure walked to the front door, their dark red cloak contrasted with the white and glimmering snow as they walked and then disappeared into the house.

Another person arrived in a black limousine. The windows were so darkly tinted I couldn't see who was in the vehicle, then the same thing transpired: A hooded figure emerged, was given a suitcase, and walked to the front doors. One by one, Michael's family arrived. Some came in luxurious vehicles, some in basic forms of transportation like Lincoln Town Cars, and even a few more by horse-drawn carriages, but what really confused me, were the ones that came from the trees. They just walked through the yard like they knew where they were going. Where did they come from? It's not like Michael lived anywhere near a town.

More conventional ways were probably too ordinary for the rich. As each member arrived, the conversations and chatter coming from downstairs got louder and louder until it was a medium-sized roar.

I was about to turn and walk back to my bed and wait, but

something caught my attention. From the corner of my eye, one of the figures came from behind a tree. Unlike all the others, his hood wasn't up. His short, blond hair was slicked back. He wore jeans and black boots. His cloak was different as well: while the others were well-kept and almost new, his was black, but looked worn and tattered like it had been through a few quarrels. While the others walked with pride and purpose, his stance and demeanor was common and undignified. As he approached the castle doors, he paused, and with a slick, devilish smile, he looked straight up at me. He stared for a moment, then raised his hood, squared his shoulders, and vanished into the house. His presence was creepy and a little uncomfortable. Chills zigzagged down my spine. I shuddered.

"Arri, are you in there?" Alex's voice came from the other side of the door. Without waiting, he turned the knob and stepped in. "Michael's family has arrived. Are you coming down?" Alex's voice took a curious tone. "Is everything okay?" he asked.

I was a little preoccupied, so I didn't answer.

"Arri?" Alex grabbed my shoulder. I looked at his hand, then back at the door.

"Where is everyone?" The roar from downstairs dispersed and disappeared within seconds.

"Michael sent everyone to their rooms to get out of their traveling clothes and to get settled in before the meeting. This would be the perfect opportunity for us to slip out...unless you want to stay." I shook my head at Alex. The serious and unemotional looks on the guests' faces as they arrived somehow told me I was better off waiting until Michael was with me for the initial pleasantries.

"No thanks. I think I will pass on the introductions for now. Let's go." I stood and grabbed my heavy jacket.

As we walked out of the room, the halls were silent and eerie. The house seemed abandoned. Nothing was stirring, not a soul in the emptiness, and the warm and inviting feel of the mansion stilled, and a bare and vacant feeling consumed its halls. A shiver ran down my spine as the unnatural vibe echoed through me.

"Wow, Michael's guests are a little odd," I said, interrupting the silence, as we closed the large, front doors behind us.

"Yeah, I guess you could say that." Alex was sullen.

"I take it you don't really like them."

Alex stopped just inside the treeline and faced me. "No, it's not that I don't like them. Under any other circumstances, I rather enjoy their company, but—"

"But now that I'm involved, this changes things?" I interrupted.

"Yes, it does."

"I heard you and Michael last night. You are afraid one of them might be working for Nicholas, right?" An awkward silence fell between us. Finally, Alex spoke.

"You don't understand." Alex raked his hair back. "Although they are much like Michael, they have never actually lived among, or with, anyone like you," Alex said, pointing in my direction.

"*Like me*? As in what?" I folded my arms. My curiosity spiked and the broken rhythm of Alex's heart spoke volumes.

"Michael is..."Alex paused. "Well, *different* doesn't exactly explain him." Alex looked at me and rolled his eyes, then shoved his hands in his pockets as he kicked the ground.

"You are...more different than you think. The world we live in isn't exactly normal."

"Okay, you're losing me here. What isn't normal, besides the obvious horse-drawn carriages?" Just then, a loud crack came from behind Alex. A slight blur passed him and stopped just behind me. I came face to face with Sarah.

"Oh, there you are, Alex." Sarah's voice spoke concern, but her eyes darted back and forth between Alex and me, and her insides cursed him.

"Sarah? What are you doing here? I thought you and Jonathan were stationed in town."

"I was, but no one is there, and if anyone stops for a snack, Jonathan is more than capable of handling the situation. I was more worried about Arri." She turned her attention to me.

"Are you holding up okay? You must feel devastated." Although her smile and calculated facial expression showed she was sincere, her inner battle to keep herself in check confused me.

"Why would I feel devastated?"

"Sarah," Alex spat, "as you can see"—Alex gestured toward me, his voice grave, his eyes expressive and full of promised punishment—"Arri is just fine. Maybe you should attend to your post." Alex's anger was only a nudge away from exploding.

"I was only trying to help," Sarah said meekly. "I figured she would need a little consoling after finding out that Michael—" Her words were cut off and her eyes widened in fear as Alex let out a growl and a snap. My heart fluttered.

"Sorry to interrupt," I said, "but I promised Michael I'd have lunch with him. Do you mind if I head on back and catch up with you guys later?" I'd give almost anything and do almost anything to get out from between them.

They exchanged a tense look. When Alex looked back at me, his irritation was replaced with concern, but Sarah's annoyance doubled.

"Sure, I'll walk you back," Sarah said as she held out her hand to me.

The look on Alex's face spoke volumes, and I opted not to accept her offer.

"No thanks, I think I can make it from here. Besides, I'll need to face the troops eventually."

As I left, the quiet whispers of their heated argument floated past. As the castle came into view, I hoped more than anything, the guests were still in their rooms.

TWENTY-THREE

I entered the house and stared at the emptiness. An ominous hum filled the mansion. Although it was bright, sunny, and still the middle of the afternoon, the hallways seemed dark and dismal. As I passed the informal dining room, disgruntled voices—and my name—seeped out.

"So, the rumors are true. A human resides here!"

"What of our secrecy?"

Murmurs of agreement followed. Some of the voices were hardy and thick, while others were light and whimsical.

"Do you wish her dead, which will be her fate if she stays?" This voice was crude and deep—villainous. I imagined a well-dressed, high-status man with greased-back hair.

A silky-smooth debonair voice replied.

"No, I mean her no harm." It was the sweet sound of Michael's enchanting delivery. He steadied his voice and paced his words carefully as thought getting angry.

"She clearly doesn't belong here. She is not one of us," another voice, just as ill-tempered as the first one, said. This one was a little less vile, though, but just as angry. The tone was rustic and husky, like an old, weathered cowboy's.

Michael spoke back up. "You worry about a child while we have walked among humans for centuries?"

I didn't understand their hostility. *There is that* human *thing again. What do they all think they are, ducks?* I was almost to the door when Michael said, "I welcome your woes, but caution. I still demand your respect."

A stern but light voice interrupted—female. Although her voice was forceful, she was soft-spoken. "We are only thinking of her safety and our secret. How do you expect us to hunt or even…?" A loud crash muffled the murmuring and conceding room. What I assumed was a chair flew across the dining room and shattered against the wall. The sound of broken, hollow wood hit the floor. Everyone hushed, and the lady's voice came to an abrupt halt.

"Ryn, I would hold thy temper if I were thou. Thou art on thin ice. Our secret has not yet been told, therefore still it is safe. Thou needest no explanation." Michael's voice was angry—not loud, but full of weight and authority. I backed away from the door and sat as quietly as I could. The last thing I needed was to upset an angry mob of people who were already against me.

"With all due respect, why would you bring a human into our world?" Another female voice asked.

"Yes, why would you risk her life and bring her into your home?" There was a deafening silence, and then Michael responded.

"Thy insubordinate behavior regarding Arri disappoints me." The room hushed; the air stilled. You could hear a feather drop. "For those of you who were here in his time, you know of Steven's evils." Gasps and murmurs erupted when Michael said this name—Steven. "And those of you who have only heard of him, I will guarantee the rumors are only half as scary as the real events. This man was thought to be dead, but alas, we were wrong." More gasps. "Steven is alive and well. If hearing of his return was not enough, he has been bonded. Their little girl is now living among us. I have been living with his daughter for weeks. Please get to know her before you decide her fate. Am I understood?" His words were slow and clear in their slight English accent as he fought to speak with certainty.

There was some rustling and a unanimous, "Yes, my lord."

I stood up against the wall, bumping into a small, oval table as I moved. A vase, full of newly cut, vibrant sunflowers, tumbled. The sound echoed in the hallway, but I caught it inches from the floor. Panic rose, and I jumped when hands settled on my shoulder and over my mouth.

Michael. He was not amused, but seemed rather disappointed.

A black cape hung over his shoulders, attached by two chains that draped across his upper chest only allowing the purple satin lining to peek through by the waist. A white, long-sleeved shirt shone through the holes of his black velvet vest. Brown fur lined the vest at the bottom and the armholes; embroidery adorned the opening of the garment. His thin black pants were tucked into his brown leather knee-high boots. All in all, it looked like Michael had stepped right out of a Shakespearian play. It would have been over the top on someone else, but it seemed to suit him somehow.

"Arri, you're just in time. I want you to meet my family." He kissed the back of my hand, then ever so softly pulled me closer and whispered in my ear. "You have some explaining to do."

I had some explaining to do? He was the one talking about me! I tried to pull away, but Michael whispered in my ear again. "Now…is…not…the…time."

I reluctantly agreed. Making a scene now would only make me look worse. These people had something against me. I didn't want to give them anything else to dislike me over. Gesturing toward the door, I took Michael's hand, and we walked in together.

The room was expansive and had several high windows, but it felt cramped. A broad rectangular table and chairs dominated the room, and all the seats were taken. Everyone sat shoulder to shoulder. Even with additional chairs, some of Michael's guests were still left standing. Michael and I stepped over the splintered wood from the crashing chair. Everyone stood as we entered, and all eyes focused on me: some with no emotion, others with horror.

Had I walked into a masquerade or a Halloween party? The attire was wild and varied. Some of the ladies were in dresses and corsets and wigs with white makeup covering their faces. Some had short hair, sleek, flowing dresses, and small hats. It was such a menagerie of people. Men in suits with vests over white dress shirts, their sleeves rolled up a notch, and bowler hats. Others with long-tailed tuxes and white powdered wigs; some men even wore skirts, tights, and hats with feathers. Everyone looked like they jumped right out of the past; some from the eighteenth century, others the 1970s. I was the only one wearing contemporary clothes.

"Ladies and gentlemen, this is *la belle* Arri. Arri, my friends, and family." Michael gestured to everyone in the room.

"Hi, it is nice to meet you." My meek and tiny voice barely carried.

"*Bonjour, salut...*" They all responded in what seemed like every language.

One by one, they all rose, greeted me formally, and left. The ladies curtsied, and the men kissed the back of my hand and bowed. Finally, it was just Michael and me. He kissed me on the cheek and sat me down in one of the chairs. He then left the room.

I was nervous in his absence. A few moments ago, this very room was overflowing with anti-Arri guests. But he was back soon enough, with a plate of lasagna that he placed in front of me. Then he poured himself more wine.

Silence stretched for long moments. Michael spoke first.

"I apologize for my family's reactions to your presence. You were not expected." He picked up his wineglass and moved to sit next to me, setting a small, simple silver-wrapped box next to my place setting. I opened the lid. Inside was a small, delicate silver necklace with a large, amber center stone, scrollwork adorning the sides and holding it in place.

My heart leaped at the sight of Michael's satisfied smile. I threw myself into his arms, excited. I melted into his warm, firm kiss. Shocked by my own behavior, I pulled away. His hands met both sides of my face and he pulled me closer, almost asking for my permission. I leaned in as his mouth parted slightly, and his tongue traced my upper lip. He held me close as his hands ran from my face down my arm stopping at my waist, pulling me in even closer. I pushed toward him, tightening my hold, running my fingers through his soft wavy hair. As we deepened our lustful kiss, we were almost one.

Suddenly, the moment was interrupted by a small sound in the background. A woman softly cleared her throat. Michael pulled away, but kept me close.

It was Nana. I burned crimson and looked away. Up until now, our affection had been hidden.

"I'm sorry to interrupt, but there is a phone call for you. It is

Steven. He said you are expecting him." Nana's voice was professional and showed no acknowledgment of me. Michael gave me an apologetic look.

"Hold that thought."

As he left, I blushed, giggling like a school girl after her first kiss. Shortly after he left, Nana came back in.

"Michael asked me to tell you he would be a while. If you want, you can wait here, or he will meet up with you later." Her voice was dull, emotionless.

"I'll just head back to my room, thanks."

With a short bow, she picked up our dishes and left.

I gathered my courage to face his family. I paused at the doors. A few muffled voices echoed through the wood. From what I heard and felt earlier, they weren't too excited about me being here. Taking a deep, resolute breath, I opened the door. I passed by a few of Michael's friends and family huddling in small separate groups. They were talking among themselves and barely noticed me at all—or so I thought.

"Hello. I'm Patrick McCleary." One of Michael's guests smiled at me—tall, swarthy, and dressed like a lumberjack, with orange-reddish hair and an Irish accent almost too thick to understand. "Arri, is it?" His hand engulfed mine as we shook.

"Yes."

"Are you really Steven's daughter?"

I stood for a moment and thought. "No, I'm sorry. My father's Roger." When I looked around, I noticed I had an audience. Everyone looked at me with fascination.

"Ah. Well, if I may," the man ventured, "I know you are new to our world, but how is it you know Michael?"

How did I want to answer? I didn't want to come right out and say, I was kidnapped. Michael had their respect. I breathed in, and when I exhaled, they all glanced at each other in confusion.

"Well, I met Michael through a friend of mine, Alex. I was staying in town until they brought me here."

"Why here?" someone asked. "It is so rare that someone of your nature willingly enters this house."

"I was attacked by…by someone I'm told is one of Nicholas's men." I stammered.

The crowd gasped.

"How do you know Nicholas?" another asked, undeniably shocked.

"I don't. He just seems determined to get me I guess."

The crowd nodded.

"My dear, I think you're a little naive," said a tall, thin brunette looking down her pointy nose at me, her English accent dripping with disgust. "How is it you know nothing of your father, but know of Nicholas?"

"I *don't* know of Nicholas. But how do *you* know my father?"

The brunette shook her head. "You mean you know nothing of your father's and Nicholas's involvement?"

"What involvement? To kill me?" I asked with unintentional sarcasm.

"No, Steven's relationship with Nicholas. The two of them go way back."

The brunette went quiet, and the entire room stilled as everyone looked behind me. Their postures drew up straight and their quaint mask-like expressions were neatly in place as they didn't dare make eye contact with me.

"Sorry about the delay. Your father does seem to talk a lot, especially when he is talking about you."

Michael had drawn to my side. He was being gentle with me, but his annoyance toward his guests was more than noticeable.

"My father? I thought you were talking to Steven?"

Michael's certainty fell slightly. "Can we go for a little walk? I want to show you something."

Michael's family bowed to him as we walked through the stunned crowd hand in hand.

In the courtyard, a full and vibrant moon shone brightly in the sky. Shadows danced as the breeze blew through the cold winter air.

How had it gotten so late? I thought as the night air bit at my arms.

Michael seemed unaffected by the cold weather. I, on the other hand, was shaking from head to toe, and my teeth chattered. Michael pulled me in closer, and we walked a little further 'til we came to a glass building.

The structure was vast and enormous, towering over me. It was circular and made entirely of monumental frosted glass panels. The seamless roof was transparent, as if there was no roof at all.

Michael opened the fogged doors, and a blast of warm moist air blew past me like I'd stepped into a giant humidifier. He put one hand in front of my eyes, and flipped a switch somewhere behind me. A motor whined. Then the noise stopped, and Michael turned me around.

A perfect garden lay before me.

But this greenhouse was not just a garden. It had a pebble walkway, a gazebo in the center, grass, planters, and a strong flowery fragrance that hung in the air.

"Do you like it?"

I walked toward the bench in the gazebo. "This is…" I laughed and shrugged. "Wow," was all I could say.

"I'll take that as a yes," Michael said from somewhere in the background.

The flowers were rare and delicate. I marveled at birds-of-paradise, orchids, and rare, luscious lotuses, all growing wild and untamed.

The tiny silver box was still clenched in my hand. Michael took it from me and opened it. The necklace glittered in the light.

"Here. I didn't have a chance to put this on you." Michael held up the chain, and I pulled back my hair so he could place it around my neck. He stepped away to admire it. "It is an heirloom, given to my grandmother by her husband only a few years before he passed. It was handed down to my mother. When my mother died, I took it as a reminder of her love."

"Thank you." I looked down to admire it myself, only for Michael to place his finger under my chin and lift it so we were eye to eye.

"You did more than say thank you, and you are welcome."

He leaned forward. I closed my eyes as our lips met. He placed his hands on either side of my face, gentle but sure. My heart fluttered, and my head flew dizzily as I pulled his firm frame to mine. He parted his mouth, and his tongue traced my lips. Michael guided me to lie on the grass. Hovering over me, he thrust his lips against mine, exploring further. I paused, panting, but he pulled me back in. His breath was intoxicating. Yet I knew it was time to stop and gently pushed him away. Warmth rose in my face, and I turned my head, hiding my nervousness. Michael laughed and lay down next to me.

"Now *that* was a thank you," Michael teased. Again, I felt my cheeks turn scarlet. I'd dated Mark, but I never felt desire for him like I did for Michael.

Michael propped himself up on one arm, studying me. His stare was scrutinizing, enough to still my heart. His mouth turned up into that adorable smile, and he nodded as if he knew—knew how badly and fiercely I desired him.

For what seemed like forever, Michael and I laid there in silence. The clouds rolled in and lightning struck. The sky lit up in a brilliant gleam. Thunder followed. The rain pittered and pattered against the glass, and, with Michael's arm under my head, we watched the storm.

The rain fell harder and harder. Lightning flashed continuously, and the thunder never stopped. Completely content and comfortable, I closed my eyes.

TWENTY-FOUR

The storm was over, and the only remaining sign of the roaring and thunderous tempest was the damp, wet earth that surrounded the lustrous garden. The brilliant morning light drifted through the leaves in the trees, creating dancing rays of light against the glass. The sun shone and lit the beautiful garden. I was so content. I would have rather been struck by lightning than leave the comfort of his embrace. Sleepily and groggily, I turned over on my back and rested close to Michael, staring up at the clear, blue sky.

"Good morning," Michael said as we both sat up. I put my fingers through my hair, trying to tame it, and then rested one hand on the necklace Michael gave me and took a deep, heartwarming breath.

The garden was just as magnificent during the day. The kaleidoscope of color was more beautiful than I ever could have imagined. The sun reflected off the glass windows, casting rainbows as the light hit the droplets left by the rain. The flowers were bright and effulgent as the sun hit the delicate petals. The redolence of blossoms filled the air. Everything around me could not have been more perfect than this moment.

Leaving the greenhouse, I smoothed my wrinkled clothes. Michael, of course, looked like he did last night. Not a hair was out of place, and his shirt and slacks were just as pristine as ever. It just wasn't fair.

When we entered the manor, the house hummed with buzzing conversations and gossip. Slowly and gradually, with each step we took toward the stairs, the room quieted. Each member bowed to Michael, but the looks on their faces made me nervous. Their eyes shot back and forth between Michael and me, then to our intertwined fingers. A look of curiosity and shock covered each and every face.

When we got to my room, Michael walked in behind me and sat in the chair as he watched me gather some clean clothes. "Would you like to join my family and me for breakfast? I am afraid it is more of a meeting, but I would love you to accompany me."

Careful not to look me in the eyes, Michael fiddled with the simple gold ring my parents gave me on my sixteenth birthday. It was one of the only things I owned, besides the necklace from Michael, that I truly treasured. Last night, I placed it on the nightstand before I left my room. Finally, Michael looked up at me. He looked so hopeful, I couldn't resist.

"Of course I will. Do I have time to get ready? Or shall I scare them with my Medusa impersonation?" I tried to joke as I plumped up my hair. Michael let out a light chuckle, looked at his watch, and smiled.

"I can postpone the breakfast meeting until later, but before we meet up with my guests, we need to talk." I disappeared into the bathroom, giving him a nervous nod. Those four little words are never good. It is usually accompanied with "I think you're great, but, maybe we should see other people" or a every girl's all-time favorite, "can we still be friends?" Those four words are like the kiss of death.

I hated to think about what he wanted to say. Michael was completely irresistible. When I was around him, I wanted to be as close to him as I could. My heart would skip a few beats and I would feel light-headed. Just thinking about him made my insides giggle. But apparently that feeling was only one-sided.

Leaving the bathroom, I spotted Michael gazing out the window. Light flooded through the stained glass, casting a shadowed outline of Michael's frame. As he faced me, I could see the weight of concern and uncertainty in his eyes. This was not the confident, self-assured man Michael was. Michael took my hand and led me to the door.

"Walk with me." His curious tone raised goosebumps along my skin as his thumb traced circles on my wrist.

When we entered the library, I eyed the book-filled shelves. The suffocating smell of old polish and paper filled the room. I sneezed.

"Have a seat." Michael gestured to a chair along the side of the room next to an old varnished table. As I sank into the chair, the cool and smooth leather embraced me. Michael walked the room, cautiously keeping an eye on me. His posture was rigid with his arms still at his sides, and his expression locked with doubt. Stopping in front of me, he studied me. His eyes mirrored the uncertainty I felt. Reaching across the calculated distance between us, he took my hands in his. His touch was tender and gentle, like I was his most beloved treasure.

"Do you trust me?"

"Yes, of course," I said, but there was something in his voice that told me maybe I shouldn't. He released his grip, and slowly pulled back, inch by inch. As his fingertips met mine, he let my hands fall to my lap. He walked to an over-stuffed shelf. Scanning the bookcase, fingering a set of old leather-bound covers, he selected one, brought it back to his chair, and placed it behind him.

"You know, it wasn't until recently I actually thought about and judged who and what I am." Michael offered me a coy smile. "I merely accepted the facts. But with you, I fear that I may not have the privilege of your acceptance." Michael shifted his weight as his untarnished, porcelain features tightened with concern.

I furrowed my brows. My heart rate picked up speed, and Michael's frame stiffened. His gem-like eyes were frozen in anticipation, and his anxious and fearful heart was heavy with fear.

"There is so much of my world that is based in fiction. In a way, I am born of what you would call myth and legend." Michael ran his hands through his hair then shook his head.

"I don't understand," I said.

"I know I'm fumbling through this."

"Why don't you just tell me what's bothering you?"

Michael's emotions jumped from one to the next before I had a chance to decipher any of them. "When you first came into my life, I knew from the moment I carried you through that door, that you and I were different, and that I should have kept my distance. I told you once that I needed to tell you who—and what—I am all the time, not just when I am with you. Now I need to fulfill my promise."

Michael stood up and paced the floor, walking among the shelves, picking up books and replacing them. As he spoke, the air in the room gradually became cool and thin as I became more and more nervous.

"In my day, guns and tanks were unheard of. Wars and battles were not won with planes and tanks. They were won with warriors, arrows, and swords." What did he mean, *his day*?

"For the last several centuries, nobody outside of the covens knew of our kind. You are the first." Michael paused, trying to judge my reaction, his eyes pleading.

"Centuries? Of *your kind*?" He was starting to scare me.

"Arri, do you understand what I'm saying? I'm not like you."

I scoffed. " I know. I mean you live in a castle."

"No. My guests and I are separated from society because we are …" Michael closed his eyes and hung his head, pinching the bridge of his nose. "What you would call vampires." His beautiful emerald green eyes were sad and unsure when they opened. He was afraid of my rejection.

After a few stunned moments, I finally understood. *She is not one of us. Do you wish her dead? I think she has the right to know who you really are.* Everyone's words echoed in my head. Michael was…

"A vampire?" I didn't mean to, but I spoke the word out loud. Michael flinched at the term and backed away from me. The lump in my throat grew, and it felt like I was swallowing a bowling ball. My heart cringed, and my breath came out fast and shallow. My chest tightened, and terror spread through my veins, leaving me breathless and close to tears. I was scared.

"Everyone out there"—I gestured to the door—"they're like you? Vampires?" I asked in a quivering voice. My heart stopped.

"Yes, they are." His words were quiet and soft.

I was in a house full of vampires.

I began to shake. Emotionless and numb, I stared at Michael. Part of me was so frightened my thoughts were paralyzed. The other part remembered the man he was last night. Biting my bottom lip, I pushed my fear back.

"The red wine," I said aloud, trying to put what he just told me together. "It's blood?" I shook my head. "They don't exist. I mean, you don't exist." I shook violently as he leaned over and took my hand. The hand that was once so warm and soft felt the same, but belonged to a demon.

"I don't understand. You go out in sunlight."

Michael's mouth turned up at the corners; just enough to notice he was smiling. "Yes, we do. The turning to ash thing is just a myth."

"But you just said you were born of myth and legend," I said, with a shaking voice.

"True, but those stories are just that—stories. We are nothing like the ones you have heard, read, and seen in movies."

I tried to rationalize everything. "You can't exist," I said, just seconds from tears.

"You saw Alex, and he is a werewolf. How am I any different?"

I almost said "You drink human blood," but kept it to myself.

I threw my arms around myself and looked away. Michael sat back in his chair. I just couldn't see him being a savage monster. Anyone who could prey on others couldn't possibly be civilized, but Michael had proven to me that he was. He had shown me kindness and love. He had given me help and protection, something a monster would be incapable of. My body shook. I felt light-headed. My vision blurred and the room was swaying. My solid and firm look on life felt askew and unstable.

"Arri, honey, breathe slowly and deeply." Michael's voice echoed my nervousness. Trying to place some much-needed space between us, Michael moved to stand behind his chair. "I'm sorry I didn't tell you sooner. I was afraid. I didn't want you to leave."

I closed my eyes and steadied myself. Swallowing hard, I tried to strengthen my soul. Michael's defeated expression resolved my fears. Michael was my stabilizer. My pillar.

As the room came back into focus, I stood on wobbly legs and walked toward him. He stilled. Every bone in my body told me to run. It was like willingly approaching a vicious predator. But my mind wouldn't allow it. Instead, I steadily approached him, my fear turning into strength.

Placing my hand over his heart, I looked him in the eye.

"Does your heart beat?" I asked tentatively.

"No." Our voices were just above a whisper. I studied him for a while and he smiled when I moved closer. He didn't feel like a vampire to me. In all honesty, I didn't know what I felt. I wasn't dead, so there must have been some good in him, and the thought of losing him was devastating. I wasn't going to lie, though: I didn't want to be scared of him, but the fact that he drank people's blood terrified me.

The look on Michael's face was intense. He was staring at me with such concentration. I bit my lip.

"What are you thinking?" he asked, cupping my face.

"I don't know. I know I should be running out of here screaming, but so far, you haven't acted like a bloodthirsty vampire, biting the neck of every human you meet. Part of me says this can't be real. Werewolves were hard enough. I'm not sure how to handle vampires too." A single tear crept down my cheek. Michael's thumb brushed the tear from my face.

He leaned down and softly kissed me. His lips had barely touched mine when he stiffened as if he was scared of me. As his hands rested on either side of my face, the warmth of his touch flushed my cheeks. The kiss started out soft and timid. He shook as he held me. Then, as if he could sense my want for more, he leaned in. The kiss turned more powerful, as if he was thanking me. That was it. How could someone so vicious and monstrous be so gentle and loving? I pulled away, and Michael's eyes stayed closed. Finally, he looked back at me.

"Are you scared of me?"

"Yeah, a little," I said. "Do you have any plans on killing me?" I asked in return. If I were going to stay here with him, then this would be a clue as to whether I wanted to stay or rethink the idea of running out of here screaming.

"*No!*" He growled. I flinched. He looked startled as much as hurt. "Have I made attempts thus far?"

"Sorry. It seemed like an obvious question," I said in a small, scared voice. I'd never heard Michael so angry and offended. I tried to slowly back away. Taking small, unmeasured steps, I bumped right into the back of a tall wingback chair. I had never been scared of Michael, but just now, my heart had dropped and clenched in fear.

Michael rested his palms on my shoulders to stay my retreat. I had no idea what was coming next.

"I'm sorry, my reaction was uncalled for. I apologize if I scared you." There was a long pause, then finally, he spoke. "Please, look at me." Desperation coated his voice. A few of the tears that I had been holding back fell and stained my cheeks. "Oh, Arri, I'm so sorry." Michael leaned down and kissed my tear-streaked face. "I didn't mean to bark at you. You surprised me, *amore mio*." He grabbed me by the waist, and pulled me close, melding his body with mine, then kissed the top of my head. My trembling slowed, and I relaxed. He would never hurt me. I'd known it the whole time, but it didn't make him being a vampire any easier to swallow.

"Now what?" I asked. "Where do we go from here?"

"Well, this can go one of two ways: one, we can get some lunch, or two, I can take you home, and between Alex and myself, we'll make sure Nicholas doesn't bother you. You would never have to see me again." Michael pushed me away just enough to look at me.

I'd thought about this. I'd wanted to go home since I'd arrived here, and now that I had the chance, the offer didn't sound so appealing.

I shook my head. "I'd like to stay, if that is okay with you."

Michael looked at me with surprise and relief. "I would be honored." He kissed my forehead. "My offer still stands. Are you hungry?"

"Yes, thank you. But um, hopefully, I'm not lunch, right?" I said nervously with a grin. Michael responded by sending me a playful glare and tsking me.

The wariness followed me as we entered the dining room—the same place where, less than twenty-four hours ago, his family expressed their dislike of my arrival into their world. When we sat down, his actions were so attentive; he was cautious not to make any sudden moves. His emotional chaos and uncertainty made me even more nervous.

Michael held out my chair, then seated himself. The formality of the gesture was a little awkward.

"I took the liberty of ordering you a pizza for lunch on the hopes you would stay." His devilish grin brought a smile to my face.

"That would be perfect."

"Well, *bon appétit.*" Just then, one of the cooks placed my meal down in front of me.

"Thank you," I said, as the cook filled my Coke.

"*Siete i benvenuti,* Arri." His smooth, thick voice took me by surprise. The man bowed, then retreated back to the kitchen.

"He said you're welcome. I apologize for Signore Damon. He has yet to speak any language but Italian."

It'd been over twelve hours since I'd eaten, and my stomach growled as the smell of fresh Italian food fluttered through the air.

I picked up a slice and took a bite. The thick crust and the smooth, robust sauce had me moaning in satisfaction. It was delicious. I closed my eyes. The flavor burst with every bite. When I opened my eyes, Michael was staring at me with fascination.

"What?" I asked.

"Nothing. I'm glad you're enjoying your meal."

"Your cooks are amazing."

"Yes, well, most of them have made it into an art after several centuries of cooking."

I took another drink and watched Michael over the rim of my glass. His long, wavy hair was loosely combed back and out of his face. His contemporary shirt and slacks spoke businessman. There was nothing about him that screamed vampire. Above-average, definitely, but nothing that implied he was a bloodsucker.

"What is running through your head, *amore mio*?"

"Nothing, really." I shrugged. "It's just…you don't look like a vampire." I almost choked on the last word.

"Hm. And how exactly is a vampire supposed to look?" Michael folded his arms and leaned back in his chair, intrigued.

"Well, you know, black tux with long coattails, long fangs"—I put my fingers to my mouth demonstrating—"black cape with red satin lining, dark-rimmed eyes. You know, the whole vampire look."

"Yes, I see." He smiled. "And it disappoints you that I'm not the cliché?"

"No, that's not what I meant. I just thought vampires would look more...Dracula," I said, then bit my lip, hoping I didn't insult him.

"Yes, well, Dracula did love the dramatics, didn't he?" A smile teased the corners of his lips.

I chuckled there too, for a moment, and then my easiness faded, and so did his. "You're nervous." It was a statement, not a question. I nodded tentatively.

"Why do you say that?" I cocked my head, and Michael shrugged, a simple, non-committal gesture. "Yeah, well, I guess I am. It's just not every day you find yourself in the presence of a real-life vampire."

"Ah, but Alex didn't scare you."

"Oh yes he did, and part of me is still scared of him."

"But you have been living with me for weeks. Why would I scare you now? Does it have to do with the fact that I drink blood?" Michael looked nervously at his wineglass.

"Yeah, a little. I just don't want to become a meal, you know."

Michael chuckled. A smile curved his lips, then disappeared just as quickly. "Yes, but while you are in this house, I guarantee you are safe." Michael studied me carefully, his eyes unblinking, and his rigid posture unyielding. "You are still scared of me, though, yes?"

"Yes, I guess so." I was afraid to meet his eyes. After everything he had done for me, I would think that I could get over a simple difference like his being a vampire, but his very existence had that little voice in the back of my mind still screaming to run. Michael placed his fingers under my chin and lifted my face to meet his.

"That is reasonable. But I will never hurt you." As if to seal the statement, Michael leaned forward and kissed me softly and passionately.

The moment passed, and silence followed the kiss. The cook reappeared a few times to fill my glass or offer more breadsticks, but other than that, the quiet room echoed my every move. Picking up a napkin to wipe my mouth, I could smell the hot fresh slice of pizza Damon had just placed in front of me, which gave me a slightly uncomfortable thought. *I wonder if he can smell my blood.* My face must have given me away, because Michael cocked his head.

"What are you thinking that makes your eyes so curious?" Michael inched his seat closer to mine.

"Well, is it any blood, or just *human* blood that you crave?" I bit into my slice of pizza. It sounded appalling. To hunt for blood? I shivered.

"Both, although we prefer the latter." He rubbed the back of his neck, not meeting my eyes.

"Is it true that you can smell our blood?" I feared what I would smell like. *Dirty socks, fine wine, something candy-coated?* My own thoughts horrified me.

"Yes, normally we can smell mortals before we even attempt our hunt. Each person has a simple savor, a simple taste. Their smell gives us everything we need to know: health status, gender, age. It tells us everything." Michael took a sip of his wine—or not. It was better not thinking about what it really was. He peered at me over his glass.

"What do I taste like?"

Michael almost choked on his drink, then picked up his napkin from under his glass and wiped the red from his mouth. I cringed. I lost my appetite and moved my plate away from me and tried really hard not to gag.

"Ah…that is an interesting question;" Michael let out a nervous chuckle and slowly rubbed the back of his neck again as he avoided my gaze. "To be honest, you have no smell, no taste. You are scentless." He glanced up at me, but only just. "At first, I thought it was just me, but when I heard my guests' reactions to your scent, then I knew that I was not alone. I must apologize for my family. You are somewhat of an oddity to them. You are different. You make them very nervous because they cannot feel your presence or smell you, and in general, vampires have control over their surroundings."

"What do you mean, they can't feel my presence?"

Michael looked down as he adjusted his wine glass. "It means they can't feel where you are. In our minds, we can place a person up to a few centimeters of where they are just by their smell, the sound of their pulse, and sensing their body heat. You, on the other hand, elude our most powerful gifts. Our only way of knowing you are there is by the sight of you, and the sound of your heartbeat." Michael looked at me nervously, waiting for it to sink in. A touch of panic hit me, and my heartbeat rose. Michael smiled and nodded at me. He heard the rise in my pulse just as I had felt it.

As we finished our lunch, someone knocked at the dining room door.

"Enter." Michael's voice broke the silence.

Alex walked in and closed the door behind him. As he approached us, he bowed to me, then to Michael.

"Yes, Alex, what can I do for you?"

"Sorry for my interruption, my lord, my lady, but we are ready." Alex was acting so businesslike. It was almost weird, but he still managed to send me a questioning look—a silent query as to whether or not Michael had dropped the bomb. I nodded, and his eyes widened. I shrugged, and a small but genuine smile touched my lips. With our silent acknowledgment, Alex swept a lingering glance over me and winked.

"Ah, yes, and who have you appointed in charge?"

"Jonathan was appointed pack leader until my return."

"And he is aware of his duties?" Michael and Alex showed no emotion toward each other.

"Yes. The pack will be within calling distance."

"Good. I need this to be quick. I can't have you gone for too long."

"I understand." Alex bowed to the two of us and walked out.

"Wait, where are you going?" I got up and stood in front of Alex, blocking the door.

"Alex was kind enough to offer his assistance as a courier."

"I'm not going to be gone long. This meeting was just a formality. Besides, Jonathan will be close by." Alex came in a little closer and whispered in my ear. "Are you okay?"

"Yeah, I think." I laughed under my breath. Alex nodded and hugged me.

"I'll be home soon. Jonathan can call me at any time." Alex kissed the top of my head and smiled.

As soon as he rounded the corner, Michael grabbed my hand and pulled me to him.

"How long will he be gone?"

"I'm not sure. It could take a while. Since your identity has been exposed, Nicholas' search for you continues, and sending messages has become a problem. It's a dangerous journey. Nicholas's men have been attacking our messengers, but Alex is our best. He'll be back, I promise," Michael assured me.

After leaving the dining room and finding out Michael and his coven, well, purposefully drank blood, Michael and I were inseparable—mainly because I was scared to leave his side. The fact that they could not smell or sense me made it a little easier to swallow, but my fears still remained.

TWENTY-FIVE

Everyone seemed friendly and cordial at dinner. I almost fit in. It didn't take long for me to realize that Michael meant every word he said when he'd said dinner was more like a meeting. Plus, it was a little unnerving that I was the only one eating, and I wanted to shovel down my food just so I wouldn't look different.. That, and I was the only one with two drink choices: one glass of sparkling cider, and another mimicking everyone else's. I knew that the thin red liquid in the wineglass probably wasn't a matured glass of Michael's finest Medoc.

After I finished the cider, I fiddled with the wine glass, tracing the top with my middle finger and turning the stem as I tried to follow their conversations. It sounded like a board meeting for a big company trying to figure out the best way to advertise their business. They had a discussion on how to go about eliminating certain vampires, and how to handle—in simple terms—me. Just like at home, I lost them, and the colloquy took an awkward turn as some of them started to speak in different languages or on unrelated topics. As a result, after about ten minutes, I stopped paying attention. Something on renegade vampires, but nothing that pertained to me. The way that everyone addressed Michael as 'my lord' and 'sir' threw me. I was amazed that Michael was so respected.

As my thoughts wandered in and out, I sensed another force at work. I didn't always know how to differentiate my own emotions from those of others, but this time I did, and it seemed to come in handy. Right now, I felt someone's evil thoughts. I didn't know whose, or exactly what they were thinking, but there was uneasiness and restlessness in the pit of my stomach. My skin prickled on the back of my neck and goosebumps rose like warning flags.. It gave me the chills. Not only was this guy ominous, evil, and nefarious, but *satisfied.* He thought he had already won. At last, too tired to keep sitting there, I was about to excuse myself, hoping that Michael would follow, when the meeting came to an abrupt end.

With guests around, it was hard to talk with Michael privately. As if sensing my desire, Michael took my hand and led me out of the room. We went outside, walked to the old willow tree in the courtyard, and sat on the bench that surrounded it. People were walking in little groups discussing the results of the meeting, but to my relief, none were paying attention to us.

Michael tried to ask how dinner was, but a dark feeling nagged at me, and his voice faded into the background. The feeling had returned and grew. The intensity got stronger by the second. I tensed, and I could feel the agitation in Michael as he responded to my nervousness. We didn't have to exchange words for him to read me. Instinctively, Michael put his arm around me, ready to react to whatever it was I feared. I gave a small shudder as I looked around for the source: the garden, the extended yard, even the trees. No one there. Michael was growing nervous, too, and the sense of the two feelings mixed together was so strong that it pained me. I was ready to break down and yell at the top of my lungs. It was like being slammed by a freight train: immediate, forceful, and inescapable. Finally, off in the distance, a few people walked the grounds. He was among them I could sense it. The aggression was coming from someone in the small group.

"Michael," I whispered, not wanting the trespasser to hear me. "In the group by the barn. Someone is not who they seem."

Just as I concluded my thoughts, a loud snap cracked nearby. I jumped. An evil-eyed man stood in front of us. He snarled, revealing gleaming teeth in a sinful grin, the rest of his features in shadow. Michael shoved me behind him and growled. My heart beat painfully fast, and my breath was shaky and unsteady.

Just before Michael attacked him, the man finally spoke. His accent was a thick, greasy, English one. It felt as if he knew something we didn't.

"Michael, just hand over the half-breed and I will leave your coven alone." Despite his expression, his words were civil.

"I promise thee, that if thou but lookest in her direction, thou will not see the day's light again. And I never break a promise." Michael's voice was bitterly cold. The crisp air swirled around me, time slowing to the space between seconds.

"You don't need this pathetic excuse of a half-breed," the man went on. "Nicholas is after her, and I will be rewarded for her capture. Nothing is going to come between me and my reward." He grabbed for me, and before I could dodge, Michael tackled him. The man groaned as he hit the ground, Michael's knee on his throat. The man frantically pulled at Michael's clothing, but Michael didn't budge as his shirt ripped and the assailant clawed at his back. Michael grabbed the attacker's jaw and pulled it back. Screaming, he rolled out from under Michael's knee and reached for me again. Michael grabbed his arm and bent it back with a loud snap. I cringed and shuddered as his piercing scream reverberated off the treetops. I looked away as ripping and tearing of clothing and breaking and snapping of bones echoed in the night.

I was about to yell for help when someone drew up behind me. I spun around, hoping beyond all hope that it was Alex.

My heart dropped. I was wrong.

Whoever it was grabbed my hand and dragged me into the woods, branches and twigs scratching my arms and face. I dug my heels in, but it was no use. I was up against a vampire, not a human.

The guy Michael was fighting was only a decoy—to get Michael diverted from me so I'd be left alone. This was an ambush—a well-thought-out ambush. Someone knew I would never be left alone or without protection and that a distraction would be needed.

I tried to yell, but the man covered my mouth before I could get a sound out. Unlike Michael's soft and warm hand, this man's was quite the opposite—rough and unnaturally cool. Without thinking, I bit him. Maybe vampires surpassed me in every area—speed, strength, and experience. Maybe I was utterly helpless and incapable of fighting him, but I was not going to let him take me without a struggle. But biting him was like biting into stone. He yanked away to slap me, blood dripping from his skin.

So they bled. Just like me.

His hand came down across my face and landed a painful blow. It felt like my eye was going to explode. I struggled to get away, but he grabbed me from behind by my shirt.

"Michael!" I cried.

Michael looked over his shoulder, horrified but unable to help, caught in a fierce fight for his own life. I turned back to confront my attacker. His hood fell back and shock struck me in the chest.

It was Erik—the colleague of my dad's. He had dinner with my parents almost a year ago. The dreamy-eyed man I couldn't take my eyes off of. Erik was the snitch—the only one who knew about me besides Alex. He had not disappeared. He was with Nicholas and returned when they found out I was alive. He managed to trick not only my dad but Michael as well. He had been hiding among us the whole time.

His grip tightened.

My blood boiled. I pulled away, hard, hurting myself and Erik as well. His eyes burned with rage as he reached for me again—then stopped. Fear crossed his steel features. I stepped toward him, but he backed away. A hand on my shoulder pulled me back. With one swift move, I grabbed whoever it was, threw him over my shoulder, and shoved him onto Erik.

It was Michael. And he was looking at me with the same fear as Erik had. Erik, meanwhile, scrambled to his feet and ran in the opposite direction. Michael carefully backed away with deliberate movements. My heart stilled. I looked over my shoulder. The lowlife Michael had been tussling with was laid on the ground in lifeless pieces.

I shuddered. I had lost myself in anger and hatred. I'd let the rage consume me.

"Arri?" came Michael's tentative voice. He was nervous, not only in his heart but in his expression as well. I was still in the moment. Slowly, I was able to come back around, and Michael's features evened out as I calmed myself, the animosity and fury fading to fear that lodged in my chest. Tears filled my eyes. I felt jittery.

"What was that?" My voice was broken and cracked. Michael spoke slowly.

"I don't know. You tell me." Michael's confusion matched mine.

"How am I supposed to know? I didn't attack us," I snapped. Michael pulled me close to him, picked me up, and ran me into the house. "I'm not hurt," I protested, wondering why he cradled me carefully as he ran.

Inside, Michael took me straight to the formal living room, where he set me gingerly on the dark leather couch and called for Nana.

"Not this again," I said. "It wasn't my fault. I was being attacked just as much as you were!"

Michael glared at me, then looked me over. Nana bustled in along with a few of Michael's friends.

"He is still out there," Michael said sternly. "I need one of you to sweep the perimeter, one of you to contact Jonathan and his pack, and one to see if we can still get Erik."

"Michael?" Nana asked.

In a low voice, Michael told Nana what had happened in great detail, all the while checking me over.

"I'm not wired," I said. Michael frowned.

"I am not looking for a wire, nor are we back to you being a hostage. I am in search of cuts, bruises, any type of damage that you might have sustained before you turned." His voice was forced and harsh now. He seized my arm, surveying the scrapes from the trees. But they were almost gone. I was close to normal. He pulled a few leaves from my hair and twigs from the tears in my shirt.

"Turned? Turned into what? I was being attacked! I was simply trying to protect myself." By this time, we had gathered quite an audience.

"Arri, you were growling. Your eyes went red, and you looked like you were going to rip his arms off. I think you've been holding back on me. No one holds that much power." Michael looked stricken, like I'd betrayed him.

"I don't understand," I said. "I was just trying to protect myself. I was angry. Why are all of you staring at me like I'm lying? I don't understand what you want from me!" I was yelling not only at Michael but at the crowd as well. Everyone went blurry behind another round of tears. They saw me as a threat, not as a victim. I cast a pleading glance at Michael.

"Are you done playing monkey so I can go?" I was obviously not welcome here. Michael searched my face one last time, then let go of my hand. As I went to leave, a few of his friends stood in my way, blocking me.

"Let her go. She means us no harm." At Michael's words, they dispersed.

I needed to cool off and review what had just happened. In my room, I could smell the awful cologne stench of my attacker on my blouse. I stripped off the ripped, dirt-stained clothes and threw them in the trash. I still felt dirty, and the foul stink of Erik lingered on my skin. I shuddered. I turned on the shower and washed out the leaves and twigs that remained in my hair, dirt from my neck and legs, and any of Erik's odor that still clung me. After I showered—twice—and scrubbed my skin almost raw, I dressed, then left the bathroom. There sat Michael on the chair across from the door.

"What do you want?" I asked sharply. "Am I being accused of attacking you too, or just planning to do it?" I sat on the bed, waiting for his response.

"There are no accusations or judgments against you, but you startled me. I didn't realize you…you looked so defensive. I wasn't expecting you to take care of yourself."

Michael was holding back, and I knew it. "What do you mean?"

"I have never seen you get so angry. You were growling, and you threw me over your shoulder with no effort. Didn't that seem strange to you?"

I considered it for a moment. At the time, I had been scared, but now, it was rather weird.

"Your eyes were red, and I don't mean just filled with anger. I mean really red, the color red. There was no humanity left within you. I have seen your eyes change color before, depending on your mood, but I have never seen this side of you." Michael took a breath.

I scanned Michael's form, trying to feel if he was lying, but he was honest and sincere.

"What do you mean, my eyes changed? My eyes are gray." Then again, if werewolves and vampires existed, I guess it was possible I was my own mood ring.

"When you are happy, your eyes are a deep brown. When you are confused, your eyes are gray. When you are sad, your eyes are ice blue. When you are kissing me, your eyes match my own—emerald green."

I was bewildered that he remembered all of this. My heart fluttered.

"But now I have learned that when you are scared, your eyes are almost black, and when you are enraged, your eyes are red." He stopped there, got up from the chair, and sat down next to me on the bed.

As he neared me, Michael's emotions bounced around like ping pong balls. This was probably a bad time to tell him I could feel everything within him.

He kissed my cheek. "Arri, I was not happy when you first came into my life. I wanted nothing more than to wash my hands of you. You broke my things. You brought trouble."

"Maybe, I should leave, then," I said. "It looks like I can take care of myself. Maybe I have overstayed my welcome."

"Arri, I have fallen in love with you, and it would break my heart if you left now."

I bit the inside of my cheek and butterflies dominated my insides. Michael loved me. I felt giddy. The feeling was mutual. I leaned over and kissed him. It was overwhelming. He pulled away.

"I don't want to go, but I feel like I need to. What purpose would I serve causing chaos in your quiet world?" I said, not knowing what else to say. Did I belong here, or would I cause more damage than good? Suddenly, I was racked with sobs. Michael held me close and wiped the tears from my face.

"Arri, I love you. You will always have a place with me." He kissed me again.

"Michael?" I asked.

"Yes, my love?"

"I know who and what you are, and I know who your friends are…but who is Nicholas? And who am I?"

REVELATION, BOOK TWO IN THE PARADOX TRILOGY

Arri and Michael's story isn't over yet. If you'd like to know what happens next,
pick up your copy of Revelation now.

As Arri waits for her destiny to reveal itself, she finds a piece of the past that helps her discover her origins and the myth behind the ill-fated and infamous word, vampire.

Here is an excerpt from Forgotten Journal.

***

FALL

I've written down my thoughts and experiences as a matter of record. The best way to do this is to start from the beginning.

When I was younger, I didn't crave the thick crimson blood of others. I never abandoned my loyalties or shirked responsibilities like some of my fellows. No, I worked hard for what I got and did more than my fair share, and I never would have done what I was about to do.

The day started like any other. The sun was trying to make an appearance as the moon dominated the predawn sky. I lit the lamps before I got dressed and left. The marketplace had been busier than usual, so I wanted to get there before the sun rose, and I had hoped before the crowd. I was glad I wasn't a slave, being born from an upper-class man. Walking around the main square, I passed many shopping for their masters. I felt terrible for their working, but as my father's father had been before him, most of our ancestors began as slaves. It was a hard reality and truth, one I learned early on. They taught me to be grateful for the place I held and not to snub anyone below my status. As I picked up my supplies, I greeted the merchant and noticed a slight drain in his color. He seemed paler than usual, and the bags under his eyes confirmed his ill status.

"Sir?" I asked as I picked up my purchase. "Are you feeling well?"

His sunken gaze already told me the answer.

"I'll fetch the apothecary."

"No," the man said as he reached out his hand and grabbed my shirt. "Go. Run. Save yourself." His words slurred together and his voice was gruff, as if he were speaking through sandpaper. "Please. Pl—"

His final plea fell short as his eyes rolled back and his heavily rounded body thudded to the ground.

"Young man!" a hearty voice thundered as I cradled the merchant's head in my lap.

"Gruth! Gruth!" I called out to the merchant as he laid there, unconscious and limp.

"What have you done?"

I tried to tell him as I shook my head as stunned tears streaked my cheeks. "He told me to run and save myself, sir. What did he mean?"

"I know treachery when I see it, young man." He grabbed my arm and yanked me from the ground.

"Leave him, good man. It wasn't him," the apothecary said as he approached with a bag in his hand.

"Sir, I did nothing, I purchased my goods then realized he looked sickly. Please help him," I begged as he came to sit beside me.

"I know you did nothing. I have been seeing Gruth."

Like everyone else my age, I had hopes, dreams, and aspirations to become more than I was. I had responsibilities, and I was well on my way to becoming someone, but something happened that night that had changed my life forever. Something I will never forget no matter how long I live.

After the sun sank behind the mountains and darkness crept into the valley, my skin burned, and my heart pounded. I felt feverish, and hot chills left beads of sweat on my skin. My ears rang, and I knew. This is what Gruth had warned me of, but how? Had he known something I hadn't?

Then it hit me: the apothecary.

I ran from my bed and pounded on Romud's door. Squinting into the darkness until he saw me, he cracked it open, then pulled me in and locked the door shut behind me.

The apothecary eyed me carefully. "Did he cut or scratch you?"

I tried to think. "No, sir, not that I know of."

"Here," Romud said before pulling on my arms and lifting my shirt off over my head. Yelling in triumph, he poked at my back.

"See, here!" he said, poking again at the tender spot on my back.

"What?" I gasped for breath.

"Gruth scratched you, and now you are ill. I knew it. I knew it would work." The apothecary seemed elated by his discovery, but I did not understand why. I felt like I was dying, and he was happy?

"What worked? What have you done to me?" I accused him, but he seemed to ignore me and was writing in a book. "What have you done?" I yelled through labored breaths as I pounded my hand on his writing.

"The merchant was ill because of what I gave him when he came in with a burning heart. Maybe you will survive."

"What?" I cried as the room went black. I hit the ground. My body aches vanished, and my thundering heart stilled. Even my fever abated, but after that, I couldn't move or open my eyes. I was trapped in my body with no control. Soon after that, I heard the apothecary speaking to someone.

"Did he have someone at home?"

"No, he was the son of Mazleous."

Then that was it. After that, I remember nothing. I felt nothing, heard nothing, thought nothing. Everything was blank and black. I don't know how I came back into this world. I suppose I could hallucinate that I might have been someone of importance for this to happen, or that I am just a man down on his luck, but in all honesty, I don't have a clue. That's when it all started. I remember the excruciating pain of burning from the inside out and how no matter what I did, I couldn't escape it. I felt the torture of death drowned me in agonizing torment. Every move I tried to make felt like red hot daggers stabbing into my sides. Breathing became horrifyingly excruciating, and my eyelids felt like molten branding irons piercing my retinas. When I awoke from my painful death, this terrifying hell, I felt an inextinguishable burning along the lining of my throat every time I fought for air. I wished for the sweet release that only death could bring, but my prayers were unanswered as I fought for either life or death.

***

I hope you enjoyed your sneak peak of Forgotten Journal. To read the rest of the exclusive bonus chapter download *Forgotten Journal* from **jamieripp.com**.

For updates on new releases join me on Facebook or at **Jamieripp.com**!

DEAR READER

Hello Readers,

Thank you for reading Paradox, it means the world to me.

I'd love to hear from you.
If you enjoyed Paradox, please consider leaving a review.
Every review helps, even if it's only a sentence or two. You know us author types, we just love that sort of thing!

For reviews!
Amazon
Goodreads

For new release updates and to follow me:
Facebook
jamieripp.com

Thank You and Happy Reading,
Jamie Ripp

ABOUT THE AUTHOR

Jamie Ripp is the author behind the Paradox Trilogy. She has lived a full and adventurous life as a hostage negotiator, a referee, and a monster slayer. Jamie is the main character of her own personal safari as she fights off mountain lions, has standoffs with bears, and contains flightless aviaries and herds of hoofed wildlife. She has studied battle strategy, visited the rainforest, battled vampires, demons, and courted death with nothing more than a pen and caffeine.

Actually, while living in the mountains of Montana, Jamie has come face to face with a mountain lion, slept in a tent alongside a bear, and enjoys feeding her chickens and deer while trekking through three feet of snow. As for a referee and monster slayer, well, she is married and the mother of three.

While Jamie has never been in a hostage situation, she has been part of a group chat and has been a prisoner of war within the battalion of three teenagers.

While writing, Jamie has played the part of writer and character. She has defeated coven masters, found love among the trees, and courted the Grimm Reaper.

In short, she is Super Woman with an imagination, also known as an author and a mother.

BOOKS BY JAMIE:

PARADOX TRILOGY

Paradox
Revelation
Ascendance

EXCLUSIVE BONUS CHAPTER:

Forgotten Journal

www.jamieripp.com

www.ingramcontent.com/pod-product-compliance
Lightning Source LLC
Chambersburg PA
CBHW020524310726
48979CB00014B/2194/J

* 9 7 8 1 7 3 3 6 2 6 1 7 0 *